the Feijoa Tree

ROSEMARY WHITTAKER

The Feijoa Tree

Rosemary Whittaker

Also by Rosemary Whittaker

The Cinnamon Snail

Sunshine State

The Wattle Birds

Stopwatch Publications

First printing, 2013
Second impression, 2015
Third impression, 2022

ISBN-13: 978-1-922651-20-4

Published by Rosemary Whittaker
www.rosemarywhittaker.com

Cover design by Estella. Title lettering by Kate Forrester,
www.kateforrester.co.uk

For our parents, who loved the time they spent with us in New Zealand.

Chapter One

The sound of the school bell drags me away from the tropical beach of my imaginings and back to the morning staff meeting. Bentinck frowns at me, clearly aware I haven't been listening to his pearls of wisdom.

'As I was saying, Miss Richardson, I've decided that you will take the year ten girls for games until Miss Baldwin returns. Do you have any problem with that?'

Actually, I do. Policing teenage girls as they shuffle around the playground muttering obscenities is hardly a dream assignment. It's one of the many reasons Stephanie is currently on extended sick leave.

'No problem at all,' I lie. 'I'll be glad to get some fresh air after being stuck inside the classroom.'

He fixes me with a beady gaze, and I wish I'd just nodded. Bentinck neither expects nor engages in non-essential chat. Not for the first time, I miss our old Head, Graham Staples, who took early retirement last year after twenty-five years as an educator, police officer, counsellor, and eternal optimist.

I'm the newest member of staff, so I'm in no position to argue with Bentinck about my timetable. Mike Glover is the only other teacher with free lessons at this time, so it looks as though I'm stuck with it.

The meeting breaks up, and I walk back to my classroom. I hear a crash as I approach, and I break into a run. Looking around for the culprit, I'm not surprised to see Simon Denny jumping up and down, hurling the eraser against the whiteboard as hard as possible. I grab it from him and sweep an eye over the rest of the children. Most of them are leaning back in their chairs with their feet on the desks, laughing and talking. Those wearing earphones sway in time to the vague thumping inside their skulls.

There are three new sketches on the whiteboard – crudely drawn and anatomically incorrect as usual. I honestly don't see the point of this school's biology curriculum.

I wipe the board clean, keeping my face impassive. The pressure is building behind my eyes, and it isn't even lunchtime. But three years of teaching teenagers has taught me not to react to trivia, not to show anger or amusement, and never *ever* to fake pious disappointment because they really don't care. My pupils aren't too awful one on one, but when they hunt as a pack, it can be deadly.

I motion the whiteboard artists towards their seats, pointing to my ears until the music lovers pull out their ear-pieces. It's Friday, which is usually a day for general rejoicing. Their weekend beckons – two days of hanging out in groups, laughing at nothing in particular and staring vacantly into space. It's pretty much the same as their weekdays but without any interfering adults trying to bang the basics of an education into their heads.

My weekend beckons too – a couple of days during which I can sleep late, dress in old jeans, and drink as much as I like in the evenings without fear of throwing up during morning assembly.

Matt and I are having lunch at *The Swan* tomorrow. It's a pretty pub in the heart of the New Forest, hidden down a twisting gravel path. Its biggest attraction is that there's little or no chance of meeting any of my pupils. *The Swan* has no happy hours or live bands and definitely no pork scratchings.

Ten minutes later, the children are sitting at their desks with their books open – most of them at the correct page. The murmur of their voices is soothing as they debate the multiple-choice questions and I gaze out of the window.

My classroom is on the top floor and has an excellent view. Clouds whip across the bright sky, and autumn leaves swirl down into the playground. The summer is well and truly over now, and we've reached that awful in-between stage when the brightness of the new school year has rubbed off, but Christmas is still too far away.

This weekend with Matt will be the last time we can eat outside until at least April. It's a depressing thought. I loathe all cold weather except for a little Christmas card snow. My idea of total hell is lunchtime duty on a grey January day, with an icy wind curling around my legs and litter scooting across the playground at such a speed I can't identify who dropped it. Now that Bentinck has added to the fun with these two extra games periods, the girls won't be the only ones praying for rain each Monday and Friday.

Matt loves the winter and recently threatened to take me skiing during my February half-term holiday. My suggestion of a week in Florida made him laugh.

'Can't you lie in the sun during all your other months off work?' he asked. 'I only get four weeks' holiday, and I don't want to waste them fighting for space on a beach.'

Mum was there, and as usual she agreed with him. 'I'm afraid Anna would spend her whole life in second gear if someone paid her to do it. It's why she only works part time.'

Many, many arguments have taught me not to engage with her, so I stared past her in silence.

Rather surprisingly, Matt came to my defence.

'It isn't really part-time, Janice,' he explained, and I felt my eyelid twitch. 'Teachers do have long holidays, but the salary isn't great, and not everyone could stand the pace at our office.'

He looked at me for a supportive comment, but I shrugged and turned away. My supply of positive and admiring phrases is currently at a low ebb, and I need to save them for staff meetings.

My pupils must have noticed my diminishing enthusiasm, although there's no real reason for it. I'm doing the job I've chosen to do, and I like St. Jude's. My colleagues are fine, and the children could be worse, judging by the horrifying conversations I've had with friends from university who've ended up teaching in inner-city schools. The pay isn't great, but Dad left me an insurance policy that I put towards a starter house in a brand-new housing estate outside the town. It's more of a box than an actual house, but the street is fairly quiet, and it's close enough for me to check on Mum most days.

It's also too small for Matt to stay over very often. He's lovely, and I'm very fond of him – most of the time. But after years of living at home, I crave personal space and the freedom to lie in bed as late as I like and wander around in my ratty old pyjamas. I also want to make unhealthy snacks whenever I choose instead of having regular meals when other people decree I should.

Looking back, I can't think how I coped with living with Mum for so long. Dad died when I was sixteen, and I didn't have the heart to apply to Durham University after that. When I was approaching my A-level exams and planning my future, Mum cried and said I must do exactly what I wanted. That was why you had children – or in her case an only child. You had to give them their own wings and let them fly. She knew Dad would have agreed if only he'd been spared to her. So, I applied to Southampton instead so I could live at home.

I stayed on there to do my teacher training, the best part of which was my teaching practice at St Jude's. It was Graham Staples who suggested I apply for the job in the English department when Jane Hall announced she was moving to Spain with her husband and daughter.

Lucky woman, I think as I scribble quotations from Hamlet onto the white board. What wouldn't I give to be in the sunshine right now – eating grilled octopus, sipping Sangria, and thinking about a siesta later? I have a flabby cheese-and-tomato sandwich and a bottle of fizzy peach-flavoured water in my bag. I'll enjoy them in the staffroom at lunchtime while I mark a pile of essays on Jane Eyre. It doesn't get much better than that.

Chapter Two

Matt picks me up at noon the following day in his company car – a shining beast I secretly call the Red Monstrosity. I'm only allowed to ride in it after wiping my shoes – better still, taking them off. When he's being even more pompous than usual, I refer to it as the Skoda, which makes the edge of his cheek twitch in annoyance.

He's driving doesn't come in to collect me because he isn't happy leaving his beloved car alone outside. I've told him plenty of times it will be quite safe on our estate. The streets are too clean, and the houses, with their Georgian windows and neat front gardens, far too kitschy to attract much in the way of yobbery.

The only graffiti I've ever seen around here was last winter, after a rare night of snow. The drifts were piled almost to the top of the brick wall behind the bus stop. Neatly spray-painted above the highest drift was the word *SNOW*. It made me laugh each time I walked past it, and I was disappointed when the snow melted and the council scrubbed it clean. Matt seems convinced his car will suffer a similar fate if he leaves it unattended on my street. Perhaps someone will spray-paint *RED* on it.

The morning is mild, but I grab a warm jacket at the last minute out of sheer pessimism. As I open the car door, Matt glances at my shoes in case I've made a beeline for the nearest dog poo on my three-second journey down the front path.

He's as smartly dressed as ever. He doesn't leave his salesman persona at the office when he checks out at the weekend. To my embarrassment, he passes out business cards to anyone who will take one. I can't imagine blurring my work and personal life like that. But Matt has the sort of ambition I'll never understand, which accounts for the fact his income is now almost double mine, even before bonuses.

He lives in an enormous warehouse flat in a regenerated yuppie area right in the centre of town, with his beloved Red Monstrosity safely garaged below. I live in my tiny house and drive Daisy, my temperamental Nova, whenever she condescends to start. I take the bus on her more difficult days, which coincidentally are the same as mine. We're neither of us morning starters.

Matt hates giving names to cars, and I'm sure he flinches whenever I talk to, or about, Daisy. I've suggested plenty of other names for the Red Monstrosity – Montague, Cholmondeley, Cecil – but he ignores them all, preferring to refer to it as the Porsche. It isn't his yet, but he can buy it after the company lease runs out next year, and he's determined to keep it in perfect condition. I happen to know he has a bottle of vintage champagne on his wine shelf, all ready for the day it finally becomes his.

The drive through the forest is fantastic, and my mood lifts. Butterflies hover over the heather in the autumn sunshine, and a herd of deer pours itself over a distant hill. Matt inches the car along the final gravel road at a walking pace, watching every stone with suspicion. He's quite capable of making me get out and walk down the hill, but he wants to park where he can keep an eye on the car. Not directly beneath the oak trees, of course, or he'll spend the entire meal in a paranoid frenzy in case an acorn falls and dents the polished paintwork.

We had dinner here a few months ago to celebrate Matt's higher-than-expected bonus. We stayed until well after dark. The honeysuckle and night-scented stocks breathed their fragrance over the courtyard while I sat with my frosted glass of cider, allowing the tensions of the week to drain away.

I only half listened as Matt's voice washed over me. It was a long tale of office rivalries and eventual triumph as he landed the account everyone else had been after for months, or vice versa.

His job is as much of a mystery to me as mine is to him. He sometimes asks about my day, but there's little point in trying to explain. In Matt's opinion, my work lasts from 9am until 4pm and only involves dealing with children. It isn't nearly as real as the proper work he does, where careers are made or broken according to how much money comes into the company. After one argument about the generous length of my holidays compared to Matt's four weeks, we tacitly agreed to stop discussing work.

We sit at the same table as last time, in a sheltered corner of the courtyard. Matt orders steak, and I dither for a while between the pork and the lasagne before finally choosing the plaice. The chips here are great – hot, crisp and salty with fluffy insides.

While we're waiting for our meals to arrive, I lean over to smell a late pink rose scrambling up the weathered wall beside me. It strikes me that Matt seems more than usually serious today. He hardly spoke as we drove over, which is unusual for him. He taps his fingers on the table, looking tense.

'Everything ok?' I ask when the server has brought us our drinks.

'Sure, fine, everything's great,' he says.

I take a gulp of my over-chilled wine and cough. I look around the pub garden. 'It's lovely here, isn't it? The New Forest is wonderful, especially in the summer.'

Matt looks at me for a long moment. 'Would you ever think of moving?'

'It's never felt like an option,' I say. 'Mum isn't going anywhere, and I suppose I feel responsible for her. She hardly ever gets out. If I lived further away, I'd have to drive down to see her all the time, and I don't see much point doing that.'

He nods. 'I was going to wait until after we'd eaten, but this seems as good a time as any. I brought you here today so we could talk.'

I'm surprised by the intensity of his frown. 'Go on.'

'Paul called me into his office on Tuesday – Paul Clark, my manager,' he adds, noticing my vacant expression. 'You met him at the Christmas party last year.'

My mind flickers back to the famous Christmas party when Matt came to pick me up and asked me to change into something a little smarter. Instead of telling him exactly where to go, I did as he asked, which still bothers me.

I remember ignoring him for most of the evening, drinking quite a bit, flirting with the guy who turned out to be Matt's chief sales rival, and finally spilling a plate of asparagus rolls down Paul's wife's rather daring cleavage. Matt and I didn't speak much for a few weeks afterwards.

Thankfully, he doesn't seem to be thinking about this. 'Paul wanted to speak to me because he's leaving next month, which means his job will be vacant.'

I lean over to kiss him. 'And he's offered it to you? That's fantastic, Matt. Congratulations!'

'Of course, he didn't!' says Matt. 'I'm nowhere near senior enough. But you're half right. The guy replacing Paul is coming down from Manchester, and Paul has offered me his job. It's a great compliment.'

'Manchester?' I say blankly. 'As in *millions of miles up north* Manchester?'

'Yes, as in Manchester,' he says. 'Naturally, I told him it's a big decision, and I'd need a few days to talk it over with you.'

'You're seriously considering it?' I ask.

'Of course!' he says. 'It's a *huge* promotion. It means lots more money and the chance to travel abroad occasionally. I think you'd like it, Anna. I've been talking to an estate agent, and we could afford a larger flat up there. Property prices are lower, and it would be a good investment. We could buy a house in a nearby village if you prefer. The agent tells me it's very pretty countryside, and I think it would suit us both well.'

I stare at him in silence. What on earth is he talking about, and who does he mean by *us*?

'You're not suggesting I go to Manchester *with* you?' I say at last.

He gives me a puzzled look. 'It's too far for us to see each other regularly if you don't. I've been thinking for a while that it makes good financial sense for us to move in together. You could sell your house. With what I get for my flat, we'd have enough for a sizeable deposit. So, a mortgage won't be a problem.'

I'm stunned by this. It isn't just Manchester, although to be honest, it's never been on my list of must-live places. Neither is it Matt's calm assumption that my life isn't as important as his, and I'll drop everything and move wherever he goes. It's more that I've never thought about our future at all. Now that he's forcing me to consider it, I wonder what I really want.

The idea of moving in with Matt isn't appealing, although it's difficult to say why. I have to settle down sometime, and Matt's a really nice guy. He's easy to talk to, has a steady job and gets on with Mum, which is a miracle in itself. He and I have been together for four years – on and off – since we met during our final year at university. It's never occurred to me until now to question where he and I are headed, which is odd in itself. But the thought of moving in with him is unsettling.

I try to think of something tactful to say. 'This is a pretty big decision for you. You shouldn't take me into consideration. You have to decide what *you* want.'

Matt looks puzzled and a little hurt. 'I have to take you into consideration, Anna. We're a couple. You'd have been upset if I hadn't consulted you.'

I feel even guiltier as I realise I wouldn't have consulted him in the same situation. That may be because I've never thought of us as a proper couple. Our relationship was great at first, but now he's just someone to spend time with, take to parties or use as a weapon whenever Mum talks about me finding a direction in life. He's someone to take on holiday to avoid the single supplement and crushing sense of failure at eating alone.

Faced with the thought of spending every evening together, chatting about our days, and choosing furniture for our new place, I feel cold inside. I've always felt that the secret of our relationship is that if Matt annoys me, or I him, we don't have to see each other again until we've forgotten what happened. I thought he saw things the same way. It seems that he doesn't, which makes me feel terrible.

'Manchester is out of the question for me,' I say. 'You know I can't move so far away from Mum. She'd never manage alone.'

His face clears. 'If that's all, I'm one step ahead of you. I've already thought about that.'

This makes me feel even worse, so I don't comment.

'Janice could come with us,' he goes on. 'We can help her with the move and finding herself a little place to live. She may even prefer to live with us. We could have a granny flat added on to wherever we decide to buy.'

I recoil from this truly awful thought, tipping back my wine glass to make sure I inhale every single dreg.

'That's kind of you,' I say at last, 'but Mum couldn't face a move at her age.'

'How old *is* she?' he asks. 'I mean, you're only twenty-six.'

This question comes as a shock. In my head, I know Mum is only fifty-nine. But I've spent so many years explaining her situation to everyone and making excuses for why I can't go away on the spur of the moment with friends that I've almost come to think of her as being in her late seventies. If other people get the same impression, it's easier all round and saves explanations. She really can't cope on her own, so what difference does it make?

I need to be honest and not string Matt along. 'It isn't only Mum. I don't feel ready to move in with you – or with anyone at all, really.'

I add this last part to stop him from taking my statement personally. But it seems to make things worse. His face is expressionless, but it usually is when I've upset him.

'I knew it would be a bit of a shock,' he says, 'but I thought you'd be pleased when you'd had time to think about it. It's been four years now, and you must have been wondering about our next step.'

'Not really,' I say. 'I could have suggested it myself if I'd wanted to. It's not the 18th century.'

We sit in silence until our meals arrive. Matt pushes his steak around his plate before laying down his cutlery. 'That's it, then – I just won't go. I'll explain to Paul how you feel about it, but I warn you he'll be horribly disappointed.'

I feel the familiar disapproval and guilt pressing down on me, but I'm determined not to give in. A few days' discomfort is a small price to pay to escape this move.

I summon up a bright smile. 'Don't be like that, Matt! I think you should go if you want to. It sounds like a wonderful opportunity for you.'

I'm aware that I sound like Miss Matson, the relentlessly cheerful careers teacher at my secondary school. She looked at my aptitude tests and personal assessment for a long time before telling me brightly that I didn't quite fit anything on her list – but not to worry because every peg has its own hole. It's just a *little* harder to place some of them.

'Now you're just being difficult,' says Matt tightly. 'How can I take the job if you're down here? It's too far for us to drive backwards and forwards each weekend.'

'We could take it in turns to visit once a month,' I suggest.

I'm not sure I really want to travel that far, but he looks hurt, and I feel responsible, which I am.

I try to find other positives. 'We'll still have the holidays. You're always saying I'm never at work.'

I say it jokingly, but it reminds me of all the times I've wanted to hit him for saying just that.

He shakes his head. 'Long distance relationships never work. We'd better forget the whole thing.'

He drains his glass, and there's an awkward silence.

'But you could easily get a job up there!' he bursts out. 'It doesn't matter where you live when you're a teacher. There will always be a school nearby.'

'Maybe I like my school,' I say. 'I have friends there, and I'm settled.'

He clicks his tongue and exhales. 'Ok, you win. Let's drop it, shall we?'

He picks up his knife and saws at his steak. I watch him, trying to read his expression. I know his face so well that I don't usually bother to look at it. He'd be anyone's definition of handsome, with his dark, wavy hair, hazel eyes and firm chin. More importantly, he's kind and stable, and he's genuinely nice to Mum. I dumped one boyfriend at university after I overheard him telling his friend I couldn't go out that night because I had to stay in and help my mother polish her broomstick. Matt is incapable of saying anything that mean.

I open my mouth to tell him I'll think about it, but I'm overwhelmed by the certainty that I won't. I know perfectly well I'm never going to move to Manchester, and he mustn't lose this opportunity because of me.

Without letting myself think about it further, in case I back down, I take a deep breath. 'Matt, I think we should talk.'

Chapter Three

So, that's just great. I'm unexpectedly and guiltily single, feeling dreadful about Matt and dreading breaking the news to Mum. I'm having lunch with her tomorrow, as I do most Sundays usually with Matt in tow. It will look suspicious if I call and cancel at the last moment, and I have to face her sometime.

I run myself a bath and soak in it miserably for an hour. I spend the evening watching old movies and feeling increasingly sorry for myself. Dad and I loved black-and-white movies and sat up watching them long after Mum had gone to bed. We quietly ripped open packs of salt and vinegar crisps as we watched. The doctor had forbidden them because of Dad's kidney problems, and Mum would have hit the roof if she'd caught us.

I feel more and more guilty as the evening wears on. Doris Day would never have dumped Cary Grant if he'd wanted to move to Manchester. She'd have been terribly supportive and gone with him and made a wonderful new life for them both. To my surprise, I sleep well and don't hear my alarm.

I wake with a start just before noon, remembering that I've promised to bring a dessert to lunch today. I'll have to drop in at the supermarket on the way over. With no chance to discard the packaging and put it into one of my own dishes, Mum will know at once it isn't homemade.

I choose two desserts in the vague hope of placating her – Death by Chocolate, which exactly suits my mood at present, and a pinkish-red mousse on a sponge base. She surely can't object to both of them. I pick up a bunch of drooping lilies at the checkout and arrive at Mum's only a few minutes behind schedule.

I wait for a while after knocking at the back door because she hates it when I let myself in. It took me forever to persuade her to give me a key after I moved out. Even then, it was on the strict understanding that I would only use it in the direst of emergencies.

Mum appears in the kitchen and opens the door. I peck her on the cheek and brandish the flowers, which she pretends not to see. She disapproves of wasting good money on flowers that will die within the week – I suspect much earlier in this case.

'Hi, Mum! I'll put these in water, shall I?' I ask, dropping the flowers into the sink and turning on the tap.

She doesn't reply but goes into the living room and plumps herself down on her recliner. I open the boxes and dump the desserts onto the draining board. I don't dare defrost them in the microwave in case the ping alerts Mum to their less-than-homemade qualities. I hope for the pink mousse's sake that lunch will be late and buy the poor thing some time.

'How's everything today?' I ask Mum as cheerfully as possible.

'Where's Matthew?' she responds. 'It isn't like him to be late.'

'I don't think you invited him this week.' I still can't lie to her without turning red.

She purses her lips. 'I rang you on Monday and told you to invite him.'

'That's right – you did. I must have forgotten. Sorry, but it's been a busy week. We've had three teachers off with flu, and I've had to cover several of their classes.' I hate hearing my breathless gabble, but I'm powerless to stop.

She waits for me to wind down before giving me a disapproving look. 'It's most annoying. I bought an extra lamb chop because I know how much Matthew likes them. You really are the most forgetful girl, Anna. I can't think how they cope with you at that school of yours.'

'Oh, I seem to scrape by all right.'

But Mum's like a terrier, worrying away at the subject. 'Give him a ring now. I daresay he's free, and he'll be glad of a good meal. A man living by himself never eats properly, and you've never been much of a cook, that's for sure.'

'I can't,' I say rather too quickly. 'He isn't around this weekend. He has a conference somewhere up north – Manchester, I think he said.'

It feels like a good idea to introduce the idea of Manchester into the conversation as soon as possible. Perhaps she'll follow it up, and I can tell her what's happened.

But Mum only returns to the buried bones I want her to ignore. 'He works much too hard,' she says. 'You wouldn't understand that, what with having weekends and holidays off and getting home by four every day.'

She's so right, I think. Every afternoon sees me skipping merrily off the school premises as soon as the bell rings, my marking and preparation finished and my classroom wall displays updated – something Bentinck is currently very keen on. There are no staff meetings, curriculum-planning meetings, departmental meetings, parents' evenings or frenzied preparations for Ofsted inspections. No records to be written or barrage of ever-changing government targets – each fresh lot arriving and contradicting the ones we've just absorbed. No meetings about troubled children with backgrounds that make even their social workers shudder. No being assaulted by a parent in the playground when the court order says they aren't allowed to pick up their child from school. Just short days and plenty of holidays, so that I sometimes wonder why they pay us at all. But I've had this conversation with so many people over the years, and it isn't worth it, especially in view of the conversation ahead of us.

Mum gives me a list of jobs, and I use the time until lunch is ready to do them. It saves having to talk. By the time I've lugged the washing downstairs, put it in the machine, hung the previous load out, wiped around the skirting boards and cleaned the lounge windows to give Mum a better view of the people passing by, lunch is ready.

We sit facing each other, and I make an appreciative face. 'This smells good.'

I fork a chop off the dish onto my plate and smother it in mint sauce.

Mum looks at me for a minute. 'What's going on with you and Matthew?'

I almost choke. I've been living away from home for three years now, and she still thinks she knows everything about me.

'I'm not sure what you mean,' I say lamely.

'You've never been able to hide anything from me, and I don't suggest you try now. Where is he this weekend?'

I'm immediately whisked back to my childhood when Mum told me she always knew when I was hiding something because I had *Liar* written right across my face. I remember going upstairs to the bathroom when I was five, peering into the mirror and wondering whether it had been written in some unfair invisible ink.

I swallow my mouthful of lamb. 'Matt and I have agreed to take a break for a bit while we think about what we both want out of life.'

'I suppose that means he's dropped you,' she says. 'He's found someone better?'

'No!' I cry, stung by the assumption that I suspect everyone who knows us will make. 'He's had a good job offer in Manchester, and he's decided to take it. I'm supportive of that. I think he should try it. He can always come back if it doesn't work out.'

'Has he got another woman?' she asks.

'It's nothing like that,' I say with what little patience I can muster. 'Neither of us has met anyone else, but we've decided we need a break. It's a mutual decision.'

I will her to drop the subject, although there's little hope of that. She chews her chop aggressively yet tidily, planning her line of attack. 'Don't you want to get married and have a nice home?'

'I'm quite happy with my house,' I say. 'And I don't want to get married unless I meet someone I can't live without – like you and Dad,' I add hopefully, if hypocritically.

She ignores this, and I don't blame her. She lays down her knife and fork and looks at me over the top of her glasses. 'I've never been one to interfere, as you know very well. All I can say is that you aren't getting any younger. You don't seem to know what you want, and you never have. It's time for you to decide what your priorities are. You have no goals, and you drift around aimlessly. If you don't want to marry Matthew and support his career, you'd better work harder at your own job and try to get up the ladder. I'm not saying anything else. I've always told you it's your life, and what you do with it is your business.'

'Thanks, Mum,' I mutter.

We finish our main course in silence, and I carry the plates to the kitchen. The pink mousse is only half thawed, but I dump it onto a plate anyway, sawing it in two to let warm air into the middle. The Death by Chocolate slumps inside its white plastic jacket, and I don't bother to unwrap it. It will give Mum a new focus for her disapproval and hopefully distract her from the subject of me and my directionless life. Anyway, now she knows about me and Matt, the worst is over. Telling everyone else will be easy by comparison.

I carry the desserts to the dining room and dump them in front of Mum.

'Pink mousse?' I ask her sweetly, plunging the knife into its icy depths. 'Or some sort of brownish cake-like thing?'

Chapter Four

As soon as the bell rings for morning break, I race to the staffroom. I want to talk to Nicole. I met her during our teacher training, and we started working here at the same time. We've become good friends, and she's the first person I go to for advice.

She should be in the staffroom by now. She doesn't have a lesson first thing, so she takes her time coming in, which I envy. Monday mornings are always pretty grim, but this one feels even more so. I'm fed up with my life, and I'm starting to wonder whether I've done the right thing in letting Matt go. Neither am I looking forward to the year ten netball lesson this afternoon. In my rush to get out of the house this morning, I couldn't find my trainers, so I'll have to jog up and down the court in heels, looking as stupid as I feel.

'*A place for everything, and everything in its place,*' is a mantra Mum has chanted at me over the years. And Matt doesn't even begin to understand the concept of disorganisation.

I do have a place for everything – usually where I last dropped it – and it's worked pretty well for me so far. I agree with whoever it was that said a tidy house is the sign of a wasted life.

The problem is that my untidy house doesn't seem to be the sign of a fulfilled one.

Was Mum right when she said I should concentrate on my career? The thought of working here for years, only to take over as head of department and grow a moustache and a nylon suit like Susie Berrow, doesn't exactly inspire me. The idea of extra meetings and more courses, where I can exchange thrilling experiences and earnest suggestions with other heads of department, leaves me equally cold.

I'm not really the meeting type. Most of the time, I prefer being in the classroom – although not when Simon Denny is on form. It's amazing how one child out of a class of thirty can require a good fifty percent of my attention. Sitting still for more than three minutes is far beyond his capabilities. Keeping his mouth shut is another skill he still hasn't mastered. There may be some good points hidden somewhere under that foul-mouthed, hostile exterior, but on a bad day he can disrupt a class before I've even taken my coat off. And he's about due for a bad day.

Nicole, as predicted, is in the staffroom when I arrive. She's sitting in the most comfortable chair, sipping coffee and reading her horoscope.

'I have to go home right now!' she announces as I walk in. 'Due to unhelpful planetary aspects, we Virgos will be the ones to feel the Monday morning blues the most. We'll find it hard to get motivated, and even more difficult to keep going. I can guess which particular unhelpful aspects they mean. That would be Jade Marbury and Sara Powiss. It says a piece of malachite will help restore my focus and flagging energy levels. Where am I supposed to get one of those? Chemistry lab, maybe?'

'I've split up with Matt,' I say, grabbing the last pink wafer from the biscuit tin before anyone else sees it and slumping into the chair next to her.

'You're joking!' she says. 'What happened? Didn't you guys have a nice weekend planned?'

I nod. 'Lunch, at that pub in the New Forest I told you about. But as soon as we got there, Matt announced he's been offered a big promotion in Manchester.'

Nicole looks startled. 'Manchester – just like that? Does he want you to go with him?'

'Yes, he does. That's the problem. He asked me to move up there and buy a house with him. He wants to take Mum too.'

She pulls a reflexive grimace, then tries to turn it into an interested look. We've had a few disagreements about me feeling I need to look after Mum so much, so now we rarely mention her.

'Goodness,' she says in a carefully neutral tone. 'And you didn't fancy it?'

I catch her eye and can't help grinning. I'd been hoping for sympathy, but she's known me for too long.

'I haven't exactly broken my heart over it,' I say, 'but I thought you might be a shoulder to cry on.'

She pulls a face. 'Well, he isn't my totally favourite person. In fact, I've never understood what you were doing with him. Don't tell me you didn't guess?'

I think back over the past few years. Nicole has usually excused herself whenever I've asked her to come out to dinner with us, and she's always checked who'll be there before she's dropped by. In his turn, Matt probably thinks Nicole is a bad influence on me, an opinion in which he's joined by Mum.

Nicole never stays with the same boyfriend for very long and thinks nothing of clubbing all night, even on school nights. She also hitchhikes to see her parents in York when funds are low.

Her life feels way more fun than mine. I envy the way she sees opportunities and grabs them without worrying. I also envy her ability to make mistakes without caring about the consequences or who might disapprove. I don't expect there's much about my life she envies. Right now, there's nothing much I envy about it either.

The bell rings, and I reach for my bag. I don't want to arrive after the year eights. If I do, obscene sketches on the board are likely to be the least of my problems.

The classroom door is wide open as I approach, and I hear shouting. Laura Willis is peering down the corridor. She waves her arms when she sees me, shrieking, 'Please hurry, Miss Richardson! It's Simon!'

When isn't it Simon? I push past her into the classroom. At first, I can't see what's happening because of the huddle of grey-sweatered backs gathered around Simon's desk. I shout at them to move, and they all melt away, giving me a horrifying glimpse of Simon Denny. His face is contorted with rage, and he's leaning on Adam Kimber, who's lying across the desk with one arm twisted up behind his back. His face is white, and his eyes are closed. No one's helping him.

As I jump forward, Simon gives Adam's arm a further twist, and I'm terrified the bone will snap. I launch myself at Simon, shrieking at him to stop, but he ignores me. I'm not even sure he hears me. I've seen him angry before, and I heard he was on the verge of suspension last year for constant fighting, but this is something else.

I throw myself on top of him, thumping his arm as hard as I can. As his grip on Adam loosens, I pull him around to face me, cracking my elbow on the wall as I do so. Adam slumps in his seat, whimpering. Simon swings his arm to hit me, and I twist away. His fist catches me on the collarbone instead of my face as he'd intended. I'm so angry now that I could easily punch him back, but some instinct restrains me.

I yell at him instead. 'Out! Right now, Simon! Get out of my classroom!'

Amazingly, he turns and walks out, knocking over several desks as he goes and deliberately slamming Laura into the door.

The room has fallen silent. I stand stock-still, battling a sudden, humiliating nausea. I swallow it down and turn back to

Adam. His arm is sticking out at a strange angle that makes me feel sick again. I assume he's dislocated his shoulder.

'Someone go down to Mr Bentinck's office,' I manage in a choked voice. 'Tell him what's happened. Ask him to find Simon, then come up here as quickly as possible. Adam, can you walk?'

He nods and stands rather shakily.

'Go straight to the sickroom,' I tell him. 'Sam, you go with him. Let Mrs Marsden have a look at your arm, Adam. I think you'll need an x-ray. Everyone else, sit down and get on with … something.'

The children drop into their seats. Fee Drewson is crying, but she'll just have to get on with it. My legs give way, and I collapse into a chair. My shoulder is hurting, and I'm starting to feel cold. No one says anything. They sit perfectly still, staring at me. Eventually, a few of them take out their books but don't look at them.

We sit in silence for five more minutes until we hear footsteps outside. Bentinck walks in, and I feel a flash of gratitude that someone – even Bentinck – is here to take over.

He leans down and speaks to me in a low voice. 'Please go and wait for me in my office, Miss Richardson.'

He straightens up, flashing his supercilious gaze around the class. 'Mr Glover is on his way up. He will stay with you until lunchtime. You will remain here when the bell rings. I wish to ask you a few questions.'

He motions to me to leave, and I pick up my bag and walk towards the door. I take a last look at the class to check they're all right, but no one meets my gaze. Bentinck is intimidating at the best of times, and these children must be suffering from shock. I'm just glad to get out of the classroom. I need to sit quietly and come to terms with what's just happened.

I walk unsteadily to the staffroom. Thankfully, no one is there. I make myself a coffee with shaking hands and carry it to Bentinck's office. I'm not sure whether Simon will be there. I really hope not.

The office is empty when I arrive. Bentinck likes the fact his entire office wall is made of glass. He says it makes him more accessible to the staff and pupils. I think he can't bear not to have his eye on everyone who walks by.

I'd hate to sit in a goldfish bowl with no privacy. There'd be no chance of playing Sudoku or slumping face down on the desk in the throes of a hangover. That wouldn't be a problem for Bentinck. He doesn't drink – something that always casts a slight pall over our Christmas meals and retirement lunches. No one is comfortable letting their hair down while Bentinck smiles tightly at whatever sycophantic remark the poor person next to him feels compelled to offer.

I wait for almost half an hour in his office before emerging to look for his secretary. Lesley is a cheerful, middle-aged woman with a huge capacity for gossip. Her face usually lights up when she sees me, and she starts straight in with the latest staff scandal, fabricating one if need be rather than miss out on a chat.

Today, she's finishing a sandwich while typing one-handed. She glances up when I appear, and I notice she looks strained and unhappy. Before she can speak, Bentinck appears. He sweeps past her and ushers me into his office. He's as unsmiling as ever, but I've grown used to that. He waves me to a seat, and the first uneasy curls of foreboding swirl around my stomach.

'This is a most serious situation, Miss Richardson,' he begins.

'Yes,' I say, waiting for him to ask me how I am. It was a frightening experience, and my elbow is still throbbing from its contact with the wall. But I'm determined not to show weakness, however terrified I may have been. I resolve to say as little as possible. I'll just tell him the facts and let him deal with the awful Simon and his equally awful parents.

He gives me a glassy stare. 'Simon's mother has called to inform me he is safely at home. You'll be glad to know he isn't badly hurt.'

'You mean Adam?' I say. 'He's the one whose arm was hurt, not Simon. Simon was the one doing the twisting.'

Bentinck's face doesn't flicker. 'I was, in fact, referring to Simon. His mother intends to have his arm looked at by a doctor. She tells me there is bruising and some swelling, but the bones appear to be intact.'

He pauses for a second. 'For which piece of information you are no doubt profoundly grateful?'

I shake my head. None of this makes any sense. 'Adam is the one whose arm was hurt,' I repeat. 'I was scared it might be broken. It isn't, is it?'

He turns his cold eye on me again. 'Adam Kimber is fine. Apparently, he has no idea why you took matters into your own hands and struck Simon.'

My stomach does a complete flip, and for a moment I can't breathe. I stagger to my feet and make a sudden rush for the door, pushing past an open-mouthed Lesley. I only just make it to the staff toilet, where I throw up violently. I keep retching for five minutes before I feel safe enough to wash my face. I lean against the wall while I compose myself. I have classes this afternoon, but I have to see Bentinck first and straighten this out.

I return to his office and push open the door without knocking. 'Sorry about that –' I begin before realising he isn't alone.

Charles Freeman, a large, red-faced man with unpleasant bright blue eyes, is standing by the window. I've never liked Charles, but he's the chairman of the Board of Governors, so we have to be polite to him. He gives me a hostile look but doesn't speak.

Bentinck gives me his usual fish-eyed stare. 'I called Charles, who was good enough to cancel what he was doing and come straight in. I hope we can keep this quiet, but the governors must be informed. Charles has agreed to call an emergency meeting tonight for those who are able to attend. Please hold yourself in readiness to speak to them tomorrow, Miss Richardson, as and when they require you. Perhaps you could recap the facts for Charles' benefit. Be as brief as you can.'

'I don't understand!' I burst out. 'I stopped a boy from having his arm broken. I was assaulted too, but you're talking as though I did something wrong. You haven't even asked how I am.'

To my immense frustration, I start to cry. The tears slip faster and faster down my cheeks as I slump in my chair. Both men watch me, Charles a little awkwardly and Bentinck with complete passivity.

He waits for me to get myself under control before clearing his throat. 'Your version of events is at variance with the one I received from the protagonists. Therefore, I must probe deeper to discover what happened. On the one hand, I have an irate mother threatening a court case for assault against this school. The witnesses all agree that you inflicted the injuries her son's arm received during this incident.'

I can't speak. My head is whirling. Bentinck is unmoved. 'I have another boy who asserts that nothing more than tomfoolery was involved. Despite there being plenty of other children in the classroom, none of them says they witnessed any kind of assault other than the one to which you have admitted. When you are calmer, you will perhaps appreciate the seriousness of what has happened here today.'

He pauses, then carries on a little more awkwardly. 'I am, of course, prepared to give you whatever limited support I can, as a member of my staff. But it would help if we could keep the emotion to a minimum and establish the facts. I do understand that Simon Denny is not a model pupil –'

I give a derisive snort. I can't help it.

'*Not*,' he repeats, a faint tinge of annoyance showing in his pinkening ears, 'a model pupil. You are not the first member of staff to have had problems with him, and his mother is well aware of that. Indeed, I stressed as much to her during our phone call. But that, as she rightly pointed out, does not give you or anyone else the right to take the law into your own hands – quite literally in this case, it would seem.'

I'm so angry I can hardly breathe. 'Ask the children who were there!' I stammer. 'Ask Laura Willis. She was screaming at me to come quickly before Adam got badly hurt. Simon almost pushed her over when he slammed out.'

'I have spoken to Laura Willis,' he says. 'She was forced to admit that she witnessed very little of the actual events, having gone to the door to look for you. She heard someone say that Adam and Simon were fighting, but she saw nothing of what actually went on. The other pupils tell me that Simon and Adam often wrestle and fight. None of them could say for certain who started this particular altercation.'

Altercation? What a jerk the man is. He sounds as though he's rehearsing his speech for a judge.

'What about Adam?' I say with a flash of hope. 'He must have told you what Simon was doing?'

Bentinck shakes his head. 'Adam tells me that he and Simon were merely engaging in horseplay.'

Engaging in horseplay? Of course, he did. I can just hear Adam Kimber, king of the one-word answer in all my comprehension tests, using that phrase. 'I was merely engaging in horseplay with the defendant, your Honour.'

'Boys will be boys, Anna,' Charles chips in smugly, but I ignore him. We have his two boys at the school, and they're both pretty loathsome. But we have to tread carefully around them, given who their father is.

I turn to Bentinck. 'Adam isn't telling the truth. Simon is twice his size, and Adam isn't stupid enough to get into a fight with him for fun. He's too frightened to say anything in case Simon catches up with him.'

'Possibly,' concedes Bentinck. 'But is it not equally possible that you misread the situation, overreacted and acted inappropriately? Any kind of physical contact with a child is fraught with difficulty, and you are a relatively new teacher, are you not?'

'Yes, but a teacher of thirty years would have done the same. I did what I had to in order to prevent a child in my care from being seriously hurt. Perhaps you think I should have stood there while Adam had his arm broken, and then filed an accident report?'

It's his turn to ignore me, which is probably a good thing. I can't believe where this is going.

'Anna,' interrupts Charles, which annoys me. I hardly know him, and the staff members are polite enough to refer to him as Mr Freeman – at least to his face.

'Anna,' he says again with a pained expression. 'It's natural for teachers to make mistakes from time to time. The best thing to do is admit them, put them right, and learn from them. That way, we can all move on, d'you see?'

I can't believe how this clown is patronising me. I don't dare flat out ignore him, but I refuse to discuss teaching methods with Charles Freeman.

'Mr Freeman,' I say, laying a bit of a slap on the *Mr*, 'I can only say that I don't believe I made a mistake. I did what seemed to me the right thing in this situation, and I have nothing else to add.'

I turn to Bentinck. 'What should I do now? I have the year ten girls for games after lunch, so we'll have to hurry this.'

His face doesn't flicker. 'You will not be returning to your classroom today. Lesley has arranged temporary cover for your classes. I would like you to go home. You will not return to school until this incident has been resolved. You will remain on full pay until we reach a conclusion and decide whether any further action is to be taken against you.'

I restrain the urge to leap across and twist his arm behind his back. That would show him what is and isn't horseplay. Instead, I force myself to stand and walk out of the room without acknowledging either one of them.

Chapter Five

Four hours later, I'm staring out at the dark windows across the street. A light flicks on in one of them, jerking me back to the present. People are arriving home from work.

I'm almost paralysed by what happened this morning. My brain is loosening up from its stiffness, but I still don't want to think too deeply about the bewildering turn of events that's landed me here.

I consider calling Nicole, but I don't know what Bentinck has said to the staff. If Lesley's embarrassed reaction is anything to go by, most of them may not want to speak to me. I shrink at the thought of ill-considered comments flicking at the rawness and destroying whatever shreds of confidence I have left.

Nothing that happened today makes the slightest sense when I replay it in my head. All I did was break up a fight, yet I'm the one who's been suspended. What was I supposed to do instead? I remember Charles Freeman's pomposity, and everything boils up again until I want to spit.

I have no idea what to do next. I should be talking to my union, but I haven't got around to joining one. I meant to, but my mortgage has taken every spare penny, and I've been putting off paying the dues until I get on top of the bills. Anyway, Graham Staples was lovely, and we all knew he'd have jumped in traffic for any of his staff or pupils. It never occurred to me that I might need protection from the headmaster himself.

I'd like to throttle Simon Denny. As for that spineless wimp, Adam Kimber, words fail me. I understand he's terrified of what Simon will do if he squeals, but dropping me in it like this is appalling. I suppose he may change his mind and do the right thing tomorrow when he's had time to think things over. But if he doesn't, where does that leave me?

Stressful images chase around and around in my mind. I need to get out of the house, but I can't think where to go. I'm terrified of bumping into anyone from school – staff members or pupils. I'm a pariah. Everyone will know by now that I've been suspended after the serious accusation of assaulting a pupil.

A wave of shame burns me, and I feel an urge to throw some clothes into a suitcase, sling it into a car and drive off somewhere – anywhere – and never return. Even Manchester sounds pretty good right now. But Bentinck said the governors will want to talk to me tomorrow.

I mentally review their self-righteous faces. Will they take my word over that of Simon and Adam? How much will three successful years of teaching at St Jude's count for when it comes to the crunch? I don't believe I've done anything questionable during those years, but Bentinck doesn't like me much.

It occurs to me that Graham Staples would speak up for me, and I reach for my phone.

Ten minutes later, I switch it off again after speaking to Jenna, Graham's eldest daughter. Graham and Martha will be away until after Christmas. Their daughter-in-law is expecting a baby next month in Hong Kong, so they've gone over to help. They plan to stay on and spend Christmas in the sunshine, and Jenna's going out for two weeks as well. Everyone's so excited, she told me. Everyone except me, I thought, asking her to send my good wishes to Alicia and Paul. No, I said, in answer to her query, nothing special. I just wanted to say hi and see how retirement was working out.

And that's pretty much that. I pick up the phone again and dial Nicole, but there's no answer. I've been waiting all afternoon for her to call. I hope she hasn't heard about the incident and decided to avoid me. Perhaps Bentinck is keeping it quiet until after tonight's meeting.

I have a quick flash of hope that he may not have said anything to the staff because he expects nothing to come of this meeting. It could be a formality – another load of red tape to be gone through to keep the school on the right side of all the regulations. I may be back on Monday morning, with no one the wiser. My class knows about it, but they don't know what happened in Bentinck's office, and they've all seen Simon like this before. If he's suspended, as he really ought to be for attacking a pupil and a teacher, that would vindicate me.

Buoyed by this line of thought, I fill the kettle and get out the coffee. This will all work out in the end. It has to. Vague, absurd images flicker through my mind – me giving an interview to the tabloids and Bentinck being pilloried. Even better, the governors voting en masse to give me my job back and suspend Bentinck. I push away the memory of Charles' brick-red face and piggy eyes. Everyone hates him anyway.

But other thoughts soon force their way in. I imagine Bentinck calling me before the board to fire me; Simon and his parents going on television to claim assault; staff members avoiding my eye as I clear out my pigeonhole; Mum's face when I tell her I've lost my job, my boyfriend and maybe my house, all in one go. The images stream across the inside of my tightly closed eyelids, and the voices ring in my ears.

The doorbell rings, and I walk to the front door and peer through the spy hole in case it's a journalist. But it's Nicole. I open the door to see her holding a bottle of white wine in one hand and a paper bag in the other. I recognize the logo of our favourite Chinese takeaway. My stomach twists as I look at her, and my eyes prickle.

She dumps the bag on the doorstep and folds me into her arms. 'I've only just heard. Bentinck called a special staff meeting after school, but I was seeing a parent. Stupid man – what's he done to you?'

She shepherds me down the hall and steers me into the lounge. I'm crying hard now, in great shuddering gulps, as the sheer enormity of it all hits me. The tears pour down my face as she sits me down and strokes my hair.

'It's ok, Anna, we'll sort it out,' she says gently. 'I promise we'll get it fixed.'

I look through swollen eyes at her wavering outline. 'It isn't ok, Nicole. You know it isn't. I'm in real trouble here. What on earth am I going to do?'

We talk long into the night. We finish the wine Nicole has brought, followed by what's left of a box of red she digs out of my kitchen cupboard. Matt brought it over a few weeks ago along with a bunch of boring science fiction films. I stared at the screen without seeing them and worked my way through the wine while planning my dream holiday in France.

I've always wanted to sit in the sunshine at pavement cafes, sipping café au lait and watching the chattering crowds. But Matt can never get a holiday in the middle of summer, which leaves me free each year to plan the kind of holiday I'd love but will never get around to taking.

I didn't think I could eat anything, but Nicole has brought sweet and sour pork balls, and I'm suddenly starving. She doesn't have any specific suggestions, but listening to her opinion of Bentinck, couched in the sort of language I'm always too embarrassed to use, makes me feel a lot better.

By midnight, she has the wine box disembowelled and is coaxing a final half glass from the silver bag as we sketch out possibly slanderous versions of Bentinck's private life. If he has the place bugged, we're toast. Nicole tips the overflowing waste paper bin upside down to show me where the Mafia hid tiny microphones in a film she once saw.

She ends up staying over. Neither of us is in a state to remember how to use a phone to get her a taxi. She crashes on the sofa at about two o'clock, where she snores heavily for the rest of the night. Although I hardly sleep, it's nice to know there's someone friendly in the house.

Chapter Six

I wake with a start as the front door clicks shut. Nicole must have left for school. The morning light is forcing its way through my bedroom curtains, and the rain is thudding on the roof and inside my head. I groan, then roll over and sit up. I smell last night's takeaway and have to decide between rushing to the bathroom to throw up or rolling over and dying. Rolling over wins, so I curl up in a ball on the bed, pushing my face into the pillow and whimpering.

After what seems like several more hours, I force myself upright and tiptoe towards the kitchen in search of caffeine. I fill the coffee maker and poke around in the cupboard until I remember I meant to buy more filter papers at the weekend. A piece of kitchen roll does the trick, and I dreamily watch the coffee drip into the jug, keeping time with the rain spattering on the window.

The milk is two days past its use-by date and glugs into the mug, splitting into layers as it hits the hot liquid and spitting grease around the surface. I can't find any sugar, so I stir in a spoonful of honey until the contents of the cup are spinning fast enough to look almost drinkable, then tip it down my throat.

The caffeine trickles into my bloodstream, and the headache eases itself to the back of my head, where it settles, no longer pounding but whispering that it *will* be back if I don't treat it nicely. I discover some orange juice in the fridge and drink it straight from the carton. It glides icily down my throat, and my head clears even more.

As the hangover eases its insistent clamour, thoughts of yesterday's fiasco push forward to take its place. I'm usually very good at displacing unwelcome thoughts, but this disaster is something I'll have to think about soon. I decide to take a shower first.

Thirty minutes later, damp but clean, I creep outside and discover the light is still surprisingly painful, despite the thick grey clouds and rain. Daisy is in one of her moods, so I slosh through the streets to the bus stop and catch a bus into town. I no longer plan on hiding. I've done nothing wrong, and I'll go out whenever I want. Any students I run into in the town centre on a weekday will almost certainly be playing truant and will be even less eager to see me than I am to see them. I've bumped into a few of them in the past in places they have no business to be. They have an amazing ability to slide up side streets and down alleyways in the short time it takes me to look blank and decide not to recognise them.

I trudge around my favourite shops for a while. It feels strange to be out of school during term time, and I catch myself looking over my shoulder in case a parent spots me. The rain doesn't let up, and after two hours of window shopping, I'm fed up. When I find myself outside a travel agency, I push through the door and drip for a while on the mat. My eyes drift around the shelves, taking in the hundreds of brochures, all bright as Lego blocks.

I catch the assistant's eye, and she waves me towards the red chair in front of her desk.

'Good morning! Do sit down. What a dreadful day to be out shopping – but a wonderful day to be booking a holiday,' she adds, showing me gums as pink as her lipstick as she laughs.

I stare through the steamed-up windows at the rain sizzling onto the pavement outside and have to agree. It's stuffy in here and far too bright, so I shade my eyes with my hand.

'How can I help you today?' she shrieks, and I wince.

This is like one of those dreams where I haven't revised for my final exams. Worse still, we've reached the end of the school year and Bentinck says I've forgotten to teach any of this year's syllabus. At least, I seem to be fully clothed in this dream. But what am I doing in this shop, and what do I want?

I have a momentary impulse to pose as a millionaire looking for an exotic break, but my scuffed shoes will give me away. This woman seems the sort who's already priced my outfit and found it wanting. Her makeup is thickly but expertly applied, and every highlight is in its blow-dried place. She's obviously someone whose own life is sorted to her entire satisfaction.

'I have a few weeks free,' I begin. 'I mean, I may have. I thought I might get away somewhere for a bit.'

She shows me all her teeth again, swinging the screen towards her and tapping furiously.

'What a marvellous idea! It's definitely the time of year for it. You've left it a *little* late, but we must be able to find you something nice. Are you travelling alone?'

'Yes, I suppose so.'

She flashes me a quick look. I'm sure she thinks my husband has left me, and I suspect her sympathies would be with him.

'Here we are!' she says. 'Our special last-minute offers for November. Sunshine or snow?'

'I'm sorry?' I say, dragging my attention away from a poster of a tanned, rippling James Bond figure diving into the Mediterranean while bikini-clad blondes admire his muscles.

'Are you looking for sunshine or would you like to try skiing or snowboarding?' she repeats more briskly, although her lipsticked smile is still in place.

'Not snow!' I say quickly. 'I hate cold weather. I like quiet places with lots of sunshine and no one pestering me to go sightseeing all the time.'

'All right, let's see what we have here,' she says. 'Hmmm … we have a few cheap rooms down on the Costa del Sol. There's some wonderful nightlife down there. All our customers say so.'

'*Well* ...' I say, but not before she's seen my horrified grimace and taken offence. 'I'm sorry, but I don't like nightclubs. Do you have somewhere quieter – but still hot and sunny?'

'Ibiza?' she hazards.

I pull another face, then try to turn it into a smile. 'Perhaps something more scenic – with flowers and mountains, or forests?'

She gives me an odd look. 'Not at this time of year – at least not short haul. We have plenty of long haul destinations. What's your budget, by the way?'

'I haven't quite decided,' I say. 'About four hundred pounds, maybe?'

My bank manager will have a fit. I'm already heavily overdrawn.

She taps her pearly nails on the desk and sighs. 'You won't get very far on four hundred pounds. You won't find many mountains and forests, especially with the single supplement to pay.' She stresses the word *single* with a tiny smirk. 'Have you thought about a couple of days in Paris? You could go to Disneyland. Perhaps you could look at the late-booking websites.'

In the end, we agree that I'll take her brochures of Spanish holiday resorts and consider them carefully. She ushers me out of the door, probably wanting to make sure I leave. Once outside, I dump the brochures into the nearest bin and catch the bus home. My attempt to escape hasn't been a success, and it looks as though I'll still be here, freezing and unemployed, when the winter comes.

I spend the rest of the day lying on the sofa, watching the rain streaming down the windows. I'm too stressed to cook, so I nibble the last of the Belgian chocolates Matt bought me for my birthday. I ate all the liqueurs first, so now I'm left with the boring, healthy fruit ones. But it's too much effort to forage for anything else.

My phone rings at four o'clock. It's Lesley, and I can tell at once that she's embarrassed.

'Anna, it's Lesley here. He'd like to see you first thing tomorrow morning. Could you come in at seven thirty?'

Seven thirty? I'm usually in the shower at that time, slumped against the tiles with my eyes closed against the stream of water. After the way he's treated me, Bentinck has to be kidding. I'm not getting up early for him or anyone else. One perk of my suspension is that I can stay up late and sleep it off. The only perk really, I think, trying to ignore thoughts of my bank imbalance.

'I can't make it at that time,' I say. 'I have an appointment with my union rep first thing tomorrow.'

I'm surprised how easy it is to lie. I don't know where the idea of a union rep came from. Chance – and forethought, Mum says in my ear – would be a fine thing.

There's a second's silence at the other end, and I feel slightly mean. This is nothing to do with Lesley.

'I can see him now if he likes – I mean in about an hour,' I correct myself, glancing in the hall mirror at my unbrushed hair and over-sized sweatshirt I got free from a conference, which predictably blares in orange letters – *Education, Education, Education.*

'I'll just check with him …' She tails off, to be replaced by *Greensleeves.* I imagine her telling Bentinck about my meeting with the union. I like to think he's looking worried, but I doubt it. The man doesn't have an insecure bone in his body.

She breaks into the music mid-flow. 'Anna? That's lovely. He's in the office until six doing paperwork, so he says to come in anytime between five and six.'

'I'll see if I can make it,' I say curtly and ring off, feeling a stab of guilt at taking it out on her.

I slouch to my bedroom and look around for a clean outfit. The jeans I'm wearing are spotted with the remnants of last night's party and smell faintly of Kung Pao chicken. I drag a less stained pair from the back of my wardrobe and am pleased to discover a forgotten sweater lurking there. I bought it last year in the winter sales and was planning to return it, but I lost the receipt.

Five minutes later, I snatch up my keys from the flowered china tray Matt bought for me to keep them in. He said if I added it all up, I probably waste six or seven hours a year looking for my keys.

If Daisy doesn't start again, I'm ringing Bentinck and calling this off. I refuse to stand in the rain waiting for a bus, just to brave further humiliation. But the thought of him dropping in here on his way home makes me think better of cancelling. The pile of washing up in the sink is higher than usual, and there's only a narrow walkway between the stacks of magazines and yesterday's takeaway boxes. There's also a faint smell coming from the washer dryer. I programmed it to wash two days ago but forgot to add the *dry* cycle.

I stuff the bus timetable into my pocket just in case, and tumble out into the rain, where Daisy surprises me by starting first time in a supportive way. I give her gear stick a grateful pat. Despite this initial boost, I hit the rush hour traffic as I come out of the estate. I crawl through each light and queue at all the roundabouts with Daisy's wipers slashing ineffectually at the onslaught.

I plunge into Bentinck's office at five o'clock with my hair straggling down my collar and my air of injured dignity somewhat dented. He raises flinty eyes from his paperwork and gives me his version of a smile – lips turning up a few degrees and cheeks slightly bunched. I'm pleased to see Charles Freeman isn't here.

I'm happy to be spared the sight of his puffy face and knowing smirk.

Bentinck gestures towards the silvery pot of coffee that always sits on his desk, but I shake my head. I'm not accepting anything from him except an apology.

'How are you, Anna?' he asks in a pleasant tone.

I can't help gaping at him in the way my year nine pupils do when I ask them for something impossible, such as turning in a piece of work by the following day without the dog, the baby or the printer eating it. I give him a dignified nod, which could mean anything. I'll let him do most of the talking.

He doesn't give me the pleasure of looking discomfited. The guy's a robot.

'You will be pleased to hear that I've talked over this unfortunate affair with the Board of Governors,' he begins. 'They all agree with me that this is not a serious enough matter for us to proceed further. I've spoken again with various members of your class and gained a better understanding of the events of yesterday. It seems there were many extenuating circumstances, which all lend weight to my decision not to take matters further.

I have also spoken to Simon's mother and given her a somewhat fuller picture. She and I have agreed there should be no further action taken against either you or Simon, so the matter rests there. I'm sure you concur?'

The only thing that stops me from jumping from my seat and lunging at him across the desk is the adrenaline pouring through my body. It weakens my arms and legs enough to keep me pinned to my chair. Bentinck may be preoccupied with drawing a line under the incident, but he's unlikely to overlook a pot of hot coffee poured over his head.

I glare at him while I struggle for words. He sits there, his pale eyes glinting behind his tinted glasses and his hands relaxed on the desk without a trace of tension or worry. The thought of what this insufferable man has put me through over the past couple of days surges up into my throat, almost choking me.

'Are you now saying I *wasn't* to blame, Mr Bentinck?' I ask at last.

I'm determined to make him squirm if I can manage it. But there's no hope of that. His eyelids don't even flicker.

'What I am saying is that your actions, while not what I would have hoped for from a more experienced teacher, were apparently provoked by most unacceptable behaviour on the part of this pupil. While your own behaviour was not entirely appropriate, it must be interpreted in the context of this incident and excused. The governors and I are prepared to overlook this and hope very much that we can now move on, having perhaps all learned a lesson here?'

The urge to slap him doesn't subside, but I feel the familiar sense of hopelessness descend on me as I stare at his pallid face. It would take a stronger personality than mine to dent his brand of spectacular self-righteousness.

I open my mouth to ask when he wants me to start work again and am taken aback to hear my voice coming from a long way off, shaky but clear.

'Actually, Mr Bentinck, I don't think I've learned any kind of lesson except that the one person who ought to be supporting his staff has no intention of doing anything of the kind. You're arrogant and smug, and you've never given me the slightest encouragement in my job. The only reason I stayed here when Graham Staples left is because I like the children – well, most of them. And I enjoy working with the staff – well, some of them. It's been no fun working here since you arrived, and it won't be as long as you're still here, so you can have my resignation, effective as of now.'

My brain takes a few seconds to catch up with what my mouth has just said. What have I done? What will I do if he takes me seriously? I suddenly realise I want him to. If he ignores me and allows me to talk myself into staying, I know I'll regret it.

He doesn't blink. 'Am I to understand you are resigning as of Christmas?'

Not even an attempt to talk me round? I thought he might have taken a nanosecond to realize what he was losing, but clearly not.

I lift my chin, staring straight at him. 'No, Mr Bentinck. You may understand I'm resigning as of today. I assume you will waive my notice period, given that if I and my union decide to take you to court over this, you could be in considerable trouble.'

I hope he doesn't realise I'm not in a union and don't have the faintest idea of my legal position. He stares back at me, and I can almost see his brain ticking away under his greying hair. A minute slides past, and I maintain eye contact, refusing to let my mind have any say in what's happening. I'll think about the implications of this later. Right now, my body is buzzing, and I feel able to take him on in any court of the land and have him convicted and put away for several years. A good lawyer would surely find *something*.

'Very well,' he says at last. 'Under the circumstances, I think the governors will agree to waive your notice period. I find it most unfortunate that you feel this way, and I don't believe your action is in any way justified, but we will take steps to replace you at once. Make an appointment with Lesley to sort out the relevant paperwork.'

He stands and extends his hand. I consider refusing it, but that seems petty. We exchange a quick handshake, and I wonder whether his hands are always this icy. I walk down the stairs, refusing to think about what I've just done. My legs are miraculously steady as I drive home.

I manage to crash on the sofa before it hits me. I've cut myself loose from everything that's stable in my life. I have an ex-boyfriend with hurt feelings, a mortgage I have no means of paying after next month, and a bank loan for a car that only starts every other day. I try to focus on these things, but it's no use.

A bubble is forming in my chest, which forces itself out in a sudden burst of laughter. I may be unemployed, but I'm free. Given the reference I expect Bentinck to write me, it's unlikely

I'll find another job at once, so there's a possibility I'll lose both my house and my car.

However, there's also the faint possibility I might make a completely new life for myself, which seems to me a very fair exchange.

Chapter Seven

The alarm shrieks through my brain at seven o'clock on Wednesday morning. I thump my phone and stuff it under my pillow before realising I set the alarm for a reason. I'd love to sleep in, but I'm unemployed now and need to spend today job hunting. Thankfully, yesterday's rain has cleared, and the morning is fresh and bright.

I took a quick look through the Times Educational Supplement last night. I didn't see anything local except the usual desperate plea from St. Catherine's for a teacher – any teacher – not necessarily a fully qualified one. They just want someone who's prepared to turn up most days to baby sit the thugs and vandals who make up their quota of little darlings. The successful candidate must be adept at dodging missiles and flying chairs and ignoring comments about their possible parentage.

Not that they worded it quite like that.

This is a great opportunity for a newly qualified teacher to gain experience in a stimulating, sometimes challenging, environment. Friendly, supportive staff will assist your development, and ongoing training is a priority to enhance teaching skills and methods.

The staff probably *is* very supportive and friendly for the one or two terms it takes for them to burn out and decide that fighter pilots and bomb disposal experts enjoy rather more pay and rather less stress. I'll sell my house and live in a box before I take a job at that school.

I leave the house, rush back to retrieve Daisy's key from its stupid china dish, and drive into town. I skirt around my fellow shoppers and make my way through a series of side streets to the Job Centre Plus. The *Latest Information* window looks encouraging. Dozens of snowy white cards have been neatly arranged into *Temporary* and *Permanent* employment opportunities.

I waste quite a bit of time on the temporary ones, which feel more appealing just now. I study the lists of required skills. I don't know shorthand, and I can only type ten words a minute, but I'm really good at Candy Crush. I can also decipher long words containing only two correct consonants and no apparent vowels. This isn't a common skill, so I could be an invaluable PA to an illiterate Managing Director whose dog chews all his reports.

I read the ads for a while, soaking up the abbreviations so I don't sound too stupid. I push through the door, take a deep breath and approach the young girl sitting at the nearest desk and typing into her computer. I wish I could type that fast. I might get her job.

I give her my most confident smile. 'Hello, I'm looking for a job. Well, obviously I am, or I wouldn't be here. I have a variety of skills and a fair bit of experience –'

She flicks me a contemptuous look, cutting me off mid-sentence. 'Take a ticket.' Her fingers flutter as fast as ever.

'Right, brilliant, absolutely!'

I move away, wondering why I'm talking like someone from an Enid Blyton book – *Anna Flunks the Lower Fourth.*

I pull ticket number 86 from the machine, hoping it will be a winning number for me. The man behind me wrenches out a ticket, ripping it in the process. He tugs impatiently until the next one emerges, then stuffs it into his pocket.

'Like a ruddy cheese counter!' he snaps.

He moves away before I can give him more than half of a sympathetic smile. He's wearing a nice grey suit and a smart tie, and I wonder why he's here. He may have elderly parents to support, or his wife may be pregnant with twins. I suddenly stop feeling sorry for myself. At least, I only have myself and Daisy to worry about.

The numbers crawl up through the seventies while I leaf through the booklets telling me about the hundreds of allowances for which I do not and never will qualify – so don't even think about it! I try not to stare too hard at the depressed huddle of humanity slumped in the surrounding chairs. There's an incredible fug building up in here. The windows are steaming up, and the place has started to smell like the dining hall at my primary school. Not as cabbagey perhaps but with the same lingering scent of general hopelessness.

Someone calls my number, and I look up to see a lanky woman with a pleasant smile. She gestures me towards one of the booths at the edge of the room. We introduce ourselves, and I give her a quick rundown of everything that's happened over the past forty-eight hours. She looks horrified. Encouraged by her sympathy, I enlarge a little on the horrors of life under Bentinck.

Her eyes widen even more. 'I thought it was bad enough working here! You poor thing. No wonder you don't want to go back. Couldn't you take some legal advice? It sounds like unfair dismissal, and you don't always need a union for that.'

I shake my head. 'He offered me my job back, and I didn't lose any pay, so I don't think that would work. Anyway, I don't want another teaching job. I want to do something completely different. Do you have anything suitable for me?'

She frowns and taps at her computer. 'I'll print out what I've got, but none of these jobs pay half as well as your last one. The problem is that you're voluntarily unemployed, so you won't get any benefits for at least six months. It's a pity you have no transferable skills. We have plenty of temp positions, but you need Word and Excel. You could probably go on a course.'

I think about this, but the matter of my mortgage weighs too heavily. I'm fairly sure my bank manager will see me as the author of my own misfortunes and won't be too sympathetic about my non-payment of the mortgage next month.

'I'd rather not do that if I can avoid it,' I say. 'I'd like to find something this week if possible.'

She prints out everything she thinks might be within my limited skill range, and I promise to hunt online too.

I spend the afternoon reading the information she gave me and poring over the local free newspapers. There are several cleaning jobs in the classified ads. I have no objection, but the clients may when they discover how inept I am.

I read an ad from a professional couple who need a replacement nanny right away – experience essential – for their charming three-year-old twin sons and adorable nine-month-old daughter. I wonder why their current nanny left so suddenly but mark it as a possible.

Next, I call a tutoring company, who are looking for remedial maths and English tutors throughout the city – own transport required. I suppose Daisy might count.

The woman I speak to is pleasant enough, but she tells me I'll need references from my last place of employment. She asks me why I left St Jude's, and I ramble on for a while about feeling the need for a change of pace while remaining deeply committed to education in general. I finish my prepared speech when I realise I'm not convincing either of us.

I'm desperate enough to ring and ask about a position as a trainee estate agent – evenings and weekends required – but the man who answers tells me they want a school leaver with good typing and computer skills. It's obvious he wants an office slave at minimum wage, but I feel I've hit rock bottom when no one will even accept me as a trainee.

By Saturday evening, I've applied for seventeen jobs online and called to enquire about eleven more. By Sunday lunchtime, I'm in complete despair. I've had fifteen automated computer rejections, all thanking me for my interest in various positions, which have now been filled. The car hire firm has gone bust, and the Italian restaurant has put my application on file. Apparently, they had twenty-three applications from students happy to work for minimum wage. I tell the proprietor I might be happy to work for less than that, but he just laughs and rings off.

Nicole calls after school the following day. 'Have you changed your mind about coming back?'

Even though I've vowed never to return, it would make everything much easier. I'd have a guaranteed salary again, and I wouldn't have to break the news of my unemployment to Mum. I'd also know what I was doing when I got out of bed the next morning.

'No,' I say at last. 'I'm not coming back, and I'm not staying in teaching either. So, if Bentinck's asking, he can get stuffed.'

She snorts at the thought. 'He isn't. He already has a supply teacher in, and I know she's looking for permanent work. You'd better hurry if you're thinking of changing your mind.'

Bentinck's pale, disapproving face hovers over me like a miasma, but I ignore it. 'No, I've had it with him and with teaching. I want to find something I really enjoy doing.'

'Good for you,' she says. 'If that's the case, I'll come and see you this evening. I'll pick up a couple of pizzas and be there around seven. Don't make any firm plans for your future before then.'

She turns up at 7.30pm, clutching two steaming pizzas and another bottle of wine. We dive straight in and eat for a few minutes without talking. It isn't until I've poured us both a second glass of wine that my curiosity gets the better of me.

'Spill!' I say. 'What do you have planned for my life?'

She wipes her fingers on a paper napkin. 'Listen for a moment, will you, without biting my head off?'

Great! This will be another of Nicole's wonderful ideas, like the one she had after our staff Christmas party. She wanted us to resign from teaching and start a lingerie home business, with the pair of us acting as models. In her defence, it had been a grim party, and she was pretty drunk.

'Let's hear it,' I say, tucking my legs under me and preparing myself for a new career as a skydiving instructor.

She takes a slug of wine. 'I was talking to my landlady last night. You've met Lynn, haven't you? Anyway, she wanted to know when term ends. Her mother lives in New Zealand, but she'd been staying with Lynn for a couple of months. She's going home next week, and she needs someone to accompany her. She's in a wheelchair, and she can't travel alone. Whenever she comes over to visit Lynn, she pays someone to fly back with her. They take care of her on the journey and have a holiday before they come back. It's a brilliant deal for a student or anyone who just wants some cheap travel. Anyway, the girl who was taking her back has pulled out, and Lynn's mother is stuck. I'd jump at it, but we have five more weeks of term. So, I thought of you.'

She looks at me with the air of a conjuror who's just pulled a gold coin from behind my ear.

'But what does all that have to do with me?' I ask.

'You get a free trip to New Zealand!'

I'm genuinely puzzled. 'But why would I want to go there?'

Nicole wriggles her shoulders in annoyance. 'I *knew* you'd be like this. It's a wonderful opportunity. You have nothing to do right now. This woman will pay your fare, and you get to go somewhere interesting. What on earth is your problem?'

I open my mouth, but I'm not sure where to start. My mortgage, my car payments, my job hunting. Lurking at the back of it all is the spectre at the feast – my mother.

'I can't,' I say. 'Not right now. You must see that.'

'If not now, when?' she demands. 'Next year, when you have some dead-end job and can't get time off to travel? When someone leaves you a fortune and you can pay your own fare? When your mother dies?'

I sit bolt upright and glare at her. 'That's a horrible thing to say!'

She has the grace to flush. 'I didn't mean it like that. But what exactly are you waiting for?'

'I don't know,' I say hopelessly. 'I have no idea what I want to do with the rest of my life. I feel as though I'm drifting, but I can't stop.'

She claps her hands. 'And where better to spend some time doing all that thinking than New Zealand? You can sit on the beach in the sunshine and make plans. It's spring over there,' she adds temptingly.

I suppose it must be spring if they're upside down from us. I have a cousin called Mike, who lives in Australia. He sends us Christmas cards with pictures of Santa in tight Speedos, barbecuing reindeer steaks, with Mrs Claus pouting beside him in a string bikini.

Mum doesn't approve of Mike. His father was Dad's younger brother, and he and Mum didn't get on well even before he took his family to Melbourne. But she always sends his children a traditional snow scene, pursing her lips as she signs it. She's never seemed particularly keen on Christmas. But she likes everything done properly, which means snow at Christmas, not sun and sea – and definitely not string bikinis.

I'm not sure I could even find New Zealand on a map. I know it isn't too far from Australia, but that's all. And I don't care where it is. I speak firmly before Nicole can come up with three hundred reasons why I can't turn this down.

'It's impossible right now. I have to earn some money straight away or I'll lose the house.'

'Sell it!' She interrupts so quickly that it's clear she's thought of my possible objections and carefully planned her ambush.

'I'm not selling it,' I say. 'I like it, and it took me ages to get my own place. It was almost impossible to find somewhere I could afford near Mum.'

'I knew you'd feel like that,' she says. 'Then I'll rent it from you while you're away. Lynn isn't too bothered about having a lodger now. Her daughter's moving in with her after her divorce, and she could do with the extra room. I'll live here and pay your mortgage. It's a better location than where I am now, and I can afford it.'

She gives me a challenging stare, daring me to object.

I stare back. 'It isn't just that. I still have payments due on Daisy.'

'Sell her! She never starts, anyway. Put an ad in the local paper or sell her back to the garage before she packs up or kills you.'

I ignore the jibe at Daisy. 'And there's the small matter of a job. This woman might be paying my airfare, but she isn't offering me employment. How am I supposed to live all winter?'

'I've thought of that too.' Nicole sounds pleased with herself. 'There's plenty of fruit picking work in the spring. I had a boyfriend at university who did that, and he said it was the best year of his life.'

'I'm not a student,' I remind her. 'That sort of thing is great when you have no responsibilities, but you must see it's impossible for me. There's Mum, for one thing ...'

I trail off, realising I'll never convince Nicole.

'Is that all?' she asks. 'None of these things would stop you if it wasn't for her?'

'I suppose not, if you're so set on it. But she needs me to do her shopping and cleaning and check up on her.'

Nicole grins. 'What you really mean is that she wants unpaid household help. What's stopping her from paying someone? She isn't hard up, is she?'

This is true. Dad put a good chunk of his salary into life insurance to take care of Mum if he went first. She never seems to spend any money, so it's probably still intact in the bank or, knowing Mum, under the floorboards.

Nicole watches me with an amused smile as I try but fail to think of further excuses.

'That's all sorted,' she says at last. 'We'll find her someone to help around the house, and I'll call around twice a week after school in case there's anything else she needs.'

This is surreal. Nicole and Mum have never got along. As far as possible, I make sure they never accidentally meet. Mum disapproves of Nicole's loose morals and her influence on me. I imagine her face when Nicole announces she'll be popping by twice a week.

Nicole interprets my quick grin correctly. 'She'll be fine. She just needs to see more of me to appreciate my finer qualities. You'll both survive. It may even do the pair of you some good.'

I want to say no. There are a thousand reasons why this could never work. But I have to admit to a tiny flicker of excitement at the idea of dropping everything and travelling somewhere unknown. I've never done anything like that. Perhaps it's time I did.

Nicole gathers the pizza boxes together. 'Don't think about it too long or you'll talk yourself out of it before you've even begun. I have to go now. I'm meeting Marcus and Sara for a drink. I'll give you twenty-four hours to decide. I'll come round tomorrow evening, and we'll fix everything up. If you haven't come up with ten good reasons why you shouldn't go, I'm packing your bag myself. Sitting around feeling sorry for yourself is no longer an option.'

She pauses with her hand on the door handle. 'Remember, the clock is ticking!'

I spend the whole of the following day thinking and arguing with myself. This is such a ridiculous idea. If Nicole wants someone to go with this woman, why doesn't she give in her notice and go herself? I look at a map and locate half of New Zealand. Part of the east coast has been sliced off along the edge of the page. It doesn't look too far away until I count all the countries between it and the UK. This plan makes no sense.

When Nicole turns up again the next evening, I'm ready for her.

She bounces in and flops onto the sofa. 'Well?'

'Fine, thanks,' I say. 'How about you? Did you have a good day at school?'

'Don't mess with me,' she warns. 'I took your year ten girls for a cross country run this afternoon. Thanks for that, by the way. I planned a route using only the side roads, but Hannah Birken still fell into a stream halfway around, and yours truly had to pull her out. You owe me a new pair of trainers.'

'I've been thinking about your suggestion all day,' I say. 'The thing is that I can't –'

'That isn't the thing!' she bursts out in frustration. 'There is no thing! Weren't you listening to a single word I said last night? You're so frustrating, Anna. I don't know why I bother.'

I let her huff herself to a halt. 'What I'm trying to say is that I can't think of any reason not to go –'

She doesn't let me finish as she bounces off the sofa, flinging her arms around me. 'You've finally seen sense! Don't do that again! I'm in a weakened condition after the run from hell, and I'll need a drink before I forgive you. Make that a very large drink – possibly two.'

We rootle through my kitchen cupboards. I dig out the remains of last Christmas' bottle of ginger wine, wondering how on earth I've overlooked it all summer. I love ginger wine, especially with After Eights dunked in it on chilly winter days. We wash it down with the last of the beer I kept for Matt. I've never liked beer, but he insists on imported, bottled lager. After the ginger, the beer tastes less like straw than usual, and we split the last three bottles.

'A toast!' says Nicole. 'To you, Anna – the mouse that roared. May you find everything you're looking for, and more.'

'Or even *what* I'm looking for,' I add, choking on an enormous swig of beer.

'To absent friends,' she carries on without noticing. 'To absent family. May this trip make *all* hearts grow fonder.'

I drink to that, although it occurs to me I ought to protest. I know perfectly well what Nicole means, but I make the toast anyway, waving my bottle at her and splashing some of it onto the sofa. Who cares? It's Nicole's sofa from now on. She can clean it.

'To present friends,' I say. 'May they never become past friends.'

I reach out to hug her, but she flushes and snatches the bottle out of my hand.

'No more for you!' she says. 'You're getting slushy, and there's work to do.'

We spend the evening going through the details. We don't discuss how long I'll be away or how Mum will take it. I'll think about all that later.

Nicole shows me the reservation, and I'm delighted to see that it's business class. If I'm starting a whole new life, it will be encouraging to start it in the lap of luxury, however it may end.

Chapter Eight

It's lucky that I have such a short time to prepare. With everything that needs doing, there's little chance to think about anything personal. My passport is up to date, and I don't need to apply for a visa, but there are plenty of other things I have to do.

I take Daisy to the garage where I bought her, and the owner offers me three hundred pounds. He tells me condescendingly that it would have been more, but I obviously haven't looked after her. Her gearbox needs changing, and the brake pads are shot.

I tell him that she can't have been in the amazing condition he claimed when he sold her to me only ten months ago. He sucks his teeth and looks as though I've insulted his mother.

'She was in perfect condition when I sold her, love! I serviced her myself. But it's always the same with women drivers. They crash the gears, then complain when they wear out. My wife's exactly the same.'

I'm surprised he even has a wife. But I need the money, so I bite my tongue as he shuffles off to his office to get the cash. I'm pretty sure Daisy will be back on the forecourt tomorrow for twice what he's given me, and I hope Bentinck buys her. Anyway,

I have enough to pay off what's left of my car loan. I feel a shamed sense of relief as I pat Daisy*'s* yellow bonnet goodbye.

I stop at Mum's house on the way home. I've been dreading this visit ever since I agreed to go to New Zealand, but it's no use putting it off any longer. It would be terrible if she found out from anyone else.

She opens the door after a few minutes. I kiss her and put my shoes on the rack. One of the many reasons she approved of Matt was that he always took his shoes off when he visited her. He reminded me to take off mine as well, with a grin that never failed to annoy me.

We go through to the living room and sit down facing each other.

'You're later than you said you'd be. Didn't you drive over?' she asks.

There will never be a better opportunity than this, so I clasp my fingers on my lap and take a deep breath. 'Actually, Mum, I've sold Daisy. I took her to the garage this morning.'

'Who's Daisy?' she asks.

She knows perfectly well who Daisy is. She just doesn't approve of giving names to inanimate objects. Her stroppiness calms me, and my hands stop shaking.

'Daisy is my car, as you know perfectly well. I've sold her for enough to pay off what I owe, so I was quite happy. She'd never have passed her MOT without a ton of work I couldn't afford.'

'Matt's car went straight through its MOT,' she says huffily. 'He takes such good care of his things.'

And his company paid twenty times as much for it, I think. But I don't want to antagonise her further.

'Shall we have a drink?' I suggest. 'I can put the kettle on.'

'I've just had a cup of tea,' she says. 'I don't drink more than one. You know that.'

I feel the familiar grinding sensation in my stomach. How was I supposed to know she'd just had one? I bet she hasn't, anyway.

'I think I'll have one,' I say, leaving the room before she can object.

When I return with a cup of tea I don't want, my stomach knots itself again, and the cup jiggles in its saucer. Mum won't have mugs in the house because they're common.

She observes me closely as I pretend to take a sip. She's one of those people who are perfectly comfortable with silences. I hate them and rush to fill them with the sort of breathless gabble that makes me hate myself, even as the inanities pour out.

As a child, I dropped my eyes under her flinty gaze, feeling the familiar burning sensation creep up my neck before confessing to things she had no idea had even happened. I give myself a mental shake. I've done nothing wrong, and anyone other than Mum would agree.

'I have something to tell you,' I say, dropping my shoulders and holding my chin high so I can look Mum straight in the eye, just as Nicole has been coaching me all week.

She doesn't miss a beat. 'You're pregnant.'

I feel a rush of welcome anger. 'I'm not pregnant, *Mum*!' I bite out the last word, pleased to see her look startled. 'Stop assuming the worst of me every damn time!'

Her mouth opens to make her usual protest at my bringing the language of the gutter into her house, but she closes it again, which is a good start.

'I wouldn't have minded,' she says after a long pause. 'Matthew would always do the right thing. He's trustworthy like that.'

'We aren't talking about St. Matt!' I flare.

I have to get this back on track before she seizes the initiative again. I hurry on. 'I need to tell you about a few things that have happened to me over the past couple of weeks. Quite a lot of things, actually. Everything seemed pretty bad at first, but I think it's all going to work out for the best.'

I flicker my gaze towards her, but she has her face well under control, her lips pulled into their usual drawstring shape. 'Like a cat's bum,' Nicole said when she used to pick me up to go out in the evenings. She seemed to gain colour and animation as she bounced into the house, greeting Mum with enough vitality to make her wince and sigh. It was a relief when I bought Daisy and we could meet elsewhere.

I try again. 'Last Monday, two of my year eight pupils started fighting before the lesson, and I broke it up. I had to use a fair amount of force to protect one boy, and the other one accused me of assault.'

I pause to allow her to comment, but her eyes are shuttered. I'm suddenly exhausted with the effort of wading through the treacle of Mum's passivity – always her most effective weapon.

'Anyway,' I say, 'I was put on paid leave while they sorted things out. In the end, they decided it wasn't my fault after all, and Bentinck said I could come back.'

I pause again to give her another chance to speak, but there's still no reaction. I drag some breath into my exhausted lungs, rubbing my eyes. 'But I don't want to go back there. This was just the push I needed to make me take stock and realise I'm not happy with my life.'

A twitch of her eyelid stops me, but she immediately has it under control.

'I've decided I'd like to try something else,' I finish in a rush. 'I don't know what, but I'm only twenty-six, and I haven't seen much of the world or done anything except school, university and teaching. So, I'm going to try something different for a while.'

I allow the silence to lengthen into a palm-sweating aeon, hoping to smoke her out. Her predictable lack of reaction makes my muscles shrivel as I wait for the storm – so much more effective after that oppressive, false calm.

'It's an argument for male teachers,' is her surprising opening gambit. This may be an attempt at sympathy, although given her usual condescending attitude towards my profession, I don't think so.

'Actually,' I burst out, 'it could have been worse with a man involved! He'd have been stronger than me, and it would have been easier to make an assault charge stick. Anyway, it had nothing to do with who was in the classroom. Anyone would have done what I did to protect a smaller boy from being beaten up by a larger one.'

'Perhaps,' she says primly. 'So, this new life you talk of. What does it really mean?'

My voice falters. 'It means I'm going away to try something new. I don't know exactly what, but that's what makes it exciting, don't you think?'

I have no idea why I add this. Of course, she doesn't think so. As usual, I'm arming her. I'm carefully picking through and selecting all my weaknesses and meekly handing them to her one by one – my need for her unobtainable approval, my self-doubt, my lack of direction.

'I can hardly comment on how exciting it is when you haven't told me a thing about it,' she says. 'What exactly, if I'm allowed to ask, is this new idea of yours?' Her voice is crisp and controlled, in contrast to mine.

'I've told you,' I say. 'I don't know yet. I'm going away somewhere for a while – not too long – and I'll see what comes up.'

'I see,' she says. 'And does this somewhere have a name?'

My stomach goes into free fall. 'Yes, actually – New Zealand.'

Her lips thin. 'Very funny.'

'No, it's true! I have … Nicole said … I mean, there's a woman called Miriam.'

I clear my throat and try again, provoked into lucidity by Mum's faint, antagonistic smirk.

'Nicole knows a woman who lives in New Zealand. At least, she spends all her summers there. She needs someone to help her on the journey home because she's in a wheelchair. So, she's paying for me to travel with her. It's a return ticket,and I plan to get myself a job out there and have a sort of working holiday before I come home. I'm looking forward to it.'

I'm sounding lamer by the moment, so I tail off and dig my nails into my palms. I've exposed all my weak spots in turn. This will be easy for her.

'I'd have to hear some more about it,' she says at last, 'but it sounds quite a good idea.'

I stare at her, bemused, all my carefully prepared arguments crashing down inside my head before I've had the chance to use them.

She frowns. 'Don't look at me like that, Anna. It's entirely your business what you do with your life. I'm perfectly aware of that. You don't seem to have thought it through very well, but if you aren't happy with what you're doing, you're young enough to try something else. I expect you'll soon see what you've lost.'

It isn't ideal, but it's some kind of a start. I stay for another hour, explaining the arrangements I've made for my house and adding that Nicole will be on call if Mum needs anything. Mum displays a marked lack of enthusiasm for this suggestion, but we gloss over it and talk a little about where I'll be going and how I plan to keep in touch. I leave as it's getting dark, and she startles me with a chilly hug on the doorstep.

Walking home in the cold night air, this whole idea feels increasingly ludicrous, and New Zealand seems more and more distant. But I've given my word to Miriam now, so there's nothing I can do. And, as Nicole reminds me each time we talk, I have a return ticket. If I still feel like this once I get there, I can turn around and fly straight home.

Chapter Nine

I meet Miriam at Heathrow. She's driving up with Lynn and her husband, and they won't have room for me with all Miriam's luggage. I'm quite pleased about this. I want to start this adventure alone, just to prove to myself I can do it.

By 9am, I'm standing in the hall with my backpack, feeling detached from everything around me and pleasantly light-headed. I'm not thinking of the past few days or what the next few weeks and months may hold.

Nicole has arrived to take me to the coach station. She probably wants to make sure I don't change my mind at the last moment. But I no longer want to.

'It's only a couple of flights,' she says for the hundredth time. 'You can be home again in a day.'

I smile at her anxious expression. 'I know. Shall we get going?'

We sling my bags into the back of her car and drive to the coach station in silence. The greyish mist has lifted, and there's a brightness behind the haze that promises a few dribs of watery sunshine later. My hands are cold, and I stuff them into my sleeves. I'm wearing the black cashmere sweater Matt bought me one winter after I complained of the cold, and its comforting softness warms my chilled hands.

Nicole parks at a crazy angle in the *No Parking* zone and jumps out. I tell her not to stay or she'll end up with a ticket, but she insists on coming into the terminal with me. It's only now that the enormity of everything hits me, and my eyes fill with tears. Nicole gives me an enormous hug, and I'm surprised to see that she too is close to tears.

She pats my back and pushes a package into my coat pocket. 'Take care. Call me, ok?'

'I'll get to Singapore at one o'clock in the morning,' I remind her. 'I'll call and wake you up.'

'Do that!'

She kisses my cheek and throws my backpack up the steps so I have to rush after it to rescue it. As the coach pulls away, the last thing I see is Nicole racing to the parking bay, frantically waving at a man in a peaked cap who's tugging a notebook from his pocket.

I reach into my pocket and pull out the package. Inside is a large cheese roll, a vodka miniature, and a note.

If I know you, you haven't eaten breakfast, so eat this now. The vodka is medicinal. Take at once to prevent motion sickness. Repeat similar dosage at regular intervals throughout your journey. Call me the minute you get a connection. I'll miss you so much. All my love, Nic xxx.

She's scribbled a cartoon picture of Bentinck in a cap and gown. Tears roll down his cheeks, and a thought bubble says, *'I'm most disappointed in you, Miss Richardson. What about the year ten girls?'*

This is the moment I wish I could get off the coach and go back home. But we're already pulling onto the motorway, and there's no turning back. I bite into my roll, realising with surprise how hungry I am. After washing it down with several sips of vodka, I feel better. I'm starting to look forward to the trip. If I don't like it, I can deliver Miriam, turn around and come straight back. Nicole would kill me, but it's comforting to know I have a return ticket in my pocket.

After all the emotion, and a series of sleepless nights, the vodka takes effect. I doze, only waking to hear the driver shout, 'Heathrow, Terminal 2! Five-minute stop only!'

The fog is thicker here, and a chilly wind curls around my ankles as I walk across the concrete. I look over my shoulder, wanting to wave goodbye to someone, but there's no one there. It's too cold to linger outside, so I walk through the sliding doors into the light and turmoil beyond.

I thought I'd left myself plenty of time, but it takes forever to locate the coffee shop where we've arranged to meet. I arrive out of breath to find Lynn and Mike sitting at a table with a woman with wavy, greyish hair and bright blue eyes.

I hold out my hand. 'Hi, I'm Anna. I hope I'm not late.'

The woman shakes my hand, smiling warmly. 'You aren't. Lynn always gets me here ridiculously early in case of problems. I can't rush anywhere, you see.'

I glance down at the yellow-handled sticks propped against the edge of the table. 'Lynn told me. I can help with anything you need. It's nice of you to buy my ticket.'

'I like having a companion when I travel,' she says. 'It stops Lynn worrying about me, and I enjoy the company. It's a long journey all by myself, and I've met some interesting people over the years.'

'I've never flown further than Spain,' I say, 'and always cattle class. This is all new to me.'

'Then we'll work it out together.' She really does have a lovely smile. It folds her face into a mass of crinkles, but they suit her.

'Would you like a coffee?' she asks, 'or something stronger?'

I pull out Nicole's empty bottle and show it to her. 'My friend gave it to me this morning. She seemed to think I might need it.'

'Your friend sounds very sensible,' she says.

I can't help smiling at this description of Nicole.

Miriam pulls out her purse. 'The least I can do is to buy you a coffee so you're sober enough to board the plane. What would I do if they left you on the tarmac?'

I laugh and accept. This trip could be more fun than I'd bargained for.

Three hours later, we're sitting in our seats waiting to take off, and I'm exhausted. It feels as though I've spent the entire day standing in queues. First, there was the luggage check and after that an endless wait at security and passport control. Miriam has several cases, all of which are surprisingly heavy. My luggage is simple – a back pack and a small suitcase. Nicole has tied a brightly patterned scarf around the suitcase handle so I can distinguish it from all the other battered dark blue cases at the other end. I'd never have thought of that.

I should have taken a gap year. Nicole back-packed around Australia and some of the Far East, teaching English in Thailand and Hong Kong when her money ran out. I'd planned to Interrail around Europe with my friends after our A levels. But after Dad died, I didn't want to leave Mum alone, even for a few weeks. There were so many missed opportunities. But I know I made the right decision then and hope against hope I've made the right decision now.

When we land in Singapore, I settle Miriam into her hotel room for the night. It takes a while because she's so tired. Several of the hotel staff offer to help, but Miriam has already told me she hates relying on strangers.

'I'm too independent for my own good,' she said with a rueful smile. 'Lynn gets upset with me, but you have no idea how frustrating it is to be so helpless.'

So, I struggle with the unfamiliar movements until I catch the trick of gently shifting her weight. It should be easier in the morning when we're both less exhausted.

Once she's settled, I wander down to the shopping area. My body is still on UK time, which means it's nearly 2am, but I don't feel ready to sleep. It doesn't matter. All the shops and restaurants are open.

I order a hot chocolate from the nearest coffee bar and sit on a bench in a tiny oasis with real palm trees. The sound of the water is soothing as it unwraps itself from the fountain and splashes into the pool below. My head is still buzzing from the relentless roar of air rushing over the wings. Miriam dozed for most of the flight, but I couldn't sleep. At first, I watched Europe slip past beneath us, but it soon became too dark to see much.

I sip my chocolate and look around. I still have a pleasant feeling of unreality, and I'd like to hang onto it. It isn't possible that Anna Richardson has packed in her job and her boyfriend, defied her mother and started off across the world with no idea of what she'll find when she arrives. That Anna Richardson feels like an entirely different person. Her life seems several worlds away – and pretty boring too.

I suppress the occasional twinge of panic as I remember this journey is an end in itself, and not a means to an end. Once we land and I get Miriam safely to her house, I'll never see her again. I'll be entirely on my own.

I've been offered a temporary job working at a campsite on South Island. One of Nicole's useful friends from her travelling days found it for me. But I don't know how well it will work out or what I'll do after that.

I decide to stop worrying about the things I can't control. I pick up my jacket and bag and wander towards the shops. A beautiful blonde girl is gesturing imperiously towards the Hermes shop. Her much older boyfriend looks bored but follows her inside. The assistant smiles and tosses gorgeous, multi-coloured scarves across the counter, where they land in a huddle of iridescent gossamer. The girl shakes her head impatiently at each one, and her eyes dart towards the bags on the glass shelves.

The assistant notices me hovering in the doorway, trying to get a better glimpse of the swirling patterns. Her experienced eyes have already flicked over my faded jeans and unbrushed hair, and she isn't about to acknowledge me. I could be a film star travelling incognito for all she knows. I toss my hair at her as I walk away.

I buy myself some aspirin and go back to my hotel room. The whirr of the air conditioning blends with the distant hammering of workmen, and I slip into darkness.

I arrive outside Miriam's door exactly on time the following morning. She still looks tired, but she greets me cheerfully and assures me she's slept as well as she ever does at this stage of the trip. It takes me a little while to help her wash and dress, but she's far less tired than she was last night, and she's able to use her sticks to cross the room. She sinks into her wheelchair, and we set off to find some breakfast.

She directs me to a cafe near the fountain, where we study the menu.

'I recommend the pancakes,' she says. 'They come with fresh fruit and the best maple syrup I've ever tasted.'

It's way past lunchtime as far as my stomach is concerned, so I'm happy to order pancakes and tall glasses of freshly squeezed orange juice. We finish our meal with cups of strong coffee. I'm wide awake now and thoroughly enjoying myself.

'It's refreshing travelling with you,' says Miriam. 'The last girl I travelled with looked up the calories in the pancakes in a little book she always carried. Then she complained to the server because she couldn't smoke. I had the feeling she couldn't wait to get rid of me.'

'I think it's wonderful,' I say. 'I've never been this far from home before, and it's exciting. Look at all these people!'

I gesture widely, and she pushes her cup out of the way.

'Sorry!' I say. 'But don't you think it's fun to wonder where they've all come from and where they might be going?'

Miriam looks around at our fellow diners. 'I'm convinced the women sitting at that table are on the run after a bank heist.'

I look at the elderly women. One of them is pursing her lips over the menu and jabbing a disapproving finger at the prices. She must be at least seventy-five. The other is clearly much older and frowns as she scrabbles in her bag for her reading glasses.

'I'm pretty sure you're right,' I say. 'And don't forget those two drug mules over there.'

I point towards a young couple, who are obviously on their honeymoon, if the pile of brand new luggage tucked around their legs is anything to go by. That, and the way they're leaning across the table, holding hands over their sticky plates of pancakes. They're completely engrossed in each other, and I sigh.

'What happened?' Miriam asks sympathetically.

She's very sharp. I shrug and start to make a flippant remark. But her expression shows she's genuinely interested, and it would be nice to talk to someone.

'His name is Matt,' I say. 'I've been with him on and off for years. I'm not really sure what happened. I suppose it got stale. He's reliable, and he has a good job, and he would never ever let me down.'

'My dear,' she interrupts, 'that all sounds very worthy, but how does he make you feel?'

'Old!' I say, without giving myself time to think. 'He treats me like a child most of the time, but he still makes me feel old. Does that make sense?'

'It does,' she says without hesitation. 'Why were you with him for so long?'

I feel embarrassed. 'Oh, I don't know. It's nice to have someone to go out with. He's kind, and he always seems to know what's best for me, even when I don't. It can be a relief to have someone else making all the decisions so you don't have to.'

Miriam traces maple syrup rings around her plate with her fork. 'Kind, reliable, nice, decisive – that's a list of qualities. But love isn't a list, is it? It's so much more. You know that, of course, or you wouldn't have broken up with him.'

'I didn't mean for us to break up,' I admit. 'Then again, I don't mean to do most of the things I do. They just seem to happen. I often wish I was a different sort of person. It might be more fun.'

She considers. 'I think we're only the people we are because we've been put into the circumstances of our own lives. If those circumstances were changed, we might have turned into someone entirely different.'

'That's why I'm going to New Zealand!' I say excitedly. 'I'm going to change my circumstances completely and find out who I really am and what I want to do.' I whirl my arms to illustrate my determination.

Miriam looks amused. 'That's rather ambitious for one quick trip. Most people need a lifetime to discover that. Even then, many of us never succeed.'

'I agree it's ambitious,' I say, 'but once I go home, I'll never have the chance again. There's Mum, you see.'

I come to an abrupt stop. I shouldn't have mentioned Mum. No one understands why she needs me to look after her.

'How old is your mother?' asks Miriam.

I hesitate. 'She's only fifty-nine. But she's a widow, and she has mild arthritis, and she can't cope by herself. I mean, she *really* can't. She's lost without my dad. I'm their only child, and I feel …'

I trail off, red-faced. This is why I don't talk about Mum.

'You feel you're all she has,' supplies Miriam. 'Of course, you do. That's perfectly natural. And does she feel the same?'

'I don't know what she thinks,' I admit. 'She was horribly understanding when I said I was coming on this trip, which only made it worse. I probably shouldn't have come, but I've told her I'll go home at once if she needs me.'

Miriam holds out her arm for me to help her into her wheelchair. 'That's all right, then. Can I just say you're a good girl, Anna, and she's a very lucky woman?'

I look away, muttering something incoherent.

She gestures towards the honeymoon pair. 'For your information – that couple you were envying. She's left her husband and eight children for him, and he only married her for a visa. Things are never what they seem.'

She laughs at my surprised expression. 'And now, back to the important things in life. Let's investigate those shops.'

Chapter Ten

I awake with a jolt fifteen hours later, feeling disorientated. Miriam is lying next to me, her blankets rising and falling as she snores. I switch on my seatback TV and flick through the channels until I find the map of our route. There's a dotted line showing how far we've come. The line appears to be motionless, but I check it again after each film or meal, and each creeping centimetre is a fresh thrill.

We're passing over the north-west coast of Australia, and I feel a throb of excitement. We're too high to be able to see much detail, but I spend the next few hours staring out of the window anyway. The sea falls away behind us, and I watch in fascination as the land beneath me turns gold and then red.

I imagine kangaroos chasing emus over the outback, or whatever it is they do. I've read about New Zealand and can now identify a kiwi at twenty paces, but I don't know much about Australia. Maybe I'll visit while I'm over here, I think in a sudden wave of adventurousness. I could camp under the stars in the outback and watch the sun set over the Indian Ocean. Right now, anything feels possible. Yesterday, I was in London, and now I'm halfway across the world, watching everything from miles up while no one down there knows I'm here.

I watch as we approach the east coast. There will be people swimming and surfing or simply watching the sun rise over the white beaches below. Someone may be lying on the sand at this moment, looking up and watching us trail brightly across the turquoise sky.

I feel Miriam stir and turn my head to see her watching me with a faint smile. 'You're very far away,' she says.

'I was trying to imagine what everyone is doing down there,' I say.

She peers over my shoulder at what looks like a long, curved piece of creamy string snaking away from us. It must be the surf curling over the beach. Only a few more hours to go, the steward tells me as he brings us yet more orange juice.

We finally sweep over the northern tip of New Zealand, across great swathes of starry tree ferns, tipped with palest green and coming into focus as we lose height. We twist and swoop over a sparkling sheet of water. The wheels peel down the runway, and the wing tip bounces and shivers, spinning brilliant sunshine off its leading edge.

When the other passengers have disembarked, a steward appears with Miriam's folded wheelchair. We sweep through the airport on an electric buggy and join the queue for immigration. I'm fascinated by the enormous screens above us, showing films of staggeringly beautiful scenery that surely can't be real. A camera swoops across an azure sea, hovering close to several white-sailed boats threading themselves through a cluster of rocks. It pans out again to show dripping emerald forests, laced with tiny waterfalls.

We move through immigration and into an area where rosy-cheeked women, who wouldn't look out of place on a village cake stall, offer us tea and coffee. Miriam hasn't complained at all, but she has pinches of pain around her eyes I haven't noticed before. I park her in a quiet space and step outside to find the taxi rank.

White light beats off the concrete and under my tired eyelids as I take my first look at this unfamiliar country. Having left my entire life to come here, I need it not to let me down. I stand still and inhale – that first deep breath in a new location that tells you everything before you even open your eyes.

Soft spring air trickles over my face and into my mouth and nostrils. It's like drinking a glass of liquid light, rippled through with the scent of flowers I've never seen but whose brilliance I can imagine. I open my eyes and swathes of colour develop into banks of flowers, sprawling over the grass like splashes of paint. I don't recognise most of them. Their exuberance would be jarring in an English garden, but not here. I draw the perfumed air into my lungs as deeply as I can and give my shoulders an experimental wriggle. I've arrived.

When Miriam is settled into the taxi, and we're pulling away from the airport, I breathe a deep sigh of relief. It's been a long journey. I've never travelled this far, and I half expected to lose our luggage en route or end up on a connecting flight to the wrong country.

I packed more lightly for this trip than for my first independent holiday four years ago when Nicole and I celebrated our graduation by taking the Eurostar to Paris for a few days. She packed makeup, underwear, a change of clothes and a toothbrush, all tucked inside a tiny backpack. I took an oversized handbag and an enormous suitcase, which caused every taxi driver in Paris to curse me under his breath and cost me a fortune in embarrassed over-tipping.

We had a fantastic weekend, and I don't remember opening my suitcase once. We wandered around in the sweltering heat in summer dresses and sandals, eating lunch at pavement cafes with style-challenged Americans. We bought warm pastries from the bakery each morning and ate them lying on the grass near the Eiffel Tower. At night, we bought fragrant slices of pizza from street vendors and ate them while we wandered around the city.

On our final afternoon, we took the Metro to Montmartre to watch the artists sitting in the rippling heat, dreamily trying to catch the curves and shadows of Notre Dame with inadequate brushes. Nicole talked me into having our portraits done in charcoal by one of the art students. The artist drew Nicole standing on the steep cobbles, hair flying off her shoulders. He sat me on a chair and sketched me with an earnest smile. I'm determined to do things differently this time, if only to prove to myself I can be a new person.

Lost in memories of my younger self, it isn't until we're sweeping over the Harbour Bridge that I remember to look out of the taxi window. When I do, I catch my breath in delight. The sea is a vivid turquoise, and mirror calm. The city is dreamlike as it grows out of the water's edge – all chunks of mirrored glass and creamy skyscrapers.

We skim over the bridge, looking down on hundreds of tiny yachts swinging in the light breeze and cresting the sun-streaked waves. Beyond them is a fat, red ferry casually trundling from one side of the harbour to the other.

Further out, I glimpse a handful of islands appearing and disappearing into the heat rising off the edge of the horizon. I have never been anywhere this beautiful, and I watch until the seascape is lost behind us as we swing inland.

Miriam's eyes are closed, so I restrain my exclamations and wind down my window to allow the sweet salt air to wash over me. Only thirty-six hours ago, I was burrowing into my cashmere sweater.

We swish to a halt outside Miriam's house. It's on the edge of a park, overlooking the sea. It feels a shame to wake her as the driver heaves the bags onto the pavement. She stretches and yawns, looking around her with sleep-fuddled eyes before realising where we are. Her face breaks into an involuntary smile as she sees her house.

She talked about it a lot during our journey, telling me how she and Geoff bought the land when they married so they could build a place ready for the large family they planned to have. Lynn and Nathan came along in due course, but Geoff died in a car crash when he was thirty-five, and Miriam only escaped with the injuries that have left her unable to walk. It looks perfect for children, with its large sweep of lawn at the front and bottle brush trees scattered everywhere.

I help the driver heave our cases one by one to the front door. I stop for a moment under the balcony, where starry white flowers scramble over the trellis, flooding the air with a delicate, soapy scent I'm sure I recognise from somewhere. After a moment, I identify it as the winter jasmine room fragrance Nicole gave me for Christmas last year.

I'm glad when we've dragged the last of the bags inside the cool hallway. This house suits Miriam. It's tidy and spacious, with pale walls and transparent cream curtains that dip and ripple in the breeze from the balcony. Miriam's face lights up as she catches sight of the damp, garnet coloured roses clustering in a copper vase on the dresser.

'They're from Deb, my housekeeper,' she explains. 'She comes in for a few hours before I get home to make sure everything is working and put food in the fridge. She always brings flowers to welcome me back. She has the best kept garden in Auckland.'

I smile in appreciation of her housekeeper's gesture, but it makes me feel somehow alien. Miriam and I have been travelling in a cocoon for the past two days, brought together by circumstance and mutual need, and I've almost come to feel we're linked in some way. Seeing her in her own place, gently touching her memories, planning for the arrival of her son's family, I realise that's not true. Our lives, after a brief collision, are orbiting away from each other.

I settle her on the couch for a nap, then make her a cold drink and put it on the table next to her. I bend to kiss her cheek. 'Thanks, Miriam. I'd never have done this without you.'

She sounds sleepy. 'Anna, darling, it's been the best trip yet. From now on, I'm booking you every time I travel.'

I laugh awkwardly. 'I'll write to you.'

'You do that! I mean it. I want to know how everything goes. I'll be thinking of you, sweetheart. Things will work out for you. I just have a feeling.'

There's nothing I can say to that. With a last look at her immaculately ordered world, I turn and leave. Closing her front door feels even more difficult than closing my own door two days earlier. All the plans that everyone else has made for my journey are now over. I'm finally here, and I'm completely alone. I close the door with a soft click and walk down the drive to the waiting taxi.

Chapter Eleven

The following day, after a series of hair-raising flights in the tiniest plane imaginable, I arrive in Queenstown. I clutch my seat miserably as we bank sharply for the last time and weave along the valley before dropping onto the miniscule runway with a clunk and a shudder.

I emerge onto the tarmac, amazed to have survived. A hand comes from nowhere, snatches my backpack and swings it out of view. I open my mouth to shout for help.

'You're all right – I'm not mugging you this time,' says an amused voice.

A tall guy in torn jeans and a stained T-shirt is looking down at me. He gives my hand a vigorous shake.

'You're Anna, right? I'm Ethan. Jim and Helen sent me over in the van. I do odd jobs for them around the campsite. They thought you'd have more luggage than this.'

'Er … no … I didn't …' I manage feebly.

He grins. 'Good enough. Shall we go?'

I follow him to his battered van and watch him heft my suitcase lightly into the muddy interior and drop it among a heap of empty green sacks. A quarter of an hour later, we arrive at the campsite. Ethan decants me onto the grass next to a small building and waves as he drives off.

Helen emerges from the building and shakes my hand. She's in her fifties and very tanned. She has the most crooked teeth I've ever seen and tired, pale-grey eyes.

'Anna, welcome! Good trip?' She doesn't wait for an answer. 'Are we glad to see you! We're completely overrun, and Jim's only been waiting for you to get here before he leaves. His mum's had a fall, and he needs to drive up to Christchurch to see her.'

I trot after her as she strides towards a group of tents, not looking back to see whether I'm following.

'I'm sorry to hear that,' I call after her retreating back. 'Is she going to be all right?' I gasp when I finally catch up with her.

She stoops to unzip a small, blue tent, pitched a few metres from the others. 'I expect so. She's an old boot, but he loves her really. And she's eighty-two, so, you know ...'

She slings my backpack into the tent. I stick my head inside and recoil at the smell of hot canvas.

'Better keep it unzipped for a while to let some air in,' she says. 'It's pretty warm during the days, but the nights are still rather chilly. You'll be glad of that thick sleeping bag. Once you've unpacked a few things, you can lock your bags in the office. There isn't much pilfering around here, but people are coming and going all the time, and it's best to be careful. Come and see me in reception when you've unpacked, and we'll get you started.'

She disappears, and I reach for my sleeping bag and bedding roll, tuck my wash bag inside the pillow section and emerge, gasping for air, into the sunlight.

Four days after my arrival, I wake soon after dawn. The tent is full of a greenish, underwater light and already growing stuffy in the morning heat. I kick my way out of my hot sleeping bag and gratefully pull open the zip.

Fresh air floods in, and I blink as always at the ferocity of the New Zealand light. This is starting to feel like home. I think of my other home and wonder how Nicole's getting on. She'll be coming back from work about now and flicking on the lights in my house. The evenings will be cold and dark, and it's probably raining too.

I hope she's checking on Mum properly. I swiftly push that thought to the back of my mind – something I find increasingly easy to do as I wake to sunshine each morning. This part of Queenstown is unbelievably beautiful. The campsite is next to a smooth lake with pebbled beaches lying between the mountains.

I step outside and squiggle my toes through the wet grass. I walk to the edge of the lake and perch on the large chunk of driftwood I found waiting for me on my first day here. I watch the mist uncurl from the water and rise into the warm air, enjoying the feeling of freedom from all responsibilities.

I jump when I hear my alarm clock go off back in the tent. It's seven o'clock, and I need to be on duty at half past seven. Helen and Jim offer a cooked breakfast to anyone willing to pay for it. I have to be there to take the cash and help to serve and clean up.

Ethan turned up early on my first morning. I held out the cashbox for payment, only to be embarrassed by his mocking grin and shrug. Helen bustled through with a steaming tin of bacon, waving the box aside. 'You get a free breakfast if you work here.'

She dumped the tin on the table and rushed off again for the eggs. Ethan grabbed a plate and started shovelling bacon slices and fried tomatoes out of the greasy juice and onto his buttered toast. Helen raced in with dozens of fried eggs stacked in an uneven heap on a tray, and Ethan took three. He waded through his breakfast in a couple of minutes, dumped his plate in the serving hatch and disappeared, waving to me as he left.

The work isn't hard. After breakfast duty, I help Helen clean the shower and toilet blocks. I go to reception at lunchtime, when most of the campers and caravanners check in. I sort the bookings, show them their pitches and help them hook up to the electricity and water. By mid-afternoon, I'm free again until the evening, when I have to check the shower block again and make sure the self-caterers have cleaned up after themselves.

My tent, like Ethan's cabin, has a flag outside so everyone knows where to find me if they have a problem during the night. Thankfully, no one has needed me so far. I can take alternate weekends off work while Helen covers for me, and I can have two evenings off each week, as long as I clear them with Jim or Helen first. In return, I get minimum wage, a discount in the shop and as many hot showers as I want, plus free use of the washing machines.

All in all, I'm more than happy with this arrangement for a while. I haven't been off the campsite yet. Central Queenstown is a bus ride away, and I plan to visit the town tomorrow.

Jim returned yesterday. He's the polar opposite of Helen. He's plump and slow spoken with a salt-and-pepper beard speckled with ginger and a great fondness for standing around chatting, as though time means nothing. I watched him check in a group of hitchhikers last night, looking up their journey on a map and showing them the best route for the next leg, just as though there were no other people waiting in line.

No one seemed to mind. He processed them all eventually, telling them with slow chuckles all about his mum and her leg and how she sent him straight home with a flea in his ear because she refused to be his excuse for a holiday while Helen was slaving away by herself. He put his mum's home-baked muffins in a glass bowl by the reception desk and insisted everyone sample them while they waited.

He stayed at his desk when everyone had gone, brushing crumbs out of his beard and asking me about my life in the UK and what I'm doing in New Zealand. I told him far more than I'd planned to, explaining how I lost my job and didn't want it back.

He nodded understandingly, giving me a description of his previous life as a government accountant. 'Too boring, love! Who wants to be stuck at a desk all day when you can be outdoors? So, we bought the campsite, left Wellington and haven't looked back. Helen's so much more relaxed these days.'

He said it without a hint of a smile. If this is Helen in relaxed mode, I wonder what on earth she was like as a hospital administrator in Wellington. Perhaps this place casts its own magic on those who live here. If so, I hope it works for me too.

Chapter Twelve

I get up late on Saturday, take a long shower and sit outside my tent to let my hair dry in the clear, morning sunlight. It's lovely not being on breakfast patrol. The campers are mostly in their twenties and pack away amazing amounts of food considering they've rolled home in the early hours after the local bars have shut.

On Thursday, an Irish guy sat by the lake until three in the morning, strumming his guitar and singing raucously, ignoring the rain of missiles and abuse from the neighbouring tents. Ethan appeared at last, sent over by an irate Helen. I had to admire the tactful way in which he persuaded the man to return to his tent, encouraging him to finish his lament to the Old Country in the morning. I deliberately tripped over his guy ropes on my way to breakfast, grinning to myself at the muffled curses.

Ethan and I are the only two employees working full-time on the site at the moment, so we're seeing quite a lot of each other. He's friendly and easy-going, and I feel more relaxed around him than I do with most people. I've agreed rather warily to meet him this afternoon to try the luge – the go-kart run that spins down the mountainside. He assures me it's a must-try for all new Queenstown residents.

I dump a load of washing into a machine, check with Helen that it's all right for me to leave, then walk along the track towards the road. It's hot, and I pull my hat down to shade my neck. By the time the bus arrives, the heat is beating up from the road and prickling my face.

I've soon seen all there is to see of the Queenstown shops, and I head to the lake with a packet of sandwiches and a coffee. The heat, the blue sky and the glassy water take me back to the last fishing trip I took with Dad, only a couple of months before his diagnosis. We parked the car at the base of Marble Hill and scrambled through the bushes to the flooded quarry. It was mid-morning, and the heat was already intense. It shimmered off the stones and over the bracken, promising us plenty of sleepy fish aimlessly cruising towards our fishing lines. We sank our bottles of lemonade up to their necks in the water, where they sat fizzing coolly until we opened them an hour later. It was the last time Dad and I ever fished together.

I drag my thoughts from the past and focus on the jet boats on the lake. They skim and weave over the water, and the tourists scream in unison as they flick and spin. Their distant shouts blend with the chatter of the children near me, who are trying to build gritty sandcastles. I slump, half-asleep in the shimmering heat, allowing time to wash over me without meaning.

I arrive at the luge an hour later. I start to have second thoughts when I see the gradient of the mountain, but Ethan has already arrived, so it's too late to back out. He's lounging against the ticket kiosk, finishing a beer. He slings the bottle into the bin when he sees me and straightens up.

'Great, you made it! Are you ready for this?'

'I'm not too keen on heights,' I say nervously.

'It isn't high,' he says, pulling me through the turnstile before I can protest further.

We reach the chairlift and scramble onto a double seat. I try to pull the bar down, but the chair swings forward and lurches drunkenly towards the mountain's edge. I scream and drag at the metal arm, but it won't click into place.

'You're kidding?' says Ethan, looking amused.

I shake my head and clutch at the side of the chair. He drapes an arm around me, holding my shoulder. 'Is that better? Come on, Anna, look down. It's no height at all.'

One glance convinces me that he's the one who's kidding, and we finish our ride in silence. He jumps off at the top and swings me down, keeping me steady until the world stops spinning.

'Sorry!' I gasp. 'I'm terrible with heights. I thought we'd be walking up.'

'We will next time,' he says. 'Are you good now? Let's find ourselves some carts.'

We start driving down the scenic slope. I steer cautiously around the bends, keeping the handbrake pulled towards me. Ethan cruises along behind, yawning loudly.

'Get your hand off the brake, Anna!' he shouts at last in exasperation. 'Stop being such a control freak, and let go! The place will be closed by the time we get to the bottom.'

Stung by his taunts, I release the brake, and suddenly I'm flying. I pull up at the end of the track, turn and give him a wave.

He seems unimpressed. 'You drive like my Nan. Next time, I'm driving in front and getting up some actual speed.'

'They should breathalyse you first,' I say.

He laughs and grabs my hand. We walk up the mountainside and line up again. We ride the advanced track four more times – racing each other, skidding around the bends, whipping over the tarmac and nearly crashing into the barriers.

I climb out when we finish, laughing and breathless. I look at the valley below and the lake stretching out in the distance. 'It's stunning, isn't it?' I say.

'I suppose so,' he agrees. 'It's even better in winter, all covered in snow. If you're still here, I'll take you skiing.'

My mind skips at once to Matt. 'I'd love to,' I say. 'Skiing sounds fun – with the right person.'

'Drink?' he suggests. 'Then you can look at your view some more.'

We make our way to the cafe and sit at a table outside, next to a low wall. I whizz my coffee into creamy whirls with the plastic stirrer.

'How long have you been here?' I ask him.

'On the campsite? Let's see – I came to Queenstown about three years ago. I worked in a bar for a while and helped on the jet boats all one summer. I hooked up with Jim and Helen about eighteen months back. They were setting up the site and needed help for a few weeks. I moved up there and just stayed on.'

'Is it permanent?' I ask.

'I hope not,' he says. 'I don't like the idea of settling anywhere – not for a long time anyway. I'm only twenty-eight.'

I give the coffee stirrer a vicious twizzle. 'I love the idea of having no one to answer to – no responsibilities, and no mortgage. But wouldn't it get to you after a while – never settling or having your own place, never making long-term friends or starting a family?'

'You mean the love of a good woman may get me yet?' he asks with a grin.

'I didn't mean it that way,' I say defensively, realising that's exactly how it sounded.

'I don't suppose you did,' he accepts. 'That's what you want, is it?'

'No, it's what I did,' I say without thinking.

'It didn't work out?' he asks.

'Not too well, no.'

'Want to tell me about it?'

I drain my coffee. 'Not really. It's a million miles away – almost literally. I'm having fun right now. I'll deal with all that stuff later.'

I look past him to the far ranges, their heads half-hidden in the clouds. 'Just gorgeous,' I breathe.

'Thanks very much, but I've heard it before,' he says.

This makes me smile, and I drag my eyes away from the scenery and study him more closely. He's nowhere near as good-looking as Matt, but his brown eyes are friendly under an uneven fringe, and his hair, curling untidily from beneath his cap, has been streaked blond by the sun. He has a freckled nose that tilts up casually at the end. It suits him. He's so much easier to spend time with than Matt. I haven't once felt the need to watch my words or check his face for signs of boredom or disapproval.

He gives me a ride back to the campsite in his van. We don't talk much during the drive. I'm tired after my day in the sun and all the adrenaline, and Ethan is singing along to the radio.

I jump out next to the main building and turn to thank him.

'Would you like to do it again sometime?' he asks. 'If you want a real rush, we could go out on the Shotover river in a jet boat.'

'Yeah, maybe,' I say.

'Yeah, maybe,' he mocks me. 'Come on, Anna – you know you're dying to. We'll have you bungee-jumping before you leave here.'

'One step at a time,' I say.

He leans over and kisses me briefly. 'I can live with that.'

He climbs into the van, leaving me standing on the grass in the sunshine staring after him as he drives off.

Chapter Thirteen

Christmas sneaks up on me long before I'm ready for it. It's difficult to associate these long, dreamy days by the lake with the usual madness of the school winter term and the classes who resent any attempt on my part to give them homework after December 1st.

Jim and Helen have decorated their house with tinsel and paper chains and put up a tiny Christmas tree in Reception. Other than that, it could be any other summer month. I raid the Queenstown shops for suitable gifts for Nicole and my other friends, barely resisting the temptation to send Matt a bag of *Finest quality chocolate sheep droppings.* I eventually send Mum the usual sweater by mail order. She isn't one to appreciate tourist nonsense.

The school holidays are nearly upon us, and the campsite is fully booked. I'm kept busy cleaning and serving the breakfasts each morning, but the afternoons are more relaxed. Ethan is building a couple of new cabins, and I volunteer to help him.

He lifts a lazy eyebrow. 'Done much construction work in a past life?'

'There's no need to be sarcastic,' I say. 'I can paint and lay flooring with the best of them. I have a house of my own in the UK.'

'You're on,' he says. 'Come by this afternoon, and I'll give you a paintbrush.'

'If I'm free,' I say, already regretting the suggestion.

He puts an arm around my shoulders. 'Just kidding. It's a very nice offer, and I could do with the help.'

I nod and walk away before he can see me smile. I could find other things to fill my afternoons, but if Ethan and I want to get to know each other better, we should spend some time together.

He seemed to imply when we spent the afternoon on the luge that this is what he'd like, and I wouldn't mind seeing where this relationship could go. Ethan doesn't know it, but he starts with one enormous advantage. He's the polar opposite of Matt, and I like him for that.

There's nothing about him of which Mum would approve, which is also an excellent beginning. He's casual, not remotely career-orientated, lives for the day and never thinks about the future. These are all promising attributes in anyone with whom I'm looking to make a fresh start and shake off my history with Matt.

I wander over to the cabins after lunch. Ethan is there, stripped to the waist and sweating as he lifts a board into position.

'Grab that hammer, will you?' he gasps.

I hand it to him, trying not to stare at his bare chest. He does a lot of his work shirtless, and he's deeply tanned. I quickly look away.

'What can I do?' I ask.

'These boards need treating before we paint them,' he says. 'Could you manage that?'

I pick up a brush and open the tin. 'I think I might be capable. How many coats?'

'Just the one.' He throws himself onto the grass and closes his eyes.

Jim wanders past as I start work. 'Hi, Anna. I didn't know you were helping.'

I gesture towards Ethan. 'If you leave it to him, it'll never get done. I take it you want these cabins done before the summer holiday rush?'

Jim grins. 'I never thought I'd see the day you were beaten by someone half your size, Ethan.'

Ethan doesn't stir, just opens one eye and mumbles something.

I push him with my foot. 'When I've finished this, shall I put up the next wall for you?'

'If you have a minute,' he says.

By mid-afternoon, I'm wilting, although I refuse to admit it. The sun has risen over the tops of the nearby trees and is beating down on us. It doesn't seem to bother Ethan, but I'd kill for a break. I finish painting the last wall and close the lid of the creosote tin.

'Would you like a drink?' he asks, pushing a window into place and noticing my face. 'Tired already?'

'No,' I lie. 'Just thirsty.'

He laughs. 'You stay here, and I'll go and blag a couple of beers off Jim. It's the least he can do.'

When he returns with the bottles of beer, I'm lying on the grass, staring up at the cloudless sky and thinking about Mum.

'Penny for them?' he demands.

I jump. 'I was remembering how far I am from home.'

'No further than you were yesterday.' He tips half his beer down his throat in one go.

'Not physically,' I agree, 'but I was thinking about Christmas. It's the first year I won't be at home, and I'm worried about Mum.'

'Do you have any brothers and sisters?' he asks.

I shake my head. 'It's just me and Mum. Dad died a while back, so I need to look out for her.'

'Maybe she'll spend the day with friends,' he suggests.

'I doubt it. She doesn't have very many. I'm scared she'll sit on her own all day and mope.'

'That's her choice,' he says. 'What does it have to do with you?'

I almost spill my beer. 'What does it have to do with me? She's my mum, and she needs me. Don't you care about your parents?'

'They split up when I was a baby,' he says, 'so I never met my dad. Mum's over in Queensland. She moved there to be near my married sister and the grandkids.'

'There you are, then,' I say. 'You're off the hook because someone else is there to take care of her for you. You're lucky.'

He looks puzzled. 'How d'you mean? Megan enjoys having Mum around, but they don't live in each other's pockets. They each do their own thing. Mum surfs a lot with her friends, and if there's one thing Megan hates, it's surfing.'

I snort at the idea of Mum on a surf board.

Ethan looks as though he knows what I'm thinking. 'What are your mum's interests?'

'Well, it's not really surfing weather this time of year,' I say to buy time. To be honest, I can't think of any interests Mum might have except for me. This of course is the problem. But I don't dare say this to Ethan. He'd probably dismiss the idea of putting your life on hold for someone else. And it isn't possible to explain about Mum.

If he came over to the UK, even for a visit, he might appreciate the situation a little more. Matt was wonderfully understanding, but he knew Mum so well, and Ethan hasn't met her yet. But I'm getting ahead of myself here. I tear my thoughts away from visions of spending next Christmas in the UK with Ethan.

Nicole would like him, even if Mum wouldn't. I wonder how Matt would react to him. Not that he has any business reacting to anything I choose to do. He and I were a wrong fit from the start, and he's probably grateful to me for seeing that and finding the courage to do something about it. Otherwise, we could have sleep walked to total disaster. I could be with him and the Red Monstrosity in Manchester right now, sheltering from the rain and wind and grumbling. Instead, I'm lying in the sunshine, chatting to Ethan and drinking beer.

Ethan tosses a handful of dry grass at me. 'Are you still with me?'

'Sorry,' I say, 'I was still thinking about my mum. She doesn't get out much because of her arthritis. She relies on me a good deal to do stuff for her – shopping, cleaning, things like that.'

'Who's doing all that while you're away?' he asks.

'My best friend, Nicole. She's promised to look in on Mum twice a week. I can't imagine how that's working out.'

'Why not?'

'Nicole's lovely,' I say, 'but she's quite impulsive, and she isn't terribly responsible.'

He grins. 'She sounds nice.'

I feel a flash of jealousy that, even at twelve thousand miles' distance, Nicole sounds more attractive than me.

'She's very nice,' I say. 'She's been a great friend to me. But I keep wondering whether it was fair to her and Mum, leaving them together like that.'

'Wouldn't you have heard by now if something had happened?' he says.

'Only something major. But I'd never know if Mum was unhappy. She wouldn't want to spoil my trip.'

I'd like to think this is true – that Mum would be so supportive of my being here, she'd do everything she could to keep my dream alive. But I'm not really sure of that. I speak to her each week on the phone, and she sounds the same as ever. Her answers are brief and to the point, giving nothing away. But Christmas on your own is a daunting thought for anyone, and I wonder whether I should use my return ticket and go home. I've been tossing the idea around for a while now. The only thing stopping me is that I'd never be able to afford to come back. Once home, I suspect I wouldn't even have the heart to try.

I'm not ready to go home yet. It took all my resolution to make it over here. I may not have found what I'm looking for, but it's early days. Looking at Ethan, lying on the grass and smiling at me affectionately, I wonder whether I have actually found what I'm looking for without realising it.

He breaks the spell as he stands and rubs his neck. 'I think you're making a fuss about nothing.'

I shade my eyes against the sun, staring up at him. 'How would you know? You'd rather stick your head in the sand than face facts.'

He looks surprised. 'How do you work that one out? All I said was that you'd hear quick enough if she wasn't fine. Until then, you have as much right to a life as anyone else.'

'And Mum would be the first to agree with you,' I lie.

'No worries, then. Are you up for more painting?' he asks.

'No, I think I'll go for a stroll now it's cooling off a bit.'

I feel his amused eyes on me as I walk away. It was my fault for talking to him about Mum and trying to explain how things are. No outsider will ever understand, least of all Ethan. He lives in his own little bubble, and nothing seems to touch him. He's an observer, not a participator. That's fine for someone like him who has their family problems taken care of. But it doesn't work for me.

I'm touched when Jim and Helen ask me over for Christmas lunch.

'More of a Christmas picnic,' says Jim when he comes to my tent to issue the invitation.

The thought of spending the day on my own has been worrying me. 'I'd love to,' I say, 'if you're sure I won't be in the way.'

'In the way?' he says. 'The more, the merrier. We don't do breakfast for the campers on Christmas Day, so you can even have a lie-in.'

I wrap their gifts in readiness. I've bought possum-fur socks and gloves for Helen and a hat and scarf for Jim. They can keep them for the winter. It doesn't seem possible that Queenstown could ever be anything less than blazing hot, but people come here to ski, so the weather must change sometime.

I'm not sure whether to get anything for Ethan. I don't know what's going on between the two of us. Some days, he annoys me with a thoughtless comment, and I end up walking away, determined not to waste any more time on him. Then he startles me with some thoughtful gesture or kind word, and my perceptions of him are tossed into the air again like the pieces of a kaleidoscope settling into a completely different image.

Perhaps I should stop over-thinking things in the way I did during my relationship with Matt. I added up his good qualities and his kindness to Mum, and I stayed with him when I shouldn't have. Now could be the time for a different approach. In the end, I settle on a bottle of whisky. I know Ethan drinks it when he can get it, and he can't read too much into it. It isn't exactly loaded with nuances and romantic overtones. At the last minute, I wrap a piece of festive tinsel around the neck of the bottle.

I wake early on Christmas morning and sit by the lake for a while, thinking of Mum and hoping Nicole is looking after her. It's Christmas Eve over there – the time Mum and I are usually staring at each other over her first and only Christmas glass of sherry while I wonder how she'll react to the latest boring scarf or jumper I've bought her before she returns it for a refund.

Seen without the romantic gloss I've tried to put on it, this Christmas can't be any worse for her than previous ones. It's a sad thought, so I put it to one side for now.

I walk over to Jim and Helen's cabin at twelve o'clock sharp to find Ethan sitting outside. I'm annoyed to realise how pleased I am to see him.

He pulls himself to his feet, giving me an enormous hug. 'I was about to come and look for you. Merry Christmas, Anna!'

'And you,' I say casually. 'I thought you might be off with friends or something today.'

He squeezes my hand. 'And miss the chance to spend the day with you?'

'I have a present for you in my tent,' I say, and he winks.

'Not now, hon. You'll shock Helen.'

I turn to greet Jim and Helen. 'Happy Christmas, and thanks for inviting me.'

They unwrap the gifts I've brought them. Jim puts his hat on straight away, but I snatch it off him. 'You'll sweat into it and ruin it. Wait until winter.'

'They're lovely,' says Helen. 'Now, we thought long and hard about what to give you two. We decided in the end that you'd probably prefer a bonus to anything else. You can't unwrap it, but you won't mind that.'

'Excellent decision,' says Ethan. 'Anyway, Anna does have something to unwrap.'

He tosses me a small package, and I feel my cheeks burn. 'Thanks very much,' I mutter, turning it over in my hands.

'Anna says she has something for me in her tent, but it's very, very private, so it has to wait until we're alone,' says Ethan, and Helen shoots me a curious look.

'Stay here!' I tell him furiously.

I jog back to my tent, hearing Ethan singing, '*In the bleak midwinter,*' as I go.

I return with the bottle of whisky, and he kisses my cheek. 'My favourite brand! But I don't understand why you made such a fuss about it having to be so private.'

'Shall we eat?' asks Helen before I can think of a suitably crushing reply.

We sit in the patch of garden behind the cabin, and I help Jim serve the cold meat and salad.

'It's all a far cry from roast turkey, isn't it?' says Helen.

I nod. 'I've been thinking of home a lot this week.'

'That's only natural,' she says. 'It's difficult being so far away from family and friends at Christmas.'

'It isn't as bad as I thought it would be,' I say.

'How's your mum?' Ethan breaks in. His eyes are warm and no longer mocking, so I smile back.

'I called her this morning. She's spending Christmas Day with my friend and her family. You were right – she won't be alone, after all.'

I try not to show too much surprise for Mum's sake. She sounded on excellent form for once. Nicole must have remembered to buy the Bristol Cream.

'I'm glad,' says Ethan. He lifts his glass. 'To present friends, and to absent friends.'

'And to the best two employees we've ever had,' says Jim, taking a swig of his wine.

'How much have you had, mate?' Ethan pretends to snatch the bottle away.

I drink a silent toast to Dad. Mum and I have always done this on Christmas Day. I wonder whether she'll think of me later today as she drinks her own toast to him.

'Pavlova?' says Helen as Ethan clears away the plates.

She goes into the house and returns carrying a silver platter. I've never seen such an enormous pavlova. She's heaped it high with kiwi fruit and strawberries, and it looks delicious.

We're halfway through our second helpings when Jim lays down his spoon. 'What did Ethan get you?' he asks me.

'Don't be so nosy,' Helen chides him. 'It may be private.'

'It isn't!' I say quickly, pulling out the package.

I don't want Jim and Helen dreaming up some kind of romance between me and Ethan and embarrassing us both. I cross my fingers as I tear open the wrapping paper, hoping it isn't something stupid like a box of fluorescent condoms. Ethan would probably find that sort of thing funny.

There's a tiny box inside. I open the lid to find an opal pendant lying on a piece of black velvet. I lift it out, and it lies in my palm like a beam of moonlight, with a flash of red at its heart.

I feel my face flush. 'It's beautiful, Ethan. Thank you so much.'

I'm embarrassed now at the thought of the whisky. If only Ethan was easier to read. Who would have guessed he'd have gone to all this trouble?

He flicks my cheek. 'No worries. It reminded me of you. Just when you think you know what colour it is, you see a different one.'

I smile at him, and he smiles back. Helen breaks the lengthening silence. 'Jim – can you and Ethan clear the plates and make the coffee while we lie here and digest.'

The men disappear into the house. Helen looks at me. 'I didn't know you and Ethan were –

'We aren't!' I say quickly.

She smiles. 'It's a lovely necklace.'

'He can be thoughtful when he tries.'

'I'm sure,' she says.

'It was a lovely lunch, Helen. Thank you.'

She accepts the rebuff. 'We won't need a lot for dinner, that's for sure.'

The four of us sit and chat until the heat of the day subsides. Ethan and I thank Helen and Jim for a wonderful day, and he walks me to my tent.

'Going to ask me in for a drink?' he says.

'No,' I say. 'Anyway, I don't have anything to drink.'

'I have this.' He waves his bottle of whisky.

I smile, despite myself. 'I wouldn't trust you in my tent, with or without the whisky. I'll take you into town one evening instead.'

'Will you wear your necklace?' he asks.

'Probably – and lots and lots of other things too.'

He laughs. 'You're on! But you aren't here forever, Anna. The clock's ticking. I'd like you to remember that.'

'I'll remember,' I promise, wondering what exactly is holding me back.

He looks at me for a moment longer, then grins and walks away.

Chapter Fourteen

The campsite cat is purring in my ear, rhythmically tapping his paw on the groundsheet next to me.

'Stop it, Jasper!' I mumble, pushing at his furry belly to move him away.

I haven't fallen asleep yet. The heat has grown steadily more oppressive all day, and I went to bed early this evening with a headache curling around my skull. Jasper purrs louder right inside my ear, licking my cheek with his wet tongue. I push at him again and lift a hand to my face. He gives another massive purr, which turns to a growl, then swells to the size of a small lion with his mouth wide open.

I scream and jerk awake. I wipe my wet face, forcing my sticky eyelids to open properly. Rain is streaming through the tent flap and pooling on the groundsheet. My pillow is soaking wet, and I shove it out of the tent. It can't get any wetter sitting out there, and I won't be sleeping on it any more tonight.

A sudden clap of thunder makes me jump. I wonder where Jasper is, then realise he would never have come outside in all this rain, being a cat with powerful instincts of self-preservation.

I must have slept for a while, after all. My headache has gone, and I'm wide awake. If the thunder wasn't rumbling and rolling across the lake, I would clamber out and let the heat of the day soak out of me into the streaming rain.

A sheet of lightning sputters and explodes right over my head. For one flickering second, it throws the trees on the far side of the lake into sharp focus. I flinch. For as long as I can remember, I've been terrified of storms.

The rain torrents more furiously against the canvas, and the guy ropes quiver beneath the onslaught. I peek out again and see what looks like a flashlight bobbing along by the water's edge. Who on earth would be stupid enough to take a walk in this weather?

The light flickers and disappears, and I wonder whether I only imagined it. It reappears and is quickly joined by another one. I watch the lights dodge and weave like sparklers on bonfire night. The wind is rising fast, and I'm almost sure I hear voices drifting towards me through the gale. I listen harder, but it's impossible to tell for certain through the shrieking and howling.

I grumble under my breath and rummage through my soaked rucksack for the least damp clothes I can find, then clamber out into the storm. I've only taken three steps before I'm wondering why I bothered with a dry top. The rain drives straight through my clothes, trailing icily over my shrinking skin. I splodge through the muddy pine needles towards the lights, vowing to make sure we kick these idiots off the camp site tomorrow. As I round the last clump of trees, Ethan cannons into me and sends me flying. He drags me to my feet, covered in mud and furious.

'I was coming to get you!' he yells through the whipping rain and wind. It's so loud I can barely hear him. 'There's someone out there on a rubber tyre!'

'Rubber what?' I gasp, and he flings up his hands.

'This pair of idiots come home from the pub all tanked up. The guy thinks it's a good idea to cool off by taking the spare inner tube from my truck and going for a sail. Then the storm hit, and he's out there now, blind drunk and passed out cold. His girlfriend can't swim, so she came running for me. I've sent her off to make herself useful and call for help. She's useless, though. She's probably got lost already. Can you swim?'

'Of course, I can!' I shriek, racing after him to the edge of the lake. 'Why, can't you?'

'Yeah, but I reckon it'll take two of us. Look – there he is! Can you see him?'

I peer through the darkness during a pause between rain squalls and can just make out a dark, lumpy shape about one hundred metres out.

'Wind's setting hard offshore!' shouts Ethan. 'He's drifted a fair way since I left him, and I can't see which way up he is. He could have his face in the water, for all I know.'

I flinch at the thought of a pale, drowned face.

'Take your clothes off!' he yells.

I jump in shock. 'What?'

'You aren't going into the lake wearing that lot, are you?'

He has a point. I remember my junior school life-saving test when we wore pyjamas and dived for rubber bricks to show the instructor how we could fill the trousers with air and use them as a float. That experience, although invaluable when diving for bricks, will be of little help in the pitch darkness on a stormy lake.

I pull off my sweatshirt and tug at my soaked jeans. They catch on my trainers. I drag at my shoes for valuable seconds, but the more I pull them, the more they tighten.

Ethan bends down and wrenches off my trainers, ripping the skin from one ankle.

'Sorry!' he shouts, pulling at my jeans until I'm free. I grab them and try to tie a knot in the ankles so I can fill them with air to make a float. But the soaked fabric flaps limply, and I can't even twist it, let alone knot it.

'What are you doing?' roars Ethan.

I drop the jeans. 'Nothing – let's go!'

He takes my hand, and we wade into the lake together. The water is no colder than the rain, so I bend my knees and swim as soon as it's deep enough, to avoid the sharp stones slashing at my feet. We strike out towards the dark shape drifting far ahead of us, and I try not to imagine what will happen if the lightning hits the water while we're in it.

It's hard going, with the wind gusting and the rain sheeting into my face. I'm soon swallowing what feels like a bucketful of lake water each time I gasp for air, and my stomach cramps.

Ethan is a fair way ahead of me, and I try to speed up. He reaches the tyre first, hanging on to it with one hand while he lifts the man's head with the other. I arrive in time to see Ethan slap the man's face and yell at him. For one horrible moment, I think he's dead. Then he rolls towards us, leans over and vomits on Ethan, who ducks under the water.

'Let's get this idiot home!' he shouts. 'Keep your head up, will you, mate?'

He heaves the man onto his back to stop him from slumping into the water.

The journey back to shore is far more difficult. I'm exhausted from my swim, and my legs dip ever lower as I clutch the tyre and try to kick. I try to keep my own head up, combatting the urge to lie down and go to sleep. Ethan is still kicking strongly, but it takes an age of struggling against the icy wind before we reach shallow enough water for us to stagger to our feet.

Headlights are streaming through the trees. Three men in fluorescent suits wade out to us. Two of them reach out to catch the tyre while the other one lifts me from the water just as my legs give way. He carries me to the grass and lies me on my side, where it's my turn to vomit. I heave up copious amounts of lake water, coughing and retching for what seems like hours.

'All right now?' he asks when I sit up at last.

'I think so,' I whisper. 'Where's Ethan?'

I look around for him, but I can't see much through the crowd of people and the rain still streaming into my eyes.

'In the ambulance,' he says, 'and lucky to be alive, I should say. You two had some nerve going in like that. That man should be very grateful to you. We've only just arrived. He could have been gone by now.'

'I don't mean that one!' I gasp. 'I mean *him*.'

I point to Ethan as he strides towards us, his face grim. 'Are you all right, Anna? Is she all right, mate?' he demands.

The man nods. 'We'll take her in and look her over, but she looks in pretty good shape to me. No need to worry.'

A second man comes over to us and wraps a silver blanket around me. I feel as though I'm watching myself from a distance. I'm shaking uncontrollably and only realise my teeth are chattering when I bite my tongue and flinch.

'I have to throw up again,' I whisper.

'I doubt it,' grins the ambulance man. 'You've brought up half of Lake Wakatipu right there.'

He's right. I retch for a minute, but that's all. When it's over, he takes my arm and leads me towards the ambulance. Ethan lopes along by my side and hops up beside me. The ambulance stinks of alcohol. The man from the lake is there, strapped to a stretcher. A woman in a fluorescent jacket is holding his wrist and checking his breathing.

'He'll be fine,' she tells us. 'He's thrown up what seems to be a litre of vodka, but he knew his name and where he was before he passed out again. That's always a good sign.'

'Like I care!' says Ethan, flinging his wet T-shirt over his head as she hands him another of the silver blankets.

I instinctively look away, then slide my eyes towards him again. He's glaring at the unconscious figure. 'Knows his name, does he? Well, halle-bloody-luja!'

I reach over and touch his arm. 'Ethan?'

The woman stares at him, shocked at his vehemence. 'Excuse me?'

'You heard me, lady!' snaps Ethan. 'He and his half-witted girlfriend put both of our lives at risk. We could have drowned out there tonight.'

'I know,' she tells him more sympathetically. 'But if we'd been able to speak to you first, we'd have recommended you wait for us to arrive. We have people trained to deal with these situations. If you two had got yourselves into trouble, there would have been three of you for us to worry about.'

'Fine!' he says in disgust. 'Next time, the amateurs will leave him to drown, and you professionals can swim out and get the body later. Best thing for him, I reckon.'

He relapses into a frustrated silence until we arrive at the hospital.

A doctor checks us over the following morning and gives us the all-clear to leave. Jim arrives in the truck to collect us and surprises me with an enormous hug and a bunch of pink and white daisies.

'You did good, the pair of you,' he says.

I sniff at the flowers to hide my embarrassment. 'The emergency team didn't agree. They said we should have waited for them and not put everyone at risk.'

'I'll bet that young man doesn't think so,' says Jim. 'His girlfriend's in pieces back at the campsite. She can't wait to talk to you.' He ignores Ethan's snort from the back of the truck. 'She knows how stupid they were. You won't need to tell her.'

'I wasn't planning to,' I say in surprise. 'It was my choice. No one made me go in after him – and the same goes for Ethan.'

I catch his eye and frown at him until his face softens into a reluctant grin.

'Pair of half-wits,' he murmurs for my benefit.

Jim stops outside the main building, where a fair-haired girl is sitting on the grass, her arms wrapped around her knees. She jumps up and scurries over to us.

'Are you the ones who saved Ben?' she gasps.

'Um, yes, I suppose so,' I confirm, and she bursts into noisy tears.

'I'm so, *so* sorry!' she gulps.

I put an arm around her shoulders until she shudders to a halt. I raise an eyebrow at Ethan. He walks over and pats her on the shoulder.

'It's all over now,' he says. 'They told us this morning that he's fine. Just a crashing hangover.'

'Which serves him right!' she says. 'Don't think I don't know that. I'll give him such a slap when I see him. Are you going to tell his parents?'

Ethan looks bewildered. 'His parents?' he echoes. 'Do you want us to?'

The girl flinches at the thought. 'Please, please don't! His mum was against us camping together. She already thinks I'm a bad influence on him …'

She trails off, and I look at her in amusement. She's small and slim, with a quirky gap between her top teeth. Right now, she's also extremely pale. She doesn't look as though she'd be a corrupting influence on anyone.

'All mothers think their children need help to choose their partners,' I tell her. 'And Ben's the one who got blind drunk, not you.'

'That's only because I'm on antibiotics for an ear infection,' she confesses. 'I can usually drink him under the table.'

Ethan bursts out laughing and looks at her with fresh interest. I'm ashamed to feel a stab of resentment at her appealing fragility.

She wipes her eyes. 'I'm going over to the hospital to see him now. But I wanted to thank you first. I know what a risk you both took.'

'Ah, go on, it was nothing,' says Ethan.

She runs across the grass, turns, waves and disappears towards the bus stop.

'Well, there's a turnaround!' I can't help my accusatory tone. 'What happened to wanting to drown them?'

He shrugs. 'They're just a couple of kids. Come on, Anna, weren't you ever young and stupid?'

This strikes me like a blow between the ribs. I turn to walk away, but he reaches out and holds me. 'I was kidding. What's wrong?'

I sigh. 'Nothing. I'm tired, that's all, and sometimes I feel about ninety.'

I try to smile as I say this, but he's perceptive, despite his carelessness.

'I forgot you've already done all that buying a house, marriage and having kids stuff,' he says. 'I wasn't digging at you.'

'I've never been married!' I say, shocked. 'What gave you that idea?'

'When we were up on the mountain,' he says. 'I thought you said … well, what does it matter? No kids, either?'

I can't tell whether he's joking. 'I haven't left a husband, and I haven't left my children. Do you really think I could do something like that?'

'People do,' he says. 'It isn't a criminal offence, and you do seem to be running away from something.'

'Well, it isn't children,' I say. 'If I'm running away from anything, it's me.'

He gives me a sympathetic smile. 'How's that working out for you?'

'I'm still here,' I say. 'But I keep hoping I'll change enough so that one day I'll look in the mirror and see an entirely different person.'

He looks amused. 'Is that right? Well, I'm glad there's no irate husband chasing after you. It gives me a much freer hand.'

I look away, and he laughs. 'It's fine. You've already told me – one step at a time. I'll wait, like a giant spider in his web.'

I force myself to meet his gaze. 'You can wait if you want to, but I don't know what you're waiting for.'

He smiles. 'I'm free this evening, if you are?'

'I expect so,' I say. 'Come by my tent at seven to check – if it's dried out by then. Otherwise, I'll have moved in with Lynn and Jim.'

'Why would you do that?' he counters. 'I have a perfectly good cabin over there. Double bed, shower, hotplate, and a roof that never leaks when it rains.'

I walked into that one. 'Let's see, shall we?' I say calmly, although my legs feel unsteady, much like they did after the rescue. I lift a hand in careless farewell and walk away, not wanting to look back.

Jim looks hurt when I find him that afternoon and ask for the evening off. 'Sweetheart, no one expects you to work right now. You should take a break. Going out with Ethan?'

He asks it a little too casually, and I feel my face turn pink.

'Yes, but I'm not sure where. He knows this town a lot better than I do.'

'He does,' agrees Jim. 'Helen and I met him on a rare night off when we were getting this place up and running. We went to see a film and stopped on the way home for a drink. Ethan was in the bar, rolling cocktail shakers down his arm like he was born to it. Half the female population of Queenstown started drinking there while he was a bartender.'

He catches my eye and coughs. 'There are plenty of nice places to go in town. Ethan's bound to know most of them. Anyway, the storm's passed now, and there's a settled forecast for the rest of the week. Your tent should dry out nicely if you pin back the flaps.'

I've already spread out most of my possessions in the sunshine and thrown my sleeping bag over the branches of the nearest tree. The steam drifts off them and over the lake, which is glassy and calm under the blue sky. I can barely picture the storm-tossed fury of last night.

After my Paris experience, I didn't bring a suitcase full of smart clothes to New Zealand. I was determined to be myself. I wash and dry my favourite skirt, which is patterned with scattered daisies, and iron a matching T-shirt. I fasten the clasp of my opal pendant, and I'm ready. Even making this much effort reminds me of dates with Matt when he used to collect me from Mum's house. I would come downstairs wearing jeans before caving in to her icy silence and changing into an outfit she considered suitable.

'Matt is always so smart,' she told me approvingly. 'He's a man who takes a genuine pride in himself.'

The unspoken thought hovered between us that there was little about me of which anyone could be proud.

I suspect Ethan's idea of being smart is brushing his hair, and I'm relieved to see him appear wearing his usual jeans and open necked shirt.

He smiles when he sees me. 'You look very nice. Are you set?'

'Just let me lock the front door,' I say, slinging my dry things inside the tent and closing the zip.

We walk over to the truck, and I wave at Jim as he disappears into his house. It's a lovely drive down the valley. I open the window and lean out to watch the setting sun casting a red haze across the lake.

'Hungry?' asks Ethan, glancing at me. I nod, realising I've been too nervous to eat all day, which is irritating.

'Good,' he says. 'Me too. I thought we'd get a bite to eat at this place I know and then … just see.' He winks, but I pretend not to notice.

The restaurant is right by the water's edge. After we've ordered, we wander down and skim stones while we wait. This is something Dad taught me to do really well. He showed me how to choose the flattened stones that curve snugly into the palm, and he helped me with the exact twist and flick that sends them skipping and hopping across the waves before dropping neatly into the water.

Ethan's pebbles bounce once or twice before disappearing with a tremendous splash.

'You aren't spinning them properly,' I tell him, putting my arms around him from behind to guide his arm.

'I was a gold medallist at the last stone-skimming world championships,' he tells me. 'But this is how I finally get you to grab hold of me.'

He tries a few more times before flinging up his hands in disgust. 'Whose idea was this? Waste of time, if you ask me.'

'You're a sore loser,' I say. 'You're too impatient. Don't grab any old stone. Find the perfect one – curved but flat, and nice and smooth. That one will do.'

He ignores the pebble I show him and grabs a much larger one. He poises it in his hand for a second, then hurls it with all his strength. It crashes and sinks.

'Don't choose the biggest ones,' I insist. 'Size isn't everything.'

'Oh, believe me, size is important,' he says, and I frown.

'You don't have to do that.'

'Do what?' he asks.

'Always be such a smart arse. I can't get past it to see the real you, and I'd like to do that.'

'Anna,' he warns, 'I'm not big on this psychology and stuff. There are no hidden depths, if that's what you're after. What you see is pretty much what you get with me, like it or not.'

'I do like you,' I say. 'Very much, in fact. But there must be more underneath. There always is. No one shares everything at once. That's all I'm saying.'

He nods towards our table. 'Looks as though they've caught the fish you ordered. We're sharing a red snapper. Will that do for now?'

The meal is to die for. The fish curls crisply on its bed of salad. When I stab my fork through the charred skin, it erupts in a cloud of salty steam. We finish our main course, and the chilled chocolate soufflés arrive, dusted with icing sugar like the mountains we saw last week. Even Ethan hesitates before diving in.

'It's so pretty,' I say. 'I don't want to ruin it.'

He plunges his spoon into my soufflé, cracking open the crust so the fluff inside oozes out.

'There you are,' he says. 'Go ahead. What are you waiting for?'

I lean over and pick up his untouched soufflé before he can react. 'I'll do it my own way, thanks.' I shield it from him with my arm.

Ethan's dessert disappears in two enormous bites, and he sits back to watch me eat mine. I'm determined not to feel self-conscious as I tap the crust with my spoon and delve into the soft centre. I eat slowly, savouring the bitterness fighting with the sweetness. I finally push my plate away, defeated, and Ethan eats the rest of my soufflé and scrapes the plate clean.

'You shouldn't have waited and thought about it for so long,' he says. 'You should have gone for it.'

'Ah, a metaphor for life, Ethan style. You're being just the tiniest bit obvious, aren't you?'

'Maybe,' he says, 'but there's something so buttoned-up about you, Anna. It makes me want to grab you and shake you and push you over the edge – in the nicest possible way, of course.'

He relapses into his usual calm, and I nurse a secret feeling of pleasure. He must feel something for me if I'm able to bug him like this.

'Of course, in the nicest possible way,' I say. 'I seem to have that effect on several people. It forced one of them to send me halfway across the world.'

'Send you?' he queries. 'You aren't a parcel. How can anyone send you anywhere?'

'I'm still wondering that,' I admit, 'but I'm glad she did.'

He takes my hand, and this time his eyes are serious. 'Me too. I've never met anyone quite like you, Anna, and I've met hundreds of girls. I don't know what it is, but you somehow manage to irritate me and attract me in equal quantities.'

'It's a start,' I say.

We leave the restaurant and stroll back to the truck. I'm surprised to find we've been here for three hours.

Ethan asks if I want to go on to a bar, but I shake my head. 'I'm tired. I think I need to go to bed.'

His eyes flicker, but he bites back the comment. He swings the truck around and scrunches it over the gravel and out onto the highway. We drive along the Frankton Road in silence, but it's no longer uncomfortable. I feel that I'm getting a handle on this guy. He's far more complex than he wants anyone to believe.

He scrapes to a halt outside his cabin and opens my door for me. He holds out his hand. 'Are you coming in? It's your call, Anna.'

'Of course, it is,' I agree, ignoring his offered hand and jumping down beside him.

Chapter Fifteen

We're lying in bed one morning, watching the sun sneak over the horizon and begin its steady climb towards the middle of what I can see will be another scorching day.

Ethan stretches and yawns. 'Those roses won't water themselves. I'd better get onto it.'

'Already?' I say. I'm far too comfortable to contemplate moving.

'Rather now than when it gets too hot,' he says. 'I have a list of jobs as long as your arm. I can't lie in bed all day with beautiful young women – or with you either.'

He dodges the slap I aim at him and slips out of bed. I sit up and watch him as he pads around the room, looking for a clean T-shirt.

'Why do you have such a long list?' I ask. 'Does Jim have to visit his mum again?'

Is it me or is he avoiding my eyes as he rummages through the drawer?

'Ethan?' I press.

He turns around. 'Nah, she's fine, as far as I know. But I'm thinking of moving on. It's about that time.'

'About what time? What are you talking about?'

'The police are after me,' he says.

I give a gasp of shock, and he grins. 'I've never known anyone rise to the bait more easily than you, Anna. Relax, no one's after me except you. It's this killer body. It's a curse rather than a blessing, I always say.'

'I'm sure you do. But why ... where ... I mean ...'

'Who, what and when?' he supplies, sitting down on the bed to pull on a sock. 'I can't exactly say. It's just time for me to move on. I can't explain any better than that. You either understand or you don't.'

'I understand you're a drifter,' I say, 'but I thought you were feeling more settled now.'

'Because of you?' he asks. 'You're a great girl, Anna, and we're having fun. But I didn't promise to change my lifestyle when we hooked up.'

I ignore the *hooked up* while I think about this. It's true that he showed me his cards up front. Now I come to think of it, there's no reason for us not to move on. The season is drawing to an end here, so we won't be letting Jim and Helen down.

'You might have discussed it with me first,' I say, 'but that's fine. I'd be happy to see more of the country. Do you have a date in mind?'

'You want to come too?' He sounds surprised.

'Of course!' I say. 'You weren't thinking of going alone, were you?'

He doesn't answer, so I press on. 'It's fine, Ethan, really it is. I understand why you were hesitant about mentioning it, but don't worry, I'm up for an adventure. It's the reason I came here, after all.'

He laces his work shoe and straightens up, the familiar grin back on his face. 'Awesome – we'll go together. We'll talk tonight. Got to get cracking now.' He blows me a kiss and disappears.

I lie for a while, watching the sun shake out the new day into bright patterns on our worn carpet. This could be fun. I didn't plan to spend the entire year in Queenstown. And there won't be much to do on the campsite when the last of the summer visitors leave. I assume we'll be heading north, which is fine with me. It will also be less daunting if I go with Ethan rather than alone.

I bump into Jim as I clear up after breakfast. He stops to chat, and I decide that now is a good time to mention he'll be losing not one but two members of staff. The summer rush is dying down, so I doubt it will make much difference to him. But I'll be sorry to say goodbye to him and Helen. They've both been so kind to me.

'I need to talk to you sometime,' I begin.

He crinkles his eyes at me. 'That's rarely a good start.'

'How do you mean?'

'It's how all my girlfriends started conversations right before they became ex-girlfriends,' he says.

I laugh. 'Their loss. I was going to say that the season is nearly over now, so it won't be a surprise that I'm thinking of moving on.'

'I suppose it shouldn't be,' he says, 'although I hadn't really thought about it. You seem such a part of the place now. Helen and I were saying only last night that it feels as though you've been here forever. We can't think how we'd have got through this summer without you – what with me coming and going to see my mum so often.'

I flush with pleasure. It's nice to be appreciated. 'I've loved being here, Jim. But Ethan's thinking of leaving –'

'You know about that?' he says.

'Of course. We've been making plans.'

I'm surprised that Jim would think otherwise. He must be aware by now that Ethan and I are together.

He looks embarrassed. 'I thought you and he were ...'

I laugh. 'Please finish that sentence before I die of curiosity.'

He looks even more embarrassed and shakes his head. 'Sorry, I wasn't trying to interfere. I thought it was a ...'

I decide to rescue him. 'A summer thing?'

He gives an uncomfortable shrug.

'It started out like that,' I say, 'but the summer's almost over, and autumn's on its way. Time for us to make fresh plans.'

'Good enough,' he says. 'But we'll miss you both. Any idea where you'll go next?'

'Not really. We're going talk about it tonight.'

He nods. 'Come and have dinner with us when your plans are clearer. Helen would love to say a proper goodbye.'

'We'd like that, but I don't imagine it will be quite yet,' I reassure him.

But Ethan, when we sit down to talk later that evening, has other ideas.

'Right,' he says, 'today's Friday. I still have a few last things to do with that fence down by the lake. But I can knock that on the head in one morning's work. Is Monday morning ok for you?'

'Monday?' I say, startled. 'That's rather rushed, isn't it?'

'Why? You only have a couple of bags. I collected you at the airport, remember? And you can't have bought much since you've been here. Queenstown is hardly the shopping Mecca of the world.'

'But what about Jim and Helen?' I ask again. 'We can't leave them in the lurch.'

'Of course not,' he agrees, 'but we won't be. We only have half the number of campers we had when you arrived. You clear the breakfast things, clean the shower block and do the general dogsbody stuff. Don't tell me Helen can't cope with that by herself, with Jim to help her when he's not doing the site work.'

I feel deflated when he says this. 'It sounds as though you think I haven't done anything since I got here.'

He gives me a swift kiss. 'Don't be daft. You work hard, and they needed you in the summer rush, but it's not rocket science. I mean, anyone could do it.'

'I suppose so.'

'I know so. Is Monday ok for you?'

'I suppose so,' I say again.

I can't think of any valid arguments to stay longer, and he's right that anyone could do the job I've done. If I want to see the country, now's the time. I won't be out here indefinitely. At least, I don't think I will. Being with Ethan might change things.

'Have you ever considered visiting the UK?' I ask.

He shrugs. 'Never say never. Right now, I'm not looking beyond Monday.'

'Good enough,' I say in my best imitation of a Kiwi accent, and he laughs.

I ask him to tell Jim what we've decided. I'm embarrassed to be leaving with so little notice, and it's Ethan's idea, so he can take the flak for it. But Jim, as Ethan reports back the following morning, is fine with it all. I may have overestimated my importance in the grand scheme of things. Nicole has always said I have a tendency to do that with Mum. Perhaps this is what she meant.

Helen asks me us over to the house on Sunday evening, and I gratefully accept. It will be nice to say goodbye properly. And there's nowhere to sit in our cabin now. Ethan piles the bags into the truck on Sunday afternoon while I sweep out and clean the cabin.

It feels forlorn when I finish, and I look around me with regret. 'I've had fun here.'

'Me too,' says Ethan. 'Do you think we'll find ourselves as comfortable a bed in the next place?'

I ignore this. 'It's been a wonderful summer, and it's where I met you. I'll be sad to leave.'

'It's exciting though?' he asks.

I consider this. 'Not for me. I've left one home this year, and now I'm leaving another.'

'Home is where the heart is,' he says. 'Don't get so attached. The more times you pack up and leave, the easier it gets. Trust me on that.'

'That can't be true,' I object. 'Pulling up roots must always hurt, however many times you do it.'

He rolls his eyes. 'Don't be so dramatic. You haven't put roots down here, have you? It's just a campsite.'

'I meant the people,' I say. 'Jim and Helen have been very kind to me.'

'There are plenty more people out there in the big, wide world,' he reminds me. 'And most of them are pretty nice.'

'I expect you're right,' I say after a moment.

'I'm definitely right,' he says with a grin. 'You need to change your outlook.'

'I'll do my best. In the meantime, I'm going to say goodbye to my friends. Employers or not, they're still friends.'

'I never said otherwise.' He clicks the door shut behind us.

Helen has cooked roast lamb, and Ethan's eyes light up when he sees it. 'My absolute favourite. This is a wonderful woman, Jim. If you two ever split up, call me at once.'

'Ignore him, Anna,' says Helen, putting a dish of vegetables on the table next to the lamb.

'It's a skill I've been honing all summer,' I tell her. 'It's the only way to cope with him.'

It's a delicious meal, and we linger over it until long after dark. Jim brings out a bottle of champagne that he tells us he's been saving for a special occasion.

Ethan laughs. 'That could have been better put, mate, but I never turn down a drink. Who's going to make a toast?'

Helen fills the glasses. 'I am. To Ethan and Anna! May you both find everything you're looking for.'

Jim nods and drinks, and Ethan waves his glass at Helen. 'That's easy in my case. I'm not looking for anything in particular. I take life as it comes. I don't know so much about Anna.'

All eyes turn to me, and I flush. 'I'm not sure what I'm looking for, either, but I hope I'll know it when I find it.'

'Or not,' says Ethan. 'Just let it happen.'

'I'm working on it,' I say. 'Maybe it comes more easily to some of us than others.'

'We're all different,' says Helen gently. 'There's no need to compare yourself to anyone else. You're fine as you are.'

'That's what I keep telling her,' says Ethan, smiling down at me.

I smile back. 'What *should* I drink to?'

'To life!' he says with his trademark grin.

I think about this for a moment. It's rather vague, but maybe that's a good thing.

'I can do that,' I say and raise my glass.

Chapter Sixteen

We leave soon after dawn on Monday. Ethan brings the truck around while I check that neither of us has left anything behind. With one last, quick glance around the campsite to imprint it in my memory, I jump in beside Ethan, and he pulls away and heads north up the Frankton road.

He doesn't glance back, not even once, and he brushes it off when I mention it. 'Live in the now, Anna. The past doesn't exist anymore.'

'But the people do.'

He grins. 'I'm not *that* self-obsessed. I don't think they've all disappeared because I'm not there any longer. But they're not a part of my life anymore.'

'That feels so callous,' I object. 'If people once meant something to you, they still should.'

'I never said they didn't. But most people belong to one part of your life, and then you move on to another part and meet the ones who belong here. The people you leave behind do the same. It's just –'

'The circle of life?' I suggest, and he gives a sputter of laughter.

'I'm not the bad guy here, Anna. I just have a different philosophy from you. Nothing's any the less valuable because it only exists for a second. Think of shooting stars and rainbows.'

'But if something's once been precious to you, how can you chuck it away?' I ask.

He sighs. 'Your word, not mine. I said, *'Move on'*, not *'Chuck away'*. Don't get so wound up about the concept of permanence. Nothing's ever permanent – not you, me or anyone else. We're all here for a bit, and then we're not. You can either waste your life kicking against that or you can go with the flow.'

'But don't some people belong in different places in your life?' I say. 'I mean the people who span the various parts of it and provide some cohesion.'

He shrugs. 'I suppose so – parents, family, that sort of thing. Anyway, this is all pretty heavy for a Monday morning. We haven't even had coffee to kick start the day. Shout out when you see a truck stop or a café, will you?'

As we get further away from Queenstown, my spirits rise. Ethan's right. I do have trouble with the concept of letting go. I'm determined not to ruin this next phase of my life by refusing to move on from the previous one.

And it's a glorious day for a new start. The mornings have become chillier over the past couple of weeks, and the early morning air is fresh and cool as it streams past my open window. By the time we stop in Christchurch for lunch, the sun is warm again, and the sky is a deep blue.

We eat lunch in a cafe on the edge of the city. Ethan doesn't want to risk driving through the centre and getting caught in traffic.

'I worked in a bar here for a few months,' he tells me.

'Of course, you did,' I say, amused. 'Is there anywhere in New Zealand you haven't lived?'

'I've been around a fair bit,' he allows. 'I doubt I'd recognise much around here now.'

'Aren't you curious to have a look?' I say.

'Nah, I have great memories of it. Why spoil them?'

'They've rebuilt, haven't they?'

'It won't be the same,' he says.

'Embrace the difference, Ethan! Don't always be harking back to the past,' I chide, and he laughs.

'Wise words, Yoda. Have you finished stuffing your face? We still have a fair way to go.'

We get ourselves some coffee and sip it as we thread our way around the outskirts of the city and continue north.

We arrive at Picton in the evening, exhausted and sticky after the journey. The campsite has a pool, so after a quick dinner, we go for a swim. I lie back in the warm water looking at the stars while Ethan lolls nearby, flipping water at me.

'It's a beautiful country,' I say.

'It is that,' he agrees. 'Godzone.'

'What?'

'God's own country,' he says. 'You've never heard that?'

'Never.'

'Makes sense, don't you think?'

I look around at the dark shapes of the trees against the backdrop of mountains. 'I can see where you're coming from. It's more beautiful than I imagined anywhere could be.'

He laughs. 'The Aussies have tried to copy the name from us, but what do they know?'

'Have you lived there too?' I ask.

He nods. 'I backpacked the whole of the East Coast a few years ago. It's spectacular, but it isn't New Zealand.'

'You don't feel cramped in such a small country?' I say.

He looks surprised. 'Why would I? Granted, it's not a vast country, but there aren't as many people here. I felt a sight more cramped in Hong Kong, I can tell you.'

'You might not like my housing estate outside Southampton either,' I say.

'I already know I wouldn't. You made the right call, coming out here.'

'But it isn't a permanent thing,' I remind him. 'You know that, right? My life is in the UK.'

'I don't see why,' he says. 'I've told you before – home is where the heart is. Where's your heart, Anna?'

'My Mum's back there,' I say, wondering which question I'm actually answering.

'Boyfriend?' he asks.

'Didn't we go through all this when you thought I had a husband and kids stashed there?'

He smiles. 'I said boyfriend, not husband. There's a massive difference.'

'True,' I admit. 'I did have a boyfriend, but we broke up before I left.'

'Is that why you left?' he asks.

'Not really. I think it was just time I tried something different. And then I had perfect storm over a few days. First, I had a catastrophe at work. Then my boyfriend wanted me to move away with him, and I couldn't because of my mum.'

'Did you want to?' he interrupts, looking genuinely interested.

'Not in the least. The work catastrophe saved me from having to go along with something I didn't want to do.'

'You needed saving from that?' he says. 'What's wrong with the word *no*?'

'Nothing,' I say. 'I know that now. But it's not a word I've used very often since Dad died.'

'I don't see the connection,' he says.

'Neither do I. Things were just going that way. Anyway, do you plan to lie out here talking all night until the ferry arrives?'

'You'd have hypothermia by morning,' he says. 'And there's a perfectly good bed in that cabin. It's a shame to waste it.'

He helps me out of the pool, and we walk towards the cabin hand in hand. I'm pleased to have had this conversation. It's the most intimate one we've ever had. It also helps to put Matt in the past, where he belongs.

Ever since I came out here, I've struggled with vague feelings of guilt about the way I treated him. Talking to Ethan, I realise I should have finished it earlier. I was wrong to allow myself to be trapped in a relationship that could never work, purely through fear of Matt and Mum's disapproval.

I sleep so well that Ethan has to shake me awake in the morning. I groan and pull the quilt over my head to shut out the bright light. 'How long until the ferry gets here?'

'Two hours,' he says.

'Then why?' I mumble.

'I thought you'd want a shower and breakfast,' he says.

I scramble out of bed and into the shower. The hot water helps soothe away the stiffness of yesterday's journey. We're aiming for Lake Taupo today. I hope it isn't too far.

We eat breakfast outside at a cafe, watching the sunbeams bounce off the Cook Strait and tangle themselves in the palm trees by the water's edge. A tiny ferry slides into sight, and we carry our bags down to the quay.

I stand on deck to say a last farewell to South Island, wondering whether I'll ever see it again. I watch the shining strait slip past while I wrestle with the growing feeling of surrealism that overtakes me whenever I think how my life has changed during these past few months.

Not only am I thousands of miles away from home, but I've broken up with one boyfriend and met another. I also haven't spoken to Mum very often since I left. This last one isn't entirely my fault. The mobile phone reception at the campsite was patchy, and we kept being cut off mid call.

I went into Queenstown several times to try. But the calls, although clearer, were less than satisfactory. Mum isn't a great phone person, and calls with her tend to be rather one-sided. I've kept most of the information strictly factual, and I haven't mentioned Ethan. Slice it whichever way you like, he'll never be Mum's type, and I don't imagine he'll be too keen on her. But I'll cross that bridge when I come to it rather than broaching the subject over the phone at this distance.

Anyway, I know she's keeping well, which will have to do for now. In keeping with my policy of containment – or avoidance – I haven't mentioned Nicole during our calls, and neither has Mum. The one and only time she mentioned Matt's name, there was an immediate and inexplicable lapse in connection, and they cut us off. There's no reason why I shouldn't call at least a few of the shots now I've escaped.

We stop in Wellington to stretch our legs before the next leg of the journey. We wander around Wellington city centre and have lunch in the Botanical gardens. They're glorious, and I wish we were staying in the city a little longer to do some sight-seeing.

We take the cable car down to Lambton Quay and set off again. We're staying in Taupo tonight, but Ethan wants to head further north tomorrow. He doesn't seem to mind where we go but says he'd like to spend some time near the sea.

I've looked at various options online, and they all look amazing. I'm happy to drift with him and see where we end up. Nicole would be proud of me, I reflect, as we traverse the Hutt Valley and head towards Lake Taupo.

'Have you ever lived in the Taupo area?' I ask Ethan.

'I spent one summer taking tourists out onto the lake to fish,' he says.

'Is there anywhere you haven't lived?'

If he notices my tone, he doesn't react. 'Stewart Island.'

'Where's that?' I ask.

'Off the south coast. It's a beaut place. There's loads of wildlife, and there are only about 400 people living there, so it's nice and quiet.'

'We could have gone there,' I offer, and he snorts.

'You almost threw up when we went out on the Shotover. It's ten times rougher on the Foveaux Strait. Anyway, it's autumn now, not spring. We're heading north for a reason.'

'I'm not bothered,' I say. 'Don't let me get in your way. I'm easy about our destination.'

'Great,' he says. 'You'll like Taupo. It's too big to see right across, so it almost feels as though you're by the sea.'

'We could stay there and set up business as fishmongers,' I suggest. 'You could catch them, and I could sell them to tourists so they can boast about their catch.'

'We could do that if you want to be arrested,' he says. 'It's illegal to sell Taupo trout. You can catch them for yourself with a license, but that's all.'

He says this as though everyone ought to know it, and yet again I feel my foreignness. Most of the time, I almost forget this isn't my country. In many ways, it feels like a cleaner, less crowded version of the UK. And then I bump up against reminders that I'm an in-comer. But that, as I always remind myself, is part of the adventure. It wouldn't have been much of a stretch if Nicole had packed me off to Birmingham.

The drive to Taupo is pretty, but I'm tired of sitting still for hours on end. Ethan hasn't insured me to drive, so I can't help him out. I fiddle with the radio, hum to myself and eventually announce that I'm hungry.

'It's like taking a toddler on a road trip,' he grumbles. 'Wait a couple of miles until we get to Mangaweka.'

'Let's hope it has toilets,' I say.

'Should have gone before we left!' he teases.

'I'm not really annoying you, am I?' I say.

'It would take a lot more than that.' He leans over to kiss me, almost landing us in a ditch.

He pulls in at the side of the road a few minutes later. 'There you go. One of these ought to do the trick.'

I stare in surprise at a large airplane perched by the side of the road. It's garishly painted with giant cookies and looks fabulous.

'Can we go in?' I say.

'If you're good,' he says, easing his long legs from the truck.

We walk over to the airplane and inspect it more closely.

'You'll have to fill me in,' I say.

'There's not a lot to fill you in about,' he says. 'It's a New Zealand landmark. You said you were hungry. One of these cookies ought to fill the cracks.'

We climb the stairs and sit by the cockpit. Ethan has an enormous cookie while I eat my way through two apple cream doughnuts.

He gestures towards my empty plate. 'Would you like another?'

I shake my head. 'That was fantastic, thanks. It will be something to put in this week's email home.'

'I noticed you always write to your mum on Sundays.'

'Not that she can use a computer,' I say. 'But I send it to my friend, and she prints it out and takes it over. It feels odd to go through a third person, but that's about par for the course for me and Mum.'

'She must look forward to hearing from you,' he says.

'I doubt it. I suspect she isn't too enthusiastic about my current life choices.'

'Me?' He doesn't sound too bothered.

'To be honest, she doesn't even know you exist,' I admit.

'Why not?'

I'm annoyed that he doesn't seem more upset, but I don't want to launch into a long, defensive speech, so I push back. 'Does your mum know I exist?'

'Not as yet.'

'There you are, then!'

'But that's because I'm a rubbish correspondent,' he adds. 'A quick text now and then, and I'm done. If I ever wrote to my mum, I'd tell her about you. But I get the feeling you're hiding me from yours. What's that all about? Is it the third leg, the hump or the string of criminal convictions?'

'I'm afraid she wouldn't need any of those to disapprove of you,' I say.

He demolishes the last of his cookie and wipes his mouth. 'Any reason?'

'It's her default mode. If you don't give her something she can actively approve of, she assumes the worst.'

'That doesn't sound likely,' he says. 'Maybe it's you that does the assuming.'

'Yeah, maybe,' I say.

Someone like Ethan could never understand Mum, and I don't intend to get into it. His lack of understanding stings a little, but short of us having the sort of conversation that would take hours and end with me in floods of tears, I'm stuck with it.

The drive along the Desert Road is fascinating enough to calm my earlier flash of resentment. Ethan doesn't seem to notice my mood, which is probably for the best. He sings and chats as we curved past the oddly shaped rocks and through miles of scrub land.

It's evening when we finally see Mount Ruapehu ahead of us, its peak lumpy and iced like a clumsily assembled wedding cake. By this time, I've put Mum well and truly out of my mind. She's where she belongs, in her pristine house in Southampton, ordering Nicole around and disapproving of me. She's welcome to it. Disapproving of me at twelve thousand miles is a far different affair from pushing her judgmental opinions into my face over lunch each Sunday.

'You look fierce,' comments Ethan.

'I'm tired, that's all. Are we nearly there yet?'

He laughs. 'What did I say? Just like a toddler. One more bend. Keep your eyes open.'

I gasp as the road swings around and Lake Taupo opens out in front of us. The water is a dazzling blue and stretches out of sight.

'It's beautiful,' I breathe.

He grins. 'It doesn't take much to impress you.'

'Which is why I'm with you,' I counter.

'Nah, I mean it. It's one of the things I like about you.'

'Low maintenance?' I suggest.

'Not too much trouble, at any rate. There are a fair few motels along this strip. Look out for any signs showing vacancies.'

We pull in at a motel right by the shore. The owners give us a room looking out over the lake, and I dump my bag by the bed. 'I never want to get into that truck again. I think I may stay here for ever.'

'You'd get bored soon enough,' he warns me.

'I wouldn't. I'd sit by the lake in the sunshine every day and enjoy the view.'

'In the winter too?'

'I don't know,' I say. 'Do they have a winter here?'

'Too right, they do! They close the Desert Road when it snows.'

'Then I'll sit indoors to enjoy the view instead,' I say. 'Anything to avoid getting in that crummy old truck of yours ever again.'

'That crummy old truck has got you this far,' he reminds me. 'And you'll need transport if you plan to eat tonight.'

'Isn't there anywhere nice nearby?' I grumble.

He sighs. 'You can stay here, buy a fishing license and catch your own supper. Or you can come into town with me and have some fish that someone's already caught.'

The doughnuts have worn off by now, so I follow him to the truck again, and he drives us into town.

The air is warm enough to sit inside. I stare out over the water as I eat my fish and chips. 'Joking aside, this is a beautiful place. Maybe we *should* stay here for a while.'

'What for?' asks Ethan. 'We're heading north, remember?'

'I know, but what's the rush? I haven't seen Taupo before, and I'd quite like a break before we drive on.'

'Sure,' he says. 'That's your choice to make, but I'm off tomorrow.'

I'm taken aback. 'You're kidding?'

He shakes his head. 'I'd like to keep going until we get to somewhere around the Coromandel.'

'Isn't the journey as important as the destination?'

'Not in this case,' he says. 'I want to get there as quickly as possible and find a job. Our money won't last forever, particularly if you insist on regular meals.'

I'm disappointed, but I see his point. I have a little money saved from my time working here, but it won't run to motels and meals out for an indefinite period.

'Fine,' I say, 'I'll come with you tomorrow.'

'Good enough. We'd better turn in soon. Then we can make an early start.'

I climb into the truck. 'You weren't serious about going on without me tomorrow?'

'I'm really glad you're coming with me, ok?' he says.

It isn't until we're on our way back to the motel that it strikes me this wasn't quite what I asked. But we've made our decision now, and there's no point in going over old ground. Ethan is simply showing me, as so often before, that it's always better to look forward rather than back.

Chapter Seventeen

The following morning sees us sweeping through glorious pine forests as we work our way towards the east coast. As we approach the base of the Coromandel Peninsula, the land flattens, reminding me of the more rural parts of England. We climb higher, and I catch my breath.

'It's stunning!' I tell him. 'Don't you want to pinch yourself sometimes?'

Ethan grins but doesn't comment. I stare out of the window, entranced by the wild clematis scrambling through the hedges, scenting the air for miles around. We stop mid-afternoon at a tiny cafe in someone's garden, where they serve us homemade herb and cheese muffins and oatmeal cookies.

When I can't eat any more, I settle back into my seat for the last part of today's journey. Ethan has promised that we'll stop in Coromandel Town for at least a couple of days, and I'll be glad to unpack and relax. He drives ever more slowly as we twist and wind up the mountain road. The sea flashes in and out of sight in streaks of peacock and emerald.

We top the ridge, and he pulls over. 'Would you like to admire the view for a few minutes?'

Far below us lies a turquoise bay, sprinkled with tiny islands scattered far out into the gulf. White-capped sailboats skip across the ripples. I pull out my phone and kneel on a grassy hillock to capture the view from several angles.

'You'll be disappointed when you look at those later,' says Ethan. 'It isn't possible to catch it.'

I switch off my phone. 'I suppose you're right. At least, not the sun and the smell of salt and flowers. But I want something to remind me of this place when I have to go back home.'

'It won't work,' he says at once. 'As soon as you try to pin anything down, it loses something. It's the same with people.'

I wonder whether he's making a point about us, but he doesn't appear conscious of having said anything too personal.

Half an hour later, we run slowly down the final hill and approach the sheet of shimmering air that rises from the hot road to meet us. We swing past several large houses, all set a long way apart from each other.

Ethan waves his arm. 'Look over there! That house on the right.'

He stops the truck next to a long, grey fence. A sign in the front garden reads *The Feijoa Tree.*

There's another sign tacked underneath. I can only just make out the words. *Rooms vacant. Help Wanted.*

Ethan swings the truck around and crunches the wheels up the long, gravel drive.

'Hang on,' I say. 'Are we looking for a room or a job?'

He grins. 'Both, if we're lucky.'

'You don't know what kind of help they want or anything about them.'

'There's only one way to find out,' he says,

We pull up in front of a large, two-storey house that's been freshly painted in a soft lavender colour. I crane my neck to look up at the attic windows, where flowered curtains flicker in and out in the breeze.

A smaller building stands to one side of the main house, inside its own patch of garden. The garden is neat and filled with flowers, but this building is shabbier than the main house and doesn't look as though anyone lives there.

A man comes around the front of the house and raises a hand in greeting. Ethan swings his long legs out of the driver's seat and walks over to him. They stand and talk together for a while. Curiosity finally overcomes my shyness, and I climb out and join them.

'Hi, I'm Anna.' I extend a hand.

'Patrick,' says the man, shaking it firmly. He has a warm smile and very muddy hands and laughs when he sees me surreptitiously rub my hand on my jeans.

'Sorry,' he says. 'I've been working in the veggie patch. I hear you're looking for temporary work. Nora will be here in a minute. She'll have the final say. It's mostly work around the house, although Ethan here could give me a hand with the new fencing.'

The front door opens, and a woman emerges. She's in her late fifties, with faded brown hair pulled back into a clumsy knot.

'Good afternoon,' she says. 'I'm Nora Kennedy. Welcome to *The Feijoa Tree.*'

'Anna Richardson,' I say. 'Nice to meet you.'

Ethan stretches out his hand. 'Ethan Manning.'

'How can we help you?' asks Nora. 'Do you want a room? We have a double all made up on the first floor.'

'They're looking for work,' Patrick tells her, and she beams.

'That's great. It's a real pain trying to get permanent help here. It's a big house, and there's always plenty to do in the summer months. We've only just arrived back after a few days away. My aunt is sick, and she doesn't have anyone living nearby. It's always difficult to leave during the season, but family has to come first. It's a pity we didn't have you here last week. We wouldn't have had to cancel the bookings.'

She pauses and exchanges a look with Patrick, who nods.

'Patrick grows all our own vegetables,' she says, 'and I look after the guests. I need help with the cleaning and laundry and breakfasts, if you can cook?'

I hope to goodness that Nora's poor guests get a better breakfast than we served at the campsite. I suppose they must or they'd never come back.

'I'm not a great cook,' I tell her, 'but I'd love to learn. And cleaning and laundry isn't a problem. It sounds as though it could be quite a good idea.'

She gives us an embarrassed look. 'We only have a single spare room, I'm afraid. Are you two a couple?'

'Erm …' I say.

Ethan cuts in. 'I can kip in my tent out the back while the weather's still warm. And we don't know how long we'll be here, so we don't need to worry about the winter yet.'

'Are you sure?' I ask him doubtfully, and he grins.

'Don't worry, hon. You can join me in my tent whenever you want.'

I turn pink and glare at him.

Patrick changes the subject. 'Come on, Anna. While Ethan gets your stuff out of the truck and finds a spot to pitch his tent, I'll show you the vegetable patch.'

'She doesn't want to see that now,' says Nora. 'She'll want to see the house.'

'No, I'm fine,' I say. 'I'd love to see the garden now it's a bit cooler.'

'Of course, you would,' Patrick tells me. 'My vegetable garden is a thing of beauty and a joy forever – much like myself, in fact.'

Nora shrugs and follows Ethan back to the van while Patrick and I inspect the garden. He points to rows and rows of beautifully tended vegetables. I can see at once why he's so proud of his garden. I've never seen anything like it. The vegetables are neatly arranged in long green lines. The ends of each row are edged with flowers – mostly marigolds and nasturtiums in different shades of orange, cream and yellow.

Around the side of the house is a garden that looks like something out of Beatrix Potter. Patrick has planted herbs between the rows of stepping stones. I recognise chives and mint, but not much else.

He gathers a few fragrant handfuls and waves them at me. 'Cilantro, parsley, basil.'

He selects tomatoes, green peppers and courgettes.

'I hope you're hungry,' he says. 'I just need a few onions and potatoes, and we're all set.'

He leads me towards the back door, where we find Nora already in the kitchen. There's a large fish on the worktop in front of her, and she's rubbing a paste into its belly.

'Ginger, lemon juice, brown sugar, peppercorns,' she chants, slapping the fish onto an enormous piece of foil and tying it up like a parcel. 'We'll give it a few minutes to marinade and then cook it.'

Patrick brushes the vegetables with a stiff brush. 'Would you like to help?' he asks.

I feel immediately nervous. I've never done much cooking. As a child, I could never get near the kitchen, which was Mum's jealously guarded territory. Even as a student, she barely let me do more than bake a cake. I only started cooking when I bought my own house – not always with great success.

This looks more fun. Patrick and Nora have a huge farmhouse kitchen with a double oven and a hob with six rings and a griddle. Patrick hands me a knife, motioning for me to chop the potatoes and onions.

I start sawing at them, and he raises an eyebrow. 'Have you done much of this before?' he asks, his tone so carefully casual that I burst out laughing.

'Hardly anything. Am I fired already?'

He shakes his head. 'Not a hope, young lady. There's nothing I enjoy more than bossing someone around. Let's start from the very beginning. Grip the knife handle firmly. No, I'm serious. That blade is sharp enough to take your finger off if you mess around with it. Now, draw the knife over the potato like this … and then back the other way. We don't want to slice them too small.'

He's right. The knife slips through the potatoes almost by itself, and they fall into neat chunks. I turn them and slice them again crosswise, feeling pleased with myself. The onions are trickier, but I soon get the hang of topping and tailing them and finally produce some quite reasonable looking crescents.

Patrick slices the tomatoes and peppers and puts them into a bowl with the potatoes and onions. He pours olive oil over the vegetables and tosses them with his hands until they're well covered. He tips everything into a baking tin, grinds salt and black pepper over the top, then slides the tin into the oven underneath the fish.

While dinner is cooking, Nora takes me upstairs and shows me the guest rooms, each with its own ensuite bathroom. She and Patrick sleep downstairs, where the whole of the ground floor except the breakfast room has been made into a self-contained flat.

The guest bedrooms are lovely. Each bed has a different patchwork cover, which Nora tells me she bought from a local business. The walls are painted in pastel colours – palest duck-egg blue, lemon, rose and mint, and the stripped-pine floors glow like pale honey in the late evening sunshine.

I've already seen the curtains floating out on the breeze. They have wide, matching ribbons to tie them back. Fluffy white towels are stacked on the end of the beds, each towel embroidered with a different flower to match the colour of the room.

As I lean out to look down at the garden, I catch a glimpse of the sea, glowing red under the setting sun.

'It's all so lovely,' I tell Nora. 'I expect people come here again and again.'

She smiles. 'We like it. And you're right. It's lovely when our guests come back year after year.'

The only access to the upper floor is by a separate stairwell. We climb the steep flight of stairs to the attic.

'It's rather small, I'm afraid,' she says, throwing open the door. 'We only offer it to guests if we're completely booked up. Will it be a problem with you being up here and him down there?'

'Apparently not,' I say as casually as possible. I'm a little hurt that Ethan doesn't seem to care whether we're together.

She nods. 'You can have a double if you're still here later in the season. The rush will be over in a few weeks. I expect Ethan realised that.'

This makes me feel more cheerful. 'I suppose so. He's a Kiwi, so he's more clued up on that sort of thing. He's been working on campsites and travelling around the country for years. I only came out here in November.'

'Are you here permanently?' she asks.

I shrug. 'I'm learning to take my life one day at a time. That's Ethan's doing. He's a good influence on me.'

'It suits some,' she says as she ushers me into the room.

It's even nicer than the guest rooms. The low ceiling slopes down on each side, and there's a dormer window with a blind. There's a narrow, single bed with another handmade cover – this one a soft red colour with blue blocks tumbling haphazardly across it. There's a small pile of towels laid over a cream rattan chair, all beautifully embroidered with sprigs of lavender. There's a tiny wardrobe built to accommodate the slanted floor and sloping ceiling. I have so few clothes that it will be perfect for me.

'This really is Green Gables!' I exclaim and blush when I realise I've spoken aloud the thought that's been with me ever since I arrived and saw the sweeping lawn with its clustering fruit trees and the weatherboard house nestled behind it.

'It's purple,' says Nora absently, and I hide a smile.

We make our way down the spiral stairs to the landing and on down to the kitchen, where Ethan is talking to Patrick. They pour us both glasses of wine – crisp and fruit-scented in slender glasses. The fish lies on its bed of silver foil, gently steaming, and a rich caramel smell fills the kitchen.

Patrick gives a satisfied nod. 'We'll eat outside if that's ok with everyone. But first, shall we drink to the new partnership?'

There's silence for a moment as no one can think of an appropriate toast.

'May our house always be too small to hold all our friends,' says Nora at last, and the four of us raise our glasses and drink.

Chapter Eighteen

The rising sun wakes me at five the following morning. I forgot to shut the blinds last night, and raspberry and apricot streaks are lighting the sky above my head. I don't mind. I got used to waking early at the campsite. I enjoyed the chill silence before the birds were sufficiently awake to open the morning with their shrill chatter.

I tiptoe to my bathroom, although I'm unlikely to disturb anyone up here, and start the shower running. The bathroom is even tinier than the bedroom. It's all white tiles and shining silver taps, and the shower is barely high enough for me to stand up, but I love it.

I rub my hair dry on one of the fluffy towels and think back to Queenstown. It seems a world away, and I wonder whether my life is destined to comprise chunks of time that never quite fit together, and whether that really matters.

I brush my wet hair behind my ears, pull on shorts and a T-shirt, and go downstairs and out of the side door. The grass is still soaking wet, so I kick off my sandals and wade across the lawn, the dew splashing over my ankles and between my toes.

There's no sign of life from Ethan's tent as I skirt silently past. It's cool in the shadows, so I make my way around to the back garden, where the sun is already tipping the herbs with gold. I crouch on the stepping stones, stroking the leaves in turn to identify the herbs. My fingers are soon a total jumble of spicy scents, and I give up.

Patrick comes around the corner of the house while I'm inspecting some bluish flowers on a spiky, green bush.

'Rosemary!' he announces.

'Anna, actually,' I say.

He wags a finger at me. 'Which herbs can you identify?'

I stare at the plants. 'I have mint and chives sorted, and now rosemary, thanks to you, but that's about it. I'd love to learn some more.'

He crouches down to join me, snapping a glossy, curved leaf off one plant. 'Have a go at this one.'

He crushes it in his palm, and I flash back to an evening with Matt, soon after we met at university. I remember wooden tables and candles stuck in wine bottles.

'Pizza?' I hazard, and he nods.

'Good going. It's basil. Great on pizza, and in plenty of other dishes too. How about this?'

This one takes longer, but I finally connect it to Mum's roast chicken on Sundays.

'Sage and onion!' I tell him triumphantly.

'Sage, anyway,' he concedes. 'You have a good nose.'

He pushes himself upright, brushing his hands together. 'Don't let me bore you too much. Gardening's *my* passion, not yours. Nora will have my guts for garters if I take you on as under-gardener and leave her without any help.'

'I promise that won't happen,' I say, 'but I'd like to learn. I have a small town house in Southampton, but there's only a bit of concrete behind it, so I've never grown anything.'

He nods. 'I can show you how to grow things in containers, and you can always grow herbs on a kitchen windowsill.'

'There might be some point if I could cook,' I say. 'How do you feel about giving me a few tips there too?'

'I will, if you're serious,' he tells me. 'Shall we start with breakfast? Nora isn't up yet. She's a little tired after yesterday's journey.'

We go to the kitchen, where Patrick shows me how the various rings work. I watch him whisk flour, eggs and milk into a creamy batter and swish a knob of butter across the griddle.

While he waits for the butter to heat, he slices open a melon, cubes the flesh and tosses it into a bowl with some velvety black grapes. He takes three glasses from the cupboard, spoons in thick Greek yogurt and drizzles maple syrup over the top.

The butter spits and sizzles, and I watch him pour neat blobs of batter into the pan. The pancakes shiver, puff up and bubble, and he flips them so the crisp, golden sides are uppermost. He slides them onto a plate and gestures to me to take over. I cautiously pour out four more pancakes, watching them spread and freeze into uneven shapes. I try to flip them, but he makes me wait until bubbles cover the entire surface. Only then does he let me turn them over.

My pancakes are more ragged than his, but each new batch comes out more even and golden, and I'm disappointed when the batter jug is finally empty.

'Do you think you could do that on your own next time?' he asks as Nora wanders in. She's still in her dressing gown and looks tired.

'Leave her alone, man!' she yawns. 'You and I can manage the guest breakfasts. Anna and Ethan can clear and wash.'

'But I'm enjoying it,' I say. 'I've always wanted to learn to cook, but I've never had the chance. I'll help with the breakfasts each day if you don't mind showing me what needs doing.'

We carry everything outside to the wooden table in the garden. Ethan is climbing out of his tent, and his face breaks into an enormous grin when he sees us.

'What perfect timing – breakfast practically in bed. This is going to be a fantastic life.'

'It's a first morning deal only,' Nora warns him as we sit down to eat under the huge, striped umbrella.

The pancakes are crisp and almost salty against the tip of my tongue. We finish with the glasses of yogurt, the fruit sliding deliciously over the glassy maple syrup. Nora disappears inside the house, reappearing with a pot of fresh coffee and a jug of cream, which she spirals into the spinning liquid with a flourish.

I give a sigh of contentment. 'If this is how you feed your guests, no wonder you're booked up. Do you cook dinner for them as well?'

'No, we're just a bed-and-breakfast,' she says. 'We point them towards the town in the evenings. There are several places to eat, and it's not too far.'

'It seems a shame,' I say. 'Patrick loves cooking, and you have this wonderful garden. You surely can't eat everything you grow?'

She shakes her head. 'We give some of it away to our neighbours, and they do the same for us in return. We get the most marvellous honey from one friend who has a few hives, and another friend collects things for us from Auckland when he goes across. He has a boat down at the harbour. Patrick can show you sometime.'

'What shall we do now that we're here?' I ask.

We talk for a while and agree on our respective jobs. Patrick needs Ethan's help with the heavier work in the garden. Nora would like help with the laundry and the cleaning, and I don't mind being up early to do the breakfasts.

Nora and I spend the entire morning airing the bedrooms and dusting ready for tonight's guests. She shows me where to find the soaps and shampoos. As we leave each room, she spritzes it with an infusion she makes herself with lavender from the garden. They're already fully booked for the next two weeks, and I'm not at all surprised.

The first guests arrive after lunch, tumbling out of their cars and looking around them appreciatively. Nora goes out to meet them and shows them to their rooms while Patrick and Ethan help carry the luggage upstairs.

By mid-afternoon, the place is full. People are sitting in groups in the garden, chatting in the sunshine and exchanging travel tips. They disappear into the town for dinner, and I hear them come in long after I've fallen into bed, exhausted. It's been a tiring day, and I'm meeting Patrick tomorrow at 6am so he can show me how to do the guest breakfasts.

This time, I remember to pull the blinds shut. I lie for a while in the heat, thinking about Mum, as I usually do while I fall asleep. Tonight, I can't manage even one guilty pang. Nicole will take care of Mum, whether she likes it or not. They'll rub along fine – if they don't kill each other. This is the first time in twenty-six years I've done anything without checking with someone else. It's probably about time.

I wonder what Dad would have said if I'd told him I was planning this trip. But if he was still with us, there would have been no problem. It was only his leaving us so early that left me with these aching responsibilities. Mum will have to survive a few months without me, I decide, as I tumble over the edge of reflection and into a deep, lavender-scented sleep.

Running a bed and breakfast is much harder work than I would ever have expected. I had assumed that as soon the guests went out for the day, we would make a few beds and run the vacuum cleaner around, and that would be it.

Nora soon sets me right. When Patrick and I have finished serving breakfast, with him cooking and me watching, there are the plates to clear and the dishwasher to load. While that's running, I tidy, dust and vacuum the breakfast room and take the table cloth and napkins to the laundry room. They go into the washing machine while we carry the clean sheets upstairs.

After that, it's on to the bedrooms, where we have two double and six single beds to strip and re-make. Like Mum, Nora has sheets and blankets beneath the patchwork covers, and I groan when I see them.

Nora whips the sheets off the large double bed in the first room. 'Sheets are more hygienic. We often have children here, and I can't be washing and drying large doonas every day. These sheets will take a boil wash if need be.'

I try to nod intelligently as I wrestle an unwieldy blanket off the bed and onto the floor. We toss the dirty sheets and towels onto the landing and turn the mattress. Nora shows me how to make hospital corners with the under-sheet. She makes me practise several times.

'Now do it for real!' she orders.

I flip up each corner in turn, tucking and smoothing it over the mattress until she's happy.

'Did you work at a hospital?' I pant.

She laughs. 'No, but everyone had to make their bed properly when I was a child. My mother came in to check each morning, and woe betide me if it wasn't perfect.'

I think back to my childhood room with its white furniture and plain curtains.

'We always had sheets and blankets,' I say. 'In fact, my mum still does. I bought a lovely, puffy quilt with a brightly striped cover when I left home. It was horribly expensive, but I didn't care. And I still use it.'

'Yet you can't make a bed?' She sounds intrigued rather than judgmental.

I feel embarrassed at owning my incompetence. 'I can't cook either,' I point out. 'Mum liked her kitchen to herself, and I wasn't a very tidy child. If I made my bed, she'd only come in and re-do it, so it didn't seem worth it. She liked to do everything herself.'

I smile as I remember laundering my favourite angora sweater before one of my early dates with Matt. By the time I'd put it through a hot wash and tumble-dried it for an hour, even my old Barbie doll would have needed a crash diet to fit into it.

Mum was incandescent at my wastefulness, but I was surprised how funny Matt found the whole thing. He came to the shops with me the following Saturday and spent the entire day helping me search out the exact deep green to replace my sweater.

Nora has finished the bed while I've been day dreaming, and we make a start on the bathroom. She watches to check I can clean a toilet properly. This is one test I can definitely pass. It was something Mum drilled into me when I first bought my house.

'I can't abide a dirty bathroom,' she told me, 'and I'm sure Matt can't either.'

So, I manage to satisfy Nora with my toilet cleaning abilities. Thankfully, the bathrooms only have showers, so there are no baths to scrub. Under Nora's eagle eye, I kneel down and scour the shower base before rinsing and drying it. I spray the glass door with white vinegar and buff it to a shine, and she nods approvingly.

We dusted the rooms yesterday morning, so all that's left is to open the windows and tie the ribbons around the curtains again. We drop a pile of fresh towels onto the beds, remembering which flowers go with each room – this one gets the pale pink rosebuds with green leaves twining up the stems – and we're finished.

'And it only took us two hours,' Nora says as we leave.

'That can't be right!' I say.

'I'm afraid so,' she laughs. 'It'll get quicker. It has to, or we can't afford you.'

I certainly hope it gets easier. My arms are aching, and my back feels as though it might break in two after all that bending and kneeling.

'No wonder you needed help,' I say. 'It's a pity I'm not better trained.'

'Nonsense, my dear, I was teasing you. You've done a splendid job, and we can each do separate rooms from now on.'

I'd prefer to shuffle up the stairs to my attic room and collapse for the afternoon, but if she can manage this, so can I.

I move on to the yellow room, remembering to select the correct pile of towels. These are embroidered with celandines, peeping out from clusters of green, crinkled leaves. I struggle with the bed for a while and eventually get it looking passable. Then I scrub the bathroom until it gleams, surprised how proud I feel of my work.

I emerge onto the landing to find that Nora has already finished the other rooms. She takes the dirty laundry downstairs while I vacuum all the bedrooms. I lug the machine to the kitchen, where I find her sitting in a chair, panting. Perhaps she finds the work more tiring than she admits.

I peg out the napkins and tablecloth while she puts the towels into the washing machine. I clip them to the line and watch them lift and billow in the breeze. Nora puts on a fresh pot of coffee while we wait for the wash and produces a tin of biscuits. I select a pink wafer and remove the top layer with my lower teeth, remembering the hundreds of times I've done this in the staff room.

Nora seems to read my thoughts. 'You're a thousand miles away.'

'Twelve thousand,' I say. 'I was thinking about my last job. I was teaching in a big secondary school. I always made a dive for the pink wafers at break time before anyone else could get to them. If they were all gone before I got there, it ruined my day. It all seems so petty now.' I laugh, aware of how stupid I must sound.

She searches in the tin for a chocolate digestive. 'It's funny, isn't it? We all have our routines and rhythms. They mean nothing to anyone else, but they shape our day for us. Pink wafers at break time is no worse than people putting their shoes on in a particular order or avoiding ladders. It gave you a sense of control, I imagine?'

That word again – it's starting to haunt me.

'Ethan often says I'm a control freak,' I say, biting into another wafer to avoid looking at her. 'It bothers me because it makes me sound like my mother, and I hate that. He doesn't want to control anything. It's what I like most about him. He just drifts, and I envy that so much.'

'It's one way,' she says, 'but it wouldn't be mine. I love change and big ideas, but Patrick's always there to rein me in if I go over the top with my plans.'

I think about this. 'That's great when you're an established couple, but what if you aren't? You have to find a middle way.'

'We all need to find our balance,' she says. 'I sometimes regret having married so young before I had the chance to get to know myself properly. But Patrick was definitely the man for me, so we had to find a road together.'

'They say owners grow to be like their dogs,' I say. 'Do you think married couples grow to be more like each other?'

She laughs. 'I honestly couldn't say. My advice is to find someone who knows who they are and is comfortable with that. That way, they'll be comfortable with you being whoever you are too.'

'I'm doing my best,' I say, feeling my face turn red. I had no intention of getting this personal with a woman I barely know.

Nora doesn't seem to notice my embarrassment. She pushes herself out of her chair. 'Time's up. That wash should be through by now, and we haven't even started on the ironing.'

Ironing has always been a complete mystery to me. I'd vaguely thought that the wind flapped the creases out of things, but it turns out it doesn't. Nora sets me up with an ironing board and one of her spray bottles of lavender water. Under her strict supervision, I get the table cloth smoother than glass.

'It's more than a business for you, isn't it?' I ask as I sweat over the steaming iron.

'Much, much more,' she says. 'It's all about creating a haven. Everyone needs little pockets of space in their lives. If I can provide one, I've done something worthwhile. At least, that's how I see it.'

'I like that,' I say. 'It's a lovely idea to make a living doing something that makes a difference. I suppose I did that when I was teaching. But there was so much other stuff – all the fuss and clutter – that the good bits often got lost.'

I fold the last napkin and show her the finished pile. For once in my life, I've created order out of chaos instead of the other way around, and it feels wonderful. This will be a good place to stay for a while. I already like Nora and Patrick, and I should get the hang of the work pretty soon. There's no reason this place shouldn't be a haven for me – and for Ethan too.

Chapter Nineteen

I wake just after dawn. My room is warm from the early morning sun, and I roll over in bed to watch the shadows of the clouds drift past my window in the pink light. Ethan drove to Auckland yesterday to pick up supplies for several projects he and Jim are working on, and I wonder what time he got home. It must have been fairly late or he'd have come up to see me. I'll wander past his tent before I serve breakfast and check whether he's awake yet.

The last three weeks have slipped by in a blur of hard work. I've enjoyed myself, although I haven't been able to spend much time with Ethan. That should change now I've settled into a routine and got the hang of my work. I want to see some more of the area and take some trips with him now the season is almost over and *The Feijoa Tree* is less busy.

I'm pretty sure I'm not in love with Ethan, but I suspect I might be perilously close, and I'm not sure whether to give in. I didn't feel like this at the beginning of my relationship with Matt. When I first realised this, I felt guilty, but now I see it as liberating. I should have known right from the start that it wouldn't work out with Matt and not wasted his time.

It's not that I haven't missed him while I've been out here. We were together for a long time, and there was a time at University when I thought he was the perfect man for me – kind, hard-working and patient with Mum.

I also fell for his air of calm assurance and belief that his future was mapped out and would be good. He seemed certain of my future too, at a time when I wasn't certain of anything. But we hadn't been together for six months before other things intruded, and we started to annoy each other more and more.

It's probably good that I didn't just fall for Ethan's looks. I fell for his attitude that he has a perfect right to take up space on this planet. I admire his unruffled skimming across the surface of life, never questioning our right to make our own choices. More than that, it's something he forces on me. I could never imagine Ethan making decisions for me, which is refreshing. Matt is so confident he's made all the right choices that he can't help inflicting them on anyone who allows it. Well, not on me – not anymore.

I slip out of bed and pull on a summer dress. I walk through the wet grass to the back of the house and tap on the tent door. There's no answer. Perhaps he didn't make it back last night, after all. If he left Auckland late, he may have stopped on the road.

I'm just turning away when the tent is unzipped, and a girl peers out, blinking in the bright morning sun.

'Hey,' she says sleepily.

I freeze for a long moment. She pushes back her tousled hair, seemingly annoyed at being woken so early. 'Was there anything in particular?'

I shake my head as I back away, then turn and run towards the house.

I burst into the kitchen just as Patrick is lifting a batch of bacon from the pan. 'Careful!' he says.

He looks at me more closely. 'Is everything ok?'

'Yeah, fine,' I say.

I walk through to the dining room, where I gather the cutlery and plates all ready for the onslaught of the guests. I put the plates onto the tables, slapping them down in rhythm and counting them in my head to squash the thoughts that bubble up.

'Anna?' says a voice.

I jump and spin around, but it's only Patrick. He's gazing at me with concern.

'Are you sure you're all right?' he asks again.

All I have left is my dignity, so I suppress the impulse to break down and howl in his arms. Instead, I nod, forcing my stiff lips into a smile. 'I just had a bad night. I'll try to get a nap when breakfast is over, if that's ok?'

'Sure,' he says, his voice filled with concern.

I realise I'm not fooling him, but I don't care. As long as he pretends to be fooled, that will have to do.

The guests trickle downstairs, and I go through the usual routine of bringing them trays of bacon, sausages and eggs, pouring coffee, refilling the pots and slopping milk into the jugs with a shaking hand.

Ethan strolls into the kitchen as I'm collecting more plates. 'Here, let me do that.'

I stare at him in shock. He could surely have had the decency to avoid breakfast today. He looks as cheerful as ever as he takes the plates from my hands. Maybe he doesn't know I came to the tent this morning. I wonder how best to wipe the smile off his face. I jump as his skin brushes against mine and hate myself for it.

'Are you all right, hon?' he asks, pouring himself a large mug of black coffee. 'Patrick says you don't seem yourself this morning.'

'Well, you seem fine enough for the both of us,' I say through clenched teeth. 'Was it a good night?'

'Yeah, great.' He clinks his mug back on the table. 'Well, if you're sure you're ok, I have to get the primer on those fences.

I'll see you later.' He smiles and flicks my cheek, then turns to leave.

'I came by this morning,' I say, watching for his reaction.

'Minnie told me,' he says. 'Why didn't you stay and say hi?'

I can hardly believe what I'm hearing. 'You knew I was there? You heard me?'

'No, I was spark out, but Minnie said someone had come and gone away again. I guessed it must be you.'

'Then, why are you asking me if I'm all right?' I hate my voice for shaking.

'I don't …' His face suddenly flashes comprehension, and he stares at me for a long, face-heating moment. 'Oh, no, Anna. You don't mean you –'

'Yes, that's exactly what I mean!' I snap, aware of my fast shredding self-control. I just want this over with, preferably ending with Ethan as hurt as I am. 'Hang on a minute, I don't mean what? What don't I mean?'

'You thought we were exclusive,' he says slowly. 'But why? We've spent a couple of weeks together, and suddenly –'

'Five weeks – not a couple!'

I flush miserably as his face starts to register amusement as well as pity.

I try to keep my voice steady. 'If you'd told me up front that you intended to sleep with every female in sight, I'd never have given you the time of day.'

'Which would have been a great pity,' he interrupts. His eyes are affectionate, which almost hurts worse than his betrayal. 'Anna, we have fun. We can still have fun. You're a lovely girl, and you're really sweet. I don't know anyone else quite like you, but I'm not sure where you got the idea it was so … restricted.'

I struggle to protect the very few shreds of dignity I have left. 'I didn't say that. I mean, I didn't think it was serious. But I tend to stick to one person at a time. Clearly you don't, so that's all there is to it.'

I try to sweep past him to the sink, but he steps in front of me. 'No, I'm not leaving it like that.'

I see three teenage girls watching us from their vantage point at the nearest breakfast table. They're checking out Ethan and giggling at each other. They stop abruptly when they catch my eye.

'I thought I knew you,' I hiss under my breath. 'I had no idea you were so shallow.'

'Many have plumbed the depths of my shallowness,' he says lightly.

I feel an almost overwhelming impulse to hit him. 'Great, Ethan, just great! Turn everything into a joke, why don't you? It saves facing up to things.'

'What things?' he asks, and I shush him, horribly aware of the girls sliding their eyes away from us.

'Are you going to tell me who she is?' I ask. 'You can't have known her long.'

He shrugs. 'She was hitch hiking to the town in the rain yesterday evening and not having much luck. Fortunately, I came along in the van.'

'Very fortunate!' I snap. 'A ride *and* a bed. Lucky her.'

'Come outside for a minute.' He grabs my arm and pulls me towards the door. We face each other, and I'm annoyed to see he's as unruffled as ever.

'Look, Anna, I don't want to fall out over this,' he says, 'and you're truly the last person I'd ever want to hurt. But you've got this all wrong. I live my life as I choose. I never pretend anything else, and I never pretended anything different with you. You live your life too, which is fine with me. I don't want to interfere.'

He hesitates. 'To be honest, I've always thought your problem is that you're scared to make your own decisions. You'd rather someone else made them for you, so you have someone to blame if things go wrong.'

I gasp in disbelief. 'You're so arrogant! Do you think you know me after just a few weeks? What you've said is *so* way off.

If either of us is scared, it's you. You float along with all that *sitting lightly on life* schtick, and now it turns out it's because you haven't got the guts to get personal.'

He inspects this statement calmly before rejecting it. 'I don't think so. But so what if that's true? Why are you pinning your happiness on trying to control what someone else does? It's pointless, and you'll always be let down.'

An image of Mum flickers before my eyes, and I choke back a fresh wave of anger.

'Controlling? You always say that, and it's such a horrible word. You know nothing at all about me. Anyway, you're only saying it to take the focus off you and your cowardly approach to life. You're the one who lets people down, Ethan, not me.'

I'm devastated to see he's still completely calm. I can't even make a dent.

'But why do you care?' he asks gently. 'Why is my approach to life so much more important than yours? It's all a bit … second-hand, isn't it?'

I'm about to lose it and start howling, and I'm determined neither to give him that satisfaction nor allow him to humiliate me any more in one day. I turn and walk away from him across the grass. As I do, Minnie emerges from the tent, rubbing her hair with a towel. She waves at me and looks surprised when I ignore her.

I skirt around the lawn and go into the house through the front door to avoid seeing Ethan again.

'I hate him! I hate him!' I repeat in my head as I stride up the stairs to the attic, holding onto the mantra to block out other thoughts. I reach my room, where I collapse in a swirl of shame and anger, pushing my hot face into my quilt, too shocked even for tears.

Ethan clearly doesn't deal in any currency I've been brought up to value, and I push aside the nagging question whether I pay too much. He's never tried to hide his philosophy. Why should he when he never thought there was anything to hide? His ultimate betrayal is that he's left me with nothing to rail against or blame. I'm fighting myself, not him, and I hate him for it.

I move through the rest of the day on autopilot, using my duties as an excuse to be anywhere that Ethan isn't. He seems to be keeping out of sight and has his meals at different times to me, so I only see him once or twice in the distance.

Nora catches me after lunch and asks whether I'd like to talk. It's kind of her, but the last thing I need is sympathetic faces and people tiptoeing around touchy subjects.

I face her head on. 'I'm sure you've both guessed what's happened, but it's one of those holiday things that wasn't meant to be. I'm chalking it up to experience.'

She nods and drops the subject.

Patrick is much worse, giving me sympathetic looks whenever I come into sight. I tackle him at breakfast the following morning.

'I'm fine, Patrick,' I say, wondering whether this is true. 'Now, please stop pulling those awful faces when I walk in and get those tomatoes out of the pan before they turn completely black.'

Oddly enough, I do feel fine. I'm shocked and extremely angry, but no longer tearful. I can't tell whether that's because I don't feel anything or because as usual I'm refusing to face it. Perhaps my therapist will tell me years from now. I seem to be falling into Ethan's habit of turning things into a joke, but whatever works right now is surely good.

'He's a great guy,' says Patrick, carefully arranging the fried tomatoes on plates to avoid looking at me directly.

I smile. 'Tell me there's a *but* in there somewhere, and you're not rubbing in what I've lost.'

'Not at all!' He looks shocked.

I stir the beans while he fumbles for whatever it is he's trying to say.

'Like I say, Ethan's a great guy,' he says at last. 'He's been a fantastic help to me with the garden. I'm getting past heavy lifting, and he isn't afraid of hard work.'

'And the downside is?' I prompt before he can make Ethan sound any more like Mother Teresa.

He pauses. 'Well, downside's not quite the right word.'

'Good talk!' I say.

I'd prefer to lighten the mood rather than discuss Ethan with someone who's still almost a stranger. I wonder whether I would have talked to Dad about Ethan and decide I wouldn't. It would have gone straight back to Mum. If I wanted to design a man who would fail to appeal to her on just about every level, I wouldn't have to look further than Ethan and his careless charm.

I'm pretty sure Dad would have liked Matt almost as much as Mum did. They were quite similar in many ways, although Matt is a more definite version of Dad, who always seemed rather obscured by the aura of inflexibility that Mum casts across everything around her.

Patrick tries again. 'There are people who are nurses and people who are patients.'

'I've heard that before,' I say.

He nods. 'What I'm trying to say is that there's also a third category – those who wouldn't dream of nursing others but who would never ask others to nurse them. I'm putting it badly, but I think Ethan's like that. He takes what he wants, but he'd never mind if someone else took it first. He looks out for number one, but he expects other people to do the same, and he doesn't resent them for it. He's amoral rather than immoral, I think. He'll always be honest, according to his own lights, and usually kind. The only people he has no time for are those who expect him to conform to their own set of expectations.'

'You have that completely wrong,' I say, stung. 'I asked nothing from him except a little loyalty. But that doesn't seem to be a word in his vocabulary.'

Patrick rubs his nose perplexedly. 'I'm not saying you asked anything from him. I'm not doing very well here, am I? Nora told me to keep out of it, and she's always right, but we've both become very fond of you.'

I relent. 'It's fine, Patrick. This was my fault. Ethan told me the score, or at least I should have worked it out for myself. As you say, he isn't someone who hides things. He just seemed such a contrast to all the people I've grown up with who always know what's best for me. Ethan doesn't care what's best for the long term, just as long as he's happy now. He isn't a great one for worrying about the future, and I envy that so much. I'd love to be more like him.'

'You can't be like someone else,' says Patrick. 'You are what you are, and what you are seems just fine to me. There's a cost to what Ethan does, even if you can't see it now. He's a rolling stone. He may not gather moss, but he may wake up one day to find he hasn't gathered other things either. It could be too late, but he'll have to live with that.'

The following week is hideously uncomfortable for everyone. Ethan has the grace to stay clear of me as much as possible, and Patrick and Nora make no attempt to discuss things further. I'm not yet ready to deal with Ethan directly, so I stay busy around the house and take long walks down to the harbour during my few free hours.

I don't know what to think about him or how he's behaved. Underneath my anger and resentment lies a suspicion that blaming him for everything isn't the answer, however satisfying it might be. He never lied to me. In fact, he told me up front exactly who he was, and I childishly refused to listen.

We weren't looking for the same things at all – me because I have no idea what I'm searching for, and Ethan because he isn't searching for anything. But I still tried to persuade myself he was the answer to everything I'd run away from back home, and there could never be a good ending to that.

I can't even feel as much anger as I'd like. I'm still oddly fond of him, even now I see him more clearly. But he'll never be the one for me. His lack of engagement is appealing on some levels, but I can't copy it. I don't even want to, however much hurt it might save me in the long run.

I can't skim the surface of life. I know that now. I wanted to believe that spontaneity was the only thing missing from my life, and I blamed Matt for that. But I see now how unfair that was. How was Matt supposed to know what I wanted when I was incapable of knowing it myself?

I've been brought face to face with the flip side of spontaneity, and I don't like what I've seen. My life in the UK was stifling me, and it needed to change. Instead, I ripped it to shreds. I wonder dispiritedly whether I'll ever find a balance.

I'm wandering along the shoreline late one evening, brooding over these things with little resolution, when a voice makes me jump.

'Planning a midnight swim in your pyjamas for old times' sake?'

I spin around to see that Ethan has crept up behind me, barefoot. I'd been hoping to avoid him for the foreseeable future. I can't think of anything we have to say to each other.

He stoops down and pulls on his trainers. 'Nora said I might find you down here.'

'I wish she hadn't,' I tell him.

'Aw, come on, Anna! Weren't you ever going to talk to me?'

I pull a face. 'About what?'

'I'm off tomorrow.'

I don't know whether to be pleased or sad when he says this.

'Tomorrow?' I say. 'Isn't that a bit sudden?'

'Not really,' he says. 'It just feels like time. I've finished all the garden stuff for Patrick, and he doesn't need me any longer. He was probably only keeping me on for your sake.'

'He needn't bother,' I say tightly.

He grins. 'I think he knows that. Anyway, I was hoping to get up towards Russell for the winter, so I'm off.'

'Have a good journey,' I say.

'You aren't coming with me?'

The sheer audacity of his question stops me in my tracks, and I swing around to face him. 'You aren't serious?'

'Why not?' he asks. 'You don't want to skivvy here for ever, do you? It was fun while it lasted, but …'

'Everything's fun while it lasts for you, isn't it, Ethan? And then you toss it all away and move on, no matter who gets run over in the process.'

'I guess that's a no,' he says. 'I'm sorry, Anna. I honestly didn't mean to hurt you. You know that, don't you?'

'The final refuge of the complete arse,' I say thoughtfully. 'I've always loved the *I didn't mean to hurt you* defence. No, I don't suppose you did – not really. But you did anyway, and I'll bet I'm not the first. Do people a favour in future and spell it out more clearly up front. Not everyone sees things quite the way you do.'

He grins. 'I promise. I'll tell them I'm a total arse – Anna says so – and I'm completely at their own risk.'

'Good,' I say. 'Well, I have an early start tomorrow, so I'm going to call it a night now. Thanks for coming down.'

'Already?' he says. 'I was going to suggest a last drink in town.'

'Thanks, but no.'

'A walk along the shore?' he suggests. 'A chance to remember the night of our extreme heroism?'

'Again, tempting, but no.'

I'm annoyed that I really want to say yes, but I'm not going there again. He's leaving tomorrow, and I don't want him complicating things.

He gives me a rueful smile. 'Rebuff accepted. All the best then, sweetheart, until we meet again.'

He wraps his arms around me, and I stand frozen for a moment before relaxing and rubbing my cheek against his shoulder. I've suddenly had enough of only remembering the things that don't hurt. Ethan was a part of my life, however briefly, and I'll keep the memories, both good and bad.

I push him away after a few seconds. 'See you around,' I say.

I stare across the water to the lights of Auckland twinkling through the dusk and barely listen to his footsteps crunching over the sand as he walks away.

Chapter Twenty

Nora and I are making beds a week later when I hear a faint cry from the other room. 'Anna!'

I race through to find her sitting doubled over on the bed in the blue bedroom. Her face is scrunched up with pain, she's breathing heavily, and she's a greyish colour.

'I'll get Patrick,' I say. 'Sit there, and I'll be right back.'

She grabs at my hand. 'Please don't! There's really no need to bother him. Can you bring my handbag from the kitchen? It has my pills in it.'

I'm not letting it go at this, but the priority seems to be the pills, so I rush down the wooden stairs and seize her leather shoulder bag. Nora rummages through it and locates a tube of tablets, which she gestures for me to open. She's still a greyish-cream colour, and she's clutching at her shoulder. I force off the lid, and she tips out a tablet and places it under her tongue.

A few moments later, the colour returns to her cheeks. She sits upright and gives me a guilty look.

'What is it?' I ask sternly. 'You can tell me it's none of my business if you like, but at least tell me whether this happens often.'

'Hardly ever,' she says. 'I always keep the pills in my pocket and take one if I feel it coming on. For some reason, I left them in my bag today and then climbed the stairs too quickly. It won't happen again, I promise.'

I think of the greyish colour of her face, and my stomach contracts. Pictures of Dad swirl through my mind, images I normally squash at once. With Nora sitting right in front of me, I can't. I finally understand why they needed someone like me to come and help.

'Is it … do you have … cancer?' I whisper miserably, and she jumps.

'No, nothing like that! I just have a touch of angina now and again. I wasn't sure whether Patrick had told you, although I made him promise not to. Whatever gave you the idea I had cancer?'

I can't trust my voice to answer.

'I had a little turn last year,' she goes on without waiting for me to reply. 'It was a very small attack, and the doctor decided I have angina. I'm fine now, though. These tablets are wonderful. They sort me out straight away.'

She gives me a half smile. 'Patrick worries himself sick. He seems to think I might keel over at any moment. That's why he insisted we get some help around the house. I'm perfectly capable of doing it myself, but there's no telling that man anything when he gets a bee in his bonnet.'

'You don't say,' I murmur as she holds out her hand for me to pull her up. 'Look, Nora, it isn't any of my business to tell him about today. That's up to you, but I wish you would. What would have happened if I'd been downstairs? I'd never have heard you, and Patrick's outside in the garden.'

'I know,' she says, 'but I usually have my tablets with me.'

I take her down to her flat, where she promises to lie down for half an hour. I settle her into her room, then wander into the garden to think.

I'm teasing a long piece of sweet corn silk through my fingers when I hear the thunk of a spade. I peer around the corner to see Patrick digging potatoes. He smiles and waves at the pile of potatoes on the grass.

'Dinner,' he tells me. 'And maybe breakfast and lunch tomorrow as well, unless you're really hungry tonight.'

'It's too hot to think about dinner right now,' I say. 'I've been making beds with Nora.'

I don't want to give her away, but I'm half hoping he'll follow this up and give me an excuse to tell him what happened.

'Good, good,' he says. 'Can you grab a lettuce and some of those tomatoes and sling them into the basket? I thought we'd have salad for lunch.'

I do as he asks, suddenly glad that I haven't interfered. It's up to Nora how she wants to live her life. I twist the fibrous stems until the tomatoes drop into my palm, then shake the dirt from a curly-leaved lettuce.

I look down at the basket. 'There's too much here for the two of you to eat. Couldn't you think about selling some of your vegetables to the local cafes?'

'I've thought about it,' he says, 'but we don't really need the money, and bartering with the neighbours works pretty well for us.'

'But it's such lovely stuff,' I say. 'It's all organic, isn't it?'

He nods.

'So there'd be a premium on it?' I pursue.

'I suppose there would, but I'd need certification,' he says. 'It's hardly worth it for one small garden. But you're right that it's good stuff.'

He snaps a pea pod from its stem and tosses it over to me. I run my teeth down the inside of the pod and roll the peas onto my tongue. They're juicy and sweet, and I wonder why we ever bother to cook them.

'Shall we have a few for the salad?' he asks, and I nod, still chewing.

We pick a small bunch of rocket, then head back to the house. A thought has been working its way around my mind for a while, and I decide to voice it. I stop abruptly, and Patrick cannons into me, dropping his basket.

'Sorry,' I say, 'but I have an idea I'd like to talk about.'

He nods. 'Go on, while I pick up these potatoes.'

'The first day I was here, I asked whether you serve dinners as well, and you said no,' I begin.

He's already shaking his head. 'We've talked about it, but it isn't right for us. This is a small operation. Nora enjoys having the guests, and it gives us an excuse to keep living in a place with a huge garden, so I'm happy. But we aren't looking for more work. We're not getting any younger, and we don't have your kind of energy anymore.'

I can tell he's thinking about Nora's health, but I'm not letting on that I know about it. Anyway, he has it all wrong.

'It isn't you I'm thinking about,' I say in a rush. 'You have that place next door that isn't doing anything. I know it needs fixing up, but couldn't we make it into a small restaurant? That way, your guests would have somewhere to eat in the evenings, and I could buy your spare vegetables and maybe even your fish when you catch it. I could put in a flat upstairs and live there. I'd pay you rent.'

'I'm stunned,' he says slowly. 'How long have you been thinking about this?'

'On and off for quite a while,' I say. 'It first came to me when I saw how many vegetables you were growing. I know I'm not a great cook yet, but I'm learning fast.'

I watch him hopefully, hoping against hope that he doesn't tell me not to be so stupid. Ideas are flooding in now, and I see the whole thing clearly laid out in front of me – snowy tablecloths, candles and big wooden bowls of salad.

Patrick sits on the wooden bench, motioning me to sit next to him. 'It isn't a bad idea, but let's break it down a bit.'

I smile. I can't help it. He sounds exactly like Dad, with his perpetual reply of, '*One step at a time.*'

He taps his teeth with one grubby nail. 'Now, what exactly are you thinking of – a full-blown restaurant or just a cafe?'

I'm stunned that he's taking me so seriously. I was braced for a brush-off or an explanation of why it would be a terrible idea. I think carefully before replying, not wanting to make any comment that might kill the idea before it's born.

'I need to do a lot more thinking and investigating,' I begin, 'but this is how I see it. You have a property you aren't using, and it's right next door. I suppose you could make it into an overflow for the bed-and-breakfast, but that wouldn't make much sense given that you've brought me in because you and Nora want to slow down.'

I carefully refrain from mentioning Nora's health, but I'm sure he takes the point. My words tumble out faster and faster as the scheme takes more concrete shape in my mind.

'What's to stop me from doing the place up and having a restaurant downstairs and a flat upstairs? That way, I could offer dinner to your guests, which would be a bonus when you're advertising. As I say, I could buy all your spare vegetables.'

I sneak a quick look at him, trying to read his face. 'You could keep on doing the breakfasts over at yours, but I could provide packed lunches for the guests. And there's no reason why people can't come in for dinner even if they aren't staying with you.'

I come to an abrupt stop, hoping my jumble of thoughts hasn't already put him off. I'm pleased to see he's looking thoughtful.

'You're looking at a heck of a lot of work,' he says at last.

I don't mind his reservations. At least, he's taking me seriously.

'I know,' I say. 'I don't mind hard work.'

He shakes his head. 'There's too much that needs doing professionally for you to do it all by yourself. A restaurant kitchen needs a licence, and you'd have to satisfy all the fire regulations and have regular health and safety inspections. Still, there's no reason why you and I couldn't do up the flat. The plumbing is in place, and I could help you fit new appliances and lay tiles. It isn't that difficult. I expect you could manage the painting and decorating yourself.'

'I think so,' I say.

My town house was a wreck when I bought it. It was so garishly decorated that Matt and I decided the previous owner had been a circus tent designer in a previous incarnation. We spent several days slapping white paint onto all the walls to hide the reds and purples. We found some cheap off-cuts of carpet, and Matt paid for them to be professionally fitted as his house warming present to me – right after I threatened to fit them myself. By the time it was finished, I loved that house. I feel a sudden pang of homesickness. I hope Nicole's looking after it for me.

Patrick interrupts my train of thought. 'You know what I think? You have some good ideas for this restaurant, but you haven't done anything exactly like this before.'

My heart sinks in anticipation of a carefully worded rejection. He reads my thoughts and shakes his head at me. 'Don't be so defeatist. I'm saying that we should take this slowly. Let's try it out on a small scale so no one loses out if you change your mind. You need to find out whether you even enjoy this sort of thing.'

'What do you have in mind?' I ask.

He thinks for a moment. 'We could let the guests know that for the rest of the season, you'll be offering afternoon teas. We'll tell them what you're thinking of doing and maybe even offer the teas at cost. That way, it'll be a bargain all round. They'll be keener to sign up, and you can use them as guinea pigs to see what works and what doesn't.'

I'm amazed that he's taking me so seriously. I feel a little worried now he's offered to help implement my idea. What if I fail?

'All right,' I say after a moment, 'but I'll need some advice.'

'Of course,' he agrees, and we'll both be happy to help. I'll put on a striped apron and be your waiter, if you like.'

'I meant help with planning and cooking,' I say, 'but don't let me stop you dressing up if you want to.'

He laughs. 'I'll give you all the advice you like, but in some ways, this is right up your street.'

I give him a puzzled look. To my mind, the biggest problem is that I've never done anything like this. I can just picture Mum's face if she even heard me suggest it.

He waves a lettuce at me. 'Yes, yes! I'd have thought that anyone who's been a teacher should be able to organise something like this very easily. Didn't you have to keep records and organise lesson plans and all that sort of thing? And what about looking after unruly children and dealing with their parents? I'd say you have a whole host of transferable skills right there. I don't think that providing the odd afternoon tea is going to throw you.'

Perhaps he's right. And I have nothing to lose by giving it a go – other than the price of a few scones and some possible embarrassment if I fail. And I ought to be able to deal with that.

'When should we start?' I ask.

Nora goes to bed early that evening. I'm not sure whether she's told Patrick about her earlier attack, but she's privately assured me she's just tired from the heat and is always fine the next day. I check she has her tablets with her and make her a cup of tea, then Patrick and I spend the evening with a pile of recipe books.

He gently talks me down from my initial ideas of a lavish spread with handmade florentines and millefeuilles.

'Keep it simple, love,' he counsels again and again as I show him pictures of hand-painted delicacies.

I eventually realise he's right, so I reluctantly abandon my ideas of tracing intricate patterns onto homemade chocolate truffles. We make a list of the sort of simple baked goods I can manage by myself and discuss sandwich fillings. By the end of the evening, I'm exhausted.

'Let's give it a week,' says Patrick. 'You'll need to practise some of these until you can make them in your sleep. We can freeze your successes for later emergencies. Pop down to the supermarket tomorrow and reckon up your costs for the three menus we've agreed. That way, you can see how much you'll have to charge. If you're using our cloths and napkins, don't forget to add in something extra for laundering them. That may sound mean, but you'll never get your own business up and running without costing it down to the last cent.'

I must look as dazed as I feel because he pats my shoulder encouragingly. 'It's a good idea, Anna, so it's worth giving it your best shot.'

'It all sounds so complicated,' I say. 'And we're only talking about afternoon teas. How would I ever manage running a whole restaurant?'

He grins. 'The same way all successful business people do – delegate, delegate, delegate, and take everything one step at a time. I think we're onto something here.'

I like the sound of this. If Patrick and Nora come on board, it may not be so daunting after all.

Chapter Twenty-One

I lie in bed for a while, flicking through recipes for ginger snaps and wondering about miniature trifles. I finally fall asleep and dream of a garden party on Patrick and Nora's lawn. Increasing numbers of people arrive, all clamouring to be fed while I stand there in my swimming costume, clutching a plate of burnt sausage rolls and some broken digestive biscuits.

Nora takes me aside after breakfast. 'You didn't say anything to Patrick. I was almost sure you would.'

'It wasn't my business,' I say. 'It's your life, not mine. But do take care, Nora. There's no point in over-exerting yourself now that I'm here.'

She pats my shoulder affectionately. 'It's made a world of difference having you here. Honestly, it has. But I'd much rather wear out than rust away. I can't imagine sitting around all day and watching everyone else work.'

'I don't suppose you can,' I say, 'but there's a balance. I can do the heavy work. I quite enjoy it now I've got used to it, and it gives me time to think.'

'Patrick told me about some of those thoughts last night,' she says. 'I think it's a wonderful idea. Don't let him discourage you. He sees all the problems before they happen.'

I smile as I think of last night's conversation. 'I need someone like that. I'm not always very practical. You should have seen the menus I tried to get past him.'

She nods. 'He's good at planning things, but don't let him squash the life out of your plans before they've even got off the ground. He and I get along so well because I have the ideas and he finds the flaws. Then I go ahead with the plans anyway, so he has to join in just to stop them getting out of hand.'

She smiles reminiscently. 'When we bought this place, I drew up plans for the guest bedrooms that would have suited Buckingham Palace. As for the solar-heated swimming pool and jacuzzi in every bedroom …'

I laugh, not sure how serious she is about these last two.

'Will you help with the afternoon teas?' I ask her. 'I don't mean doing all the work, but I could use some advice. You do the breakfasts so beautifully.'

'I'd love to help,' she says. 'Just tell me to hush up if I get too bossy.'

I show her my plans for the three different menus, and we discuss them and make a few amendments. She suggests that we base all the menus on cream teas because they're so simple.

'And everyone loves cream teas,' she says. 'I have plenty of jam that Verity sent over when they had a glut of strawberries a few months ago. You can have those if you like.'

She resists the idea of payment at first, but I tell her that Patrick was firm on that point, and she gives in. She thinks we should make up batches of scones each weekend and freeze them.

'You can make scones, of course?' she says.

For some reason, I seem to have overlooked this point. When I sheepishly admit this to Nora, she chuckles. 'Roll up your sleeves, and let's get started.'

I copy her as she rubs the flour and butter into crumbs then stirs in the egg and milk. At the end of the process, her dough sits smugly in its bowl while mine stretches and sags.

'A little more flour, perhaps?' she suggests.

I sprinkle in some more flour and gently knead the dough. This time, it ends up as a tough lump that cracks when I roll it out. We cut out circles, flip the dough and re-roll it. When we've finished, Nora beats an egg and brushes it over the scones before sliding them into the oven.

Ten minutes later, the timer beeps and she stoops down and lifts out the two trays. Her scones have risen, all golden and puffy, with a slight quirky tilt at the top. Mine are hunched on their tray, sulking, and don't appear to have risen at all.

'Perhaps your dough should be wetter next time?' she ventures politely.

I shrug rather huffily. I did exactly what she did, so why did mine turn out so badly?

She frowns. 'I must admit I didn't think it was possible to mess up scones. Try again, but perhaps make a half batch this time, just in case.'

I try again. This time, my dough is too wet to cut, and the dough slouches and slops in strands across the counter. I scrape it into the bin and read the recipe again. My third batch turns out beautifully, and the scones puff up happily in the oven.

'Marvellous,' says Nora, motioning to me to sit down. She reaches for a pot of jam, which shines in the sun like a pot of rubies. We ladle it into a glass bowl, and Nora calls for Patrick.

He appears a few minutes later, sniffing appreciatively. 'This is definitely the up-side of your idea, Anna – all these tastings.'

I wave at the tray of hardened lumps on the counter, and his eyes crinkle in amusement. 'Hmm. Well, practise makes perfect, and the chooks will love those.'

'These latest ones are an accident,' I tell him through a mouthful of crumbly scone. 'I don't know exactly what I did right, which is a bit worrying.'

'Oh dear,' he says. 'Scones every day for a week, do we think?'

'Get away with you, man!' says Nora. 'She's done a lovely job. We'll make some more this evening. If they're as good as this batch, we can freeze them for later.'

I make three more batches of scones. Although one of them is a little shaky, I finally get the feel of how sticky the dough needs to be, and I freeze two batches. The chooks get the rest and seem quite happy with them. Before I go to bed, I write down the cost of the ingredients, making a note of the failed batches too. If I keep feeding the hens like this, Nora says she'll give me the eggs for free.

Over the following days, Nora and I visit the herb garden and make an array of herb butters, which we label and put in the fridge. She also suggests various sandwich fillings we can prepare in advance. I scribble down all her ideas and recipes and store them in a red, loose-leaf notebook.

We prepare a large bowl of salmon and wrap it in cling film. Patrick promises us fresh cucumber on the day. We riffle back through the books, finally deciding on Anzac cookies and miniature chocolate and cherry muffins.

'And if they're hungry after that lot,' Nora says cheerfully, 'they can forage in Patrick's vegetable garden with the chooks.'

I practise making the muffins. The first batch is rather chewy, but it doesn't take me long to get the hang of lightly mixing the ingredients. I start to turn out light and crumbly muffins, swirled through with cherry puree and ready to be topped with melted chocolate and cream just before we serve them.

The Anzac cookies are even easier. When I first stir the dough in the saucepan, it looks pale and flabby. But ten minutes in the oven magically turns it into crisp, golden bites. I tuck them between layers of greaseproof paper in Nora's largest cake tin.

We've scheduled the first afternoon tea for Saturday afternoon. Patrick comes into the kitchen that morning, beaming. 'I've talked every single one of them into it.'

I turn pale. 'Patrick, you haven't?'

'I most certainly have,' he says. 'I told them all about your idea for a restaurant and how we plan to start small. Then I gave them all a menu for this afternoon. They couldn't sign up fast enough, especially when I told them it was all at cost. So that's six … seven … eight adults and two little boys who have hollow legs. They can finish all the burnt bits for you and stop those poor chooks getting indigestion.'

I throw the tea towel at him. 'Nothing will be burned, and you know it. Stop trying to make me nervous. Will you help?'

'Of course,' he says. 'We both will. It's almost as exciting for us as it is for you.'

He dances a mock jig, and I smile. 'What time did you tell them?'

'Four o'clock exactly. I also told them the price would double for each minute they were late, and everyone has to wash their hands and faces first.'

'If I finish the bedrooms by lunchtime, may I have the kitchen for the afternoon?' I ask.

'Of course,' he says. 'Nora will help you, and I'll set up the dining room. I'll cut some flowers and put them in vases.'

I wanted to serve tea outside, but we don't yet have enough garden tables. And as Nora points out, the weather could change, and I don't need to be worrying about flies and gusts of wind.

I clean the dining room and bring in fresh cloths for the tables. I ironed them last night, and they're perfectly flat and scented with lavender. I take the herb butters from the fridge and put them out on the counter to soften. I pull out the boxes of scones and muffins and count them carefully, wondering how much people will eat. I run upstairs and clean the bedrooms as quickly as possible, then rush downstairs again to find Nora and Patrick already eating lunch.

'Great muffins,' says Patrick with his mouth full. 'This herb butter is wonderful.'

My eyes widen in horror, and Nora taps his hand. 'You stop that right now! The poor girl is nervous enough without you carrying on. We haven't touched a single thing, love. We're just finishing up yesterday's soup so we don't make any mess cooking.'

'The girl won't miss a few scones,' grumbles Patrick, reaching his hand towards the counter.

She slaps at it again. 'Have some soup, Anna. You need something before this afternoon.'

'And I don't charge for it like you do,' says Patrick smugly.

The soup is wonderful, and I start to relax as I dip my spoon into its clear, orange depths. Carrot and coriander, fresh from the garden, is an unbeatable combination. It would be great to include it on the restaurant menu – simple to prepare and tasting of sunshine.

After we've cleared away the bowls, Patrick goes outside to cut some flowers to *pretty up* the dining room, as he mockingly puts it.

'Don't take any notice of him, will you?' says Nora. 'He pretends this is all a big joke, but he kept waking me up last night to ask whether you'd remembered everything. Now, let's just run through it all. We've made the cookies and scones, but you still have to top the muffins. We'll whip the cream nearer the time. All the herb butters are in bowls, and we have fresh bread for those who don't want sandwiches. So, it's just the sandwiches left to do. Can you get us a couple of sharp knives and a bowl of hot water?'

We use grainy, caramel-coloured bread. I fill the sandwiches and Nora slices them, dipping her knife into the hot water as she goes. We soon have a plate of salmon sandwiches, the crisp slices of cucumber lying in emerald layers against the coral of the fish. We cut more bread before sweeping the thinnest layer of mustard over it. I add honey roast ham and wafer-thin cheese and some of Patrick's curled lettuce. Finally, I make a pile of egg and cress sandwiches and grind black pepper over the filling.

'If they finish that lot, I'll be surprised,' says Nora.

She surveys the table. 'You've done a fantastic job here, Anna. I'm so proud of you.' She sweeps me into one of her enormous hugs.

'It was all three of us,' I say. 'I'll never manage any kind of restaurant without you two, so we'll need to have a talk about that soon.'

'Let's just concentrate on this wonderful spread for now,' she says. 'Can you whip the cream while I take a quick shower?'

I start the beater and watch the white liquid shiver and wrinkle, then puff into clouds of snow. I scoop it into three small bowls and make one final mental check of everything before heading upstairs to take a shower.

I've washed and ironed my daisy skirt in honour of the occasion. I wonder what Ethan would make of my new venture. I like to think he'd be pleased for me. Maybe I'll write to him this week and tell him about it. Life's too short to hold grudges.

I'm back downstairs by half past three. Nora and Patrick help me to carry the plates and bowls to the dining room and arrange them neatly on the two tables. Patrick has cut some of his precious roses and arranged them into one huge glass jug and several single-stem vases. By the time we've finished, the tables look perfect.

'Just don't tell the guests I'm a closet flower-arranger or they'll want them in their rooms too,' he whispers, poking me in the ribs as I pass.

The guests gather outside the dining room at four o'clock.

Patrick ushers them inside. 'Come in, come in! Welcome, welcome!' he booms, and everyone smiles at his courtly air. There are gasps of appreciation when they see the tables loaded with food.

When everyone is sitting down, he motions for silence.

'Thank you all so much for coming. You've met Anna already. She's worked extremely hard to produce this feast, so the best way you can show your appreciation is by trying everything and eating plenty of it.'

No one seems to need further encouragement as they help themselves to the sandwiches. Patrick and I take orders for tea and cold drinks, and I run backwards and forwards to the kitchen. I've stationed Nora discreetly in the doorway with a small notebook, and she's jotting down how much of everything is being eaten. Most of the guests are eating as though Patrick and I hadn't served them a full cooked breakfast only six hours ago.

After a few minutes, everyone is chattering and laughing and passing the plates around, trying everything. The little boys are ploughing through the salmon sandwiches and eyeing the muffins hungrily. It takes more than an hour before everyone runs out of steam. When I enter the room with the final steaming pot of tea, the guests break into a round of applause. I thank them, my face flaming, as Patrick and Nora smile proudly from the doorway.

The guests roll out into the garden, leaving us to clear up. We fill the fridge with wrapped plates of sandwiches and put the remaining cookies and muffins back in their tins. Half the scones didn't get eaten, and I vastly overestimated how much cream we'd need, but Nora says she'll make us a trifle tomorrow.

We pack the dishwasher and sit down at the kitchen table while Nora shows us her notebook. I've lavishly over-provided, and we calculate we could have got away with about half the food and still had plenty for everyone.

'Big night for the chooks,' says Patrick.

'But everybody loved it,' I say happily. 'Go on, admit it. It was a success.'

He grins at me. 'Indeed it was. You have a dazzling new career waiting for you, young Anna, if you want it.'

'*We* have a new career,' I correct him. 'I couldn't have done any of this without you.'

'Perhaps,' he says. 'But it won't be long before you're doing all this single-handed.'

Nora goes outside and reappears to tell me the guests are lying in the garden, vowing never to eat again but making afternoon tea bookings for the rest of the week. She reaches into the fridge and pulls out a gold-topped bottle. She deftly slits the foil and pours out three glasses. 'To you, Anna.'

'To *us*,' I say. 'To our joint venture. And thank you both, more than I can say.'

Chapter Twenty-Two

I'm out in the garden the evening the call comes. The air is milk-warm after the gentle heat of yet another cloudless day. I'm lying on the grass, watching the moon glide upwards between the dark mountains. The day's warmth oozes out of the flagstones. I could easily read a book in this bluish light, but I can't be bothered to fetch one from my room, so I lie and watch the stars flicker and disappear through the slight haze that forms above the mountains each night.

It's been a long day. I set my alarm very early this morning and drove out to take the funicular train up the mountain. The frondy ferns were still damp, and the cool air curled around my ankles, chilling my toes. When the train reached the top, spicy green scents enveloped us, while the bay below developed into a panorama of sapphire and gold like a Polaroid image.

Watching the scene change minute by minute, I realised that the world has always seemed very temporary to me. Each new experience feels fleeting as it slides remorselessly through my clutching fingers. The brevity that Nicole finds so exciting depresses me. I want to pin down, file away, collect and make an enduring image to remind me of my experiences.

But today, standing at the peak of the mountain, floating among the drifting clouds, I felt a flash of completeness. I watched the scene below me with a sense of unity, seeing it as a set of tiny moments strung together into a complete picture. Perhaps one step at a time makes a coherent journey after all.

I've thought much more about Dad since I've been out here. The pain hasn't entirely gone, but the physical distance has offered perspective. Since he died, I've often felt as though I'm walking underwater, with all sights and sounds dimmed. I can see the people around me and join in with their conversations, but we're separated by the invisible barrier between us.

The sense of responsibility that was Dad's legacy to me has sometimes felt so crushing as to make it difficult to breathe. But even that has lifted during these past few months, although the guilt at leaving Mum remains. I know she'll survive this time apart, but I wonder whether our relationship, already tense to the point of fracture, can ever be the same again. If she resents me for abandoning her, I'll just have to live with it. We can probably rebuild something, however unsatisfying.

But the thought of Dad being disappointed with me is something I can't bear. He would have wanted both Mum and me to be happy, and I feel that I've failed him on both counts. Neither she nor I seem to have found contentment since he left. We need to find a better way when I go home.

I'm thankful for the space that New Zealand has given me. The painful memories of Dad's last months have receded and the images lurking behind them, pictures I had thought were lost forever, have come back into focus. I see Dad laughing as often as I see him fighting the pain. My time out here has helped me to regain the bigger picture, which I had begun to think would never happen.

The grass is growing chilly, so I stand and head towards the house, wading through the scents that flood the night air as the flowers relax in the dark.

Nora steps into the pool of light thrown across the stones by the window, making me jump.

'Phone for you, love,' she says. 'Hurry – it's from England.'

I step inside and lift the phone silently to my ear.

'Anna? Anna?' says Nicole's voice. 'Oh, for goodness' sake, is anyone there?'

'I'm here!' I push the words over my stiff tongue.

She gives a gasp of relief. 'Your mobile seems to be switched off. Thank goodness I got through on the house phone.'

I speak as calmly as possible. 'What's wrong? Is it Mum?'

'Yes, but she's fine. Honestly, she is. Please don't start panicking. Just listen to me, ok?'

I lean against the wall, just outside the patch of light. I can't see Nora, but I'm sure she's standing somewhere in the shadows.

'I'm still here,' I say. 'Tell me what's happened.'

She sighs. 'I took her to the supermarket yesterday afternoon after school. We were walking through the car park when I realised I'd left my carrier bags in the car, so I went back for them while she went on ahead. Just as I opened the boot, I heard a bang and some shouting. When I turned around, she was just lying there. She'd walked straight into a car as it was pulling out. The poor driver was in a terrible state. We called an ambulance because she couldn't stand up, and she's in hospital now. Are you still there?'

'I am. So, what's the damage?' I ask as cheerfully as I can.

Nicole sounds relieved at my tone. 'She got a bit of a bang on the head. They think she had a mild concussion because she wasn't making much sense for a while. She's fine now and even talking about suing the poor driver. It wasn't his fault. I've told her that several times, but you know your mum. He was hardly moving, and she walked straight out behind him. Several people saw her do it. She'd have got away with it if she hadn't fallen awkwardly.'

She hesitates. 'Anyway, she's broken her right hip quite badly. They took her into surgery and put a pin in it. She's all slung up in one of those winch things, so they're keeping her in for a few days. She's furious about that. She told them she isn't staying there just to catch one of their nasty infections and go out in a box.'

She bursts out laughing, but I don't join her. 'Should I come back?' I ask.

'I honestly don't think so,' she says quickly, and it's quite clear she was prepared for this. 'I'm here, and I promise I'll go in and see her every day and get her whatever she needs. She'll be home in a couple of days, and the doctors say her hip will heal very well. It will just take time.'

'How much time?' I ask.

'They said it depends on her attitude and how committed she is to doing her physio.'

We both think about this for a moment. At last, I take a deep breath and speak as quickly as I can because I don't want to be tempted into listening to Nicole and staying here.

'I'll look into flights first thing tomorrow. I have a return ticket, so that shouldn't be a problem.'

'Oh, Anna!' Nicole says despairingly. But I'm not discussing this. She must have known what I'd do, even before she called me.

'I'll ring you tomorrow night for an update and to tell you when I'll be arriving,' I say. 'Thanks for letting me know so quickly.'

I ring off before she can argue. Nicole is always very persuasive, but I'm not listening to any of her rehearsed arguments. Mum needs me, and that's that. I should never have left her. I see that now. She shouldn't have been doing her own shopping. I always did it for her. It was nice of Nicole to take her, but she couldn't be expected to realise how closely she should have watched Mum.

I step into the front hall and hand the phone to Nora, who's standing behind the reception desk, tapping busily into her computer and trying to look as though she wasn't listening.

'It's my mum,' I say. 'She's broken her hip, and I have to fly back home.'

She looks sympathetic. 'Oh, dear. I did wonder if it was something like that when your friend called so late. Still, it could be worse, I suppose. Is she in the hospital?'

'Yes, for the next few days. After that, I'll have to fix something up for her. She can't go back to her house alone, so I'll have to stay with her.'

My face is stiff with misery, and I don't look her in the eye. I hate sympathetic faces – I always have. I resent feeling I need to comfort other people when I'm the one who's upset.

'I'm so sorry, Nora,' I say. 'I know I'm letting you down at short notice, but …'

She comes around the desk and gives me a swift hug. 'Don't be so silly. You get up to bed now. There's nothing you can do tonight. You can call the airline in the morning and sort something out. Patrick will give you a lift into Auckland if you need one. It won't be for long, I hope. You'll be coming back when it's all sorted out?'

I try to smile. 'That's nice of you, but I can't make any plans. I don't know how Mum will be when I get there. Thanks, anyway.'

'We understand,' she says. 'There's no need to decide anything right now. You pop off to bed now and make your calls in the morning. It might be good to call the hospital as well.'

I nod. 'Thanks, Nora.'

I walk across the hallway and out into the garden. I won't be back. I know it, and Nora knows it too. It's been a lovely dream, but reality is kicking in now, a little harder than I'd like, but this could never be permanent. When I get outside, I stand for a few moments wiping my eyes and breathing in the night scents for the last time.

Chapter Twenty-Three

Walking into Mum's house without permission feels wrong, a violation of the privacy she holds so dear. The key clicks in the lock, and I push open the freshly painted front door. Who did that, I wonder? I stoop and pick up the cluster of letters spilling across the mat, sifting through them. None of them look urgent. There are a couple of *Get Well* cards, and I separate those out to take in when I collect her. I put the rest of the post on the hand-embroidered cloth on the hall table.

Mum made a complete set of these when she was my age. There are several tray cloths and a gorgeous linen swathe, scattered with alpine flowers. It lay in a snowy drift across the table each Christmas, making the cranberry sauce and gravy a terror to me. I secretly thought of it as a winding sheet.

I bend and look more closely at the tiny flowers. There isn't a stitch out of place as they twine in intricate order around the silken stems. The doorbell rings, and I jump. I'm expecting it to be a postal worker with a parcel for Mum, but it's Nicole, waving an enormous bunch of daffodils. We hug for a long time, but I can't speak.

She drops the flowers onto the hall table, where they leave a damp patch on the white cloth. I snatch them up, and she grins. 'I thought you'd have arrived home by now. It's a good job I was right because I forgot my key.'

'You have a key?' I say.

'Of course, I do. Why ever not?'

'Mum doesn't like anyone coming in the house when she isn't here.'

'I'm not just anyone,' says Nicole. 'If she wants me to help her, she can't expect me to wait around for her to be home. She understands that.'

I raise my eyebrows, but I'm too tired to ask questions. I glance down at the flowers. 'These are lovely. Mum likes daffodils.'

'They're for you,' declares Nicole.

'Me? Why on earth?'

'It was very nice of you to fly all this way back. I thought someone should recognise that.' She hugs me again, and my eyes sting.

'Even though you think it was unnecessary, and I was over-reacting?'

She grins. 'Yes, even though. Anyway, it's your choice. What does it have to do with me? I knew before I called that you'd come home, but I couldn't not tell you, could I?'

'Absolutely not,' I say. 'Well, they're lovely. They smell of spring. Thanks, Nicole.'

'What's next?' she asks.

'I don't know. I only landed this morning, and I thought I'd better check everything here before I went to collect her. I spoke to the doctor before I flew, and he said she can come home today as long as someone stays with her. I'll be moving in for a while until she can get around. I'd better make up a bed in the spare room.'

Nicole follows me up the stairs, where I peep into each of the rooms. As usual, the place is immaculate, with that familiar whiff of lemon polish I remember from my childhood Saturday mornings.

'She must have cleaned just before she had the accident,' I say, poking around in the airing cupboard for fresh bedding.

'I expect the cleaner's been in,' says Nicole.

'What cleaner? She doesn't have one.'

She grins. 'Yes, she does. It was one of the first things we did after you left. A friend of mine was looking for a few hours a week, and Janice thought it was a great idea. Really, she did,' she adds, seeing my expression. 'Come on, Anna, you know she can afford it, and I don't have time for all that stuff. I didn't push her into it, so don't look at me like that. They get on pretty well. Jess is a bit of a perfectionist, which suits your mum down to the ground.'

If this Jess can clean to Mum's standards, she must be something special. I never could. I peek in at the bathroom where even the taps sparkle at me aggressively.

I take some sheets from the airing cupboard and toss them onto the spare bed, and we go downstairs to the kitchen, where Nicole switches on the shining new coffee maker. I'm not about to ask, but she catches my eye and grins.

'We gave it to her for her birthday. She likes coffee after dinner, and I was fed up with that horrible instant stuff she was drinking.'

Who's *we*, I wonder? After only six months, I feel like a stranger in the house in which I grew up. It's all very disorientating. But the coffee is surprisingly good, and Mum even seems to have bought new china cups. I don't allow myself more than a faint feeling of surprise when Nicole rummages in the cupboard and produces biscotti.

We sit in the living room with our cups of coffee, and I watch in resignation as Nicole sinks into Mum's special reclining chair, kicking out the foot stool and lying back. Mum will have a fit when she finds out, which she will. But Nicole doesn't seem nervous about the possibility.

We talk for ages, and I fill her in on everything that's happened since she waved me off at the coach station, right up to the moment the phone rang at Nora's, calling me back to my old life. We refill our cups and crunch our way through the biscotti.

'We'll pick up some more on our way to the hospital,' says Nicole. 'I finished the cream too. It all sounds amazing, Anna. I'm so jealous. I almost wish I'd come with you now.'

'We'd have had a great time,' I say, 'but I'm glad I did this on my own.'

She gives me a thoughtful look. 'Yeah, you've changed. I can't say how, but you have. Anyway, I've had a pretty good time too over the past few months. I love your house, by the way. I can't think why I didn't buy when I had the chance. If you're ever selling …'

'That's not likely, is it?' I say. 'It looks as though I'm home for good now, so I'll have to find myself a job soon. What's been going on at school since I left?'

'Bentinck's gone,' she says.

'No!' I gasp. 'It wasn't because of me, was it?'

Nicole laughs. 'Tragically not, although he deserved stringing up for the way he treated you. We all reckon he jumped before he was pushed. He had some spectacular rows with Charles Freeman. You could hear them all over the school.'

'I thought those two were thick as thieves,' I say, surprised. 'They gave a pretty good impression of it when they ganged up and suspended me.'

'Apparently not,' says Nicole. 'It all started with Freeman's obnoxious son – you remember the one in year nine?'

I grimace. 'I remember him. He was a nasty piece of work. Both those boys were.'

'He got caught shoplifting,' says Nicole. 'He was wearing his school uniform at the time, so Bentinck suspended him, and Freeman hit the roof. He contacted all the governors, calling in favours. He got a report from a tame specialist who said his son was suffering from stress after his parents' divorce. The governors signed a petition, but Bentinck wouldn't budge, and it all got really nasty.'

'I don't blame him,' I say, surprising myself. Bentinck is pretty high up on the list of all the people for whom I never thought I'd feel sorry.

Nicole slugs the last of her coffee and stretches out like a cat in Mum's chair. 'Anyway, we came in one morning and heard that Bentinck had resigned because of ill health.'

'Wanted to spend more time with his dead beetle collection?' I ask, surprised to discover how bitterly resentful I still feel about what happened.

Nicole grins. 'But you haven't heard the best bit. Guess who's the caretaker head for the rest of the year, and maybe even next year if they don't appoint immediately?'

I stare blankly at her before comprehension flickers. 'You don't mean …?'

'I do mean!' she says. 'Graham's back, and the school's a different place again. Even the kids seem to feel it. The staff certainly does. He didn't really want to retire, and I don't think he's in any hurry to leave now he's back. Which means that you should go in and see him before the summer term starts. You were always one of his favourites, and he went ballistic when I told him what had happened. He was really upset he'd been in Hong Kong at the time. But he couldn't understand why you didn't contact him straight away.'

'I tried,' I say, 'but he'd just had his grandson, and I didn't want to bother him too much.'

'He wants you to bother him now,' she says crisply, 'so get yourself over there as soon as possible, ok?'

My mind is struggling to keep up with this swift change of events. I hadn't considered what this could mean for me personally.

'Great idea,' I say at last. 'I'd like to see Graham again.'

She nods. 'He'll take you back like a shot. I know he will. You're an excellent teacher, and you hold plenty of winning cards. What happened to you was all over the school by the following morning, so either Bentinck or Charlie Boy must have told someone about it. I looked it all up and rang my union. They said that a temporary suspension was appropriate, pending investigation, but it should never have been spread around like that. They've offered to look at your case for you.'

I hate disappointing Nicole while she's looking so pleased about the legal technicalities, but it isn't for me.

'I can't do that,' I tell her. 'Bentinck really did me a favour. I'd never have gone to New Zealand if he hadn't been such a complete arse. Anyway, he's gone now, so I don't feel I have anything else to prove.'

'Well, think about it for a bit, then go and see Graham,' she persists. 'Don't forget that term starts a week on Monday.'

I can't help asking, 'Is that the only reason you've been having such a great time while I've been away – just work?'

She laughs. 'Oh, I've been trying all sorts of new things – meeting new people, you know ...'

'You've changed too,' I say. 'I can't quite put my finger on it, either. Are you going to tell me what it is?'

'I wish I knew,' she says, smiling to herself, and I find myself wishing the same thing.

We arrive at the hospital just as the doctor is signing Mum out. She actually smiles when she sees me walk in.

I bend over to kiss her cheek. 'How are you?'

'I'm fine,' she says. 'There was no need for you to come rushing halfway across the world.'

'Perhaps not,' I say, 'but I'm here now.'

Nicole helps Mum pack her things into a small case while I head off to the nurses' station with a box of chocolates and a bunch of roses.

'Not very original, I'm afraid,' I say apologetically, 'but thanks for looking after my mum so well. I hope she wasn't too much trouble?'

The duty nurse looks surprised. 'Mrs Richardson? She was great. We never had a word of complaint from her, although she had a couple of bad nights at first.'

It's my turn to feel surprised. If Mum had bad nights, I would have predicted she'd take it out on anyone who came near her. She'd have enjoyed having a captive audience for her complaints. But the nurse seems quite genuine as she calls for a porter to help Mum into a wheelchair and take her downstairs. She says goodbye to us all, and Mum thanks her warmly as we leave.

It takes us a few minutes to work out how best to get Mum into the car, but we manage it at last, and Nicole drives home slowly, negotiating the bends with care. We help Mum inside, and she sinks into her armchair and closes her eyes.

Nicole offers to make us a sandwich, and I follow her to the kitchen to check she knows where everything is kept.

'Of course, I do!' she says, rootling through the bread bin. 'I've cooked entire meals in here. In fact, we cooked her an extremely posh three-course birthday dinner a few weeks ago.'

'We?' I query.

'I cooked the main course, and Matt did a starter,' she says. 'He made this really impressive chocolate soufflé thing afterwards. Janice couldn't find a single thing to complain about. I think she was slightly disappointed. Next time, I may burn the edge of something, just for her.'

'*Matt?*' I can hear the outraged squeak in my voice. I see Nicole's quick grin and moderate my voice. 'I'm surprised. I didn't realise he still came down from Manchester.'

She gives me an odd look. 'He didn't go to Manchester.'

'Why on earth not?'

'I can't believe you don't know this,' she says. 'Your mum must have told you.'

I pull a face. 'We tend to avoid that particular subject. Why didn't he go?'

'Talk to him yourself,' says Nicole. 'I'm not your go-between.'

I shrug. 'Perhaps I will, if I ever see him again. Do you see him often?'

'Oh, you know, when we're both around. He's a nice guy.'

She finds a packet of ham in the fridge and digs around for tomatoes.

'I don't suppose there's any chance that Mr Wonderful bought his soufflé at the supermarket?' I ask, thinking of my ill-fated Death by Chocolate.

'Of course, he didn't,' says Nicole. 'You're always so hard on him. You don't want him – you've made that pretty clear. But you don't need to run him down all the time.'

I search for a way to change the subject and brighten as I remember *the Feijoa Tree*.

'I can cook pretty well now,' I say. 'I helped out quite a bit in the Coromandel, and Patrick often let me cook in the evenings.'

'Great,' says Nicole. 'That will stop Janice trying to do too much.'

'If she lets me.'

She sighs. 'I've told you hundreds of times – she needs handling. Don't give her so many options. I never do. I just say, *'This is what we're going to do,'* and turn suddenly deaf if she starts complaining. She always comes around.'

'I'll try,' I say doubtfully. 'But it isn't so easy for me. She still sees me as a ten-year-old.'

Nicole slices a tomato and arranges it on top of the ham. 'It's up to you now. You've left home and gone halfway around the world, and now you're back. It's time the pair of you sorted things out a bit better. Don't fall back into being her little girl. You don't need her to help you with everything.'

'*Need* her?' I gasp. 'It's entirely the other way around. She's needed me ever since Dad died. I didn't want it to be like this.'

She rips a few lettuce leaves into shreds and tosses them onto the plates. 'Put these plates on a tray, will you?'

'She won't eat in the living room. You know that. We'll have to help her into the dining room.'

Nicole isn't listening. She's already marching ahead of me, carrying the tray.

'Can you switch on the coffee maker?' she calls over her shoulder.

I follow her through to the living room, where I find Mum sitting with a tray on her lap and frowning at Nicole.

'I don't like eating in here,' she announces, and I quail.

Nicole sits down and takes a huge bite of her sandwich. 'Just for today, Janice. Great ham, by the way. I'm glad you told me about that delicatessen. I was buying it in slimy packets.'

'Oh, never in packets, dear!' says Mum, shocked. 'Always buy it loose so you can check the quality.'

'I will,' promises Nicole and winks at me as I watch the pair of them in uncomprehending silence.

She disappears after lunch, telling us she'll be back tomorrow morning. I suddenly wonder whether she'll have Matt with her.

As if she's read my mind, Mum fixes me with a sharp gaze. 'Have you seen Matthew since you got back?'

Now is clearly the time to establish some ground rules, so I keep my face impassive. 'No, and I don't expect to, so let's not discuss him, please.'

She isn't letting it go this easily. 'Did you write to him?'

I stand and collect the plates. 'I've said I'm not going to discuss him. I don't want to be rude, but I have no plans to see Matt at all. Let's drop the subject.'

'He's coming for lunch tomorrow,' she says with a smug gleam in her eye.

'He's what?' I almost shout. 'When did you arrange that?'

'He's been over here to see me fairly often since you left. He rang the hospital this morning to see how I was, and I asked him to lunch. He's bringing a nice salad, and I have a chicken in the freezer. Don't worry. We're not expecting you to cook.'

'Mum, will you just stop this ridiculous matchmaking?' I snap.

She purses her lips but doesn't answer.

I press on, trying to make her understand. 'Matt and I are over. Please get that into your head. Inviting him over to lunch when I'm here isn't fair to either of us. I don't know how he feels about our break up, but I'm completely over it. It's embarrassing throwing us together like this.'

She smiles slightly. 'Nicole is coming too.'

'Meaning?'

'I'm just saying that Matthew and Nicole will be here for lunch tomorrow,' she says.

'Are you trying to tell me they're an item?'

As usual, she avoids answering the direct question. 'Would you mind if they were?'

'Not at all,' I say. 'In fact, I'd be delighted if it got you off my back.'

She says nothing, and I slam the plates onto the tray and walk out.

Chapter Twenty-Four

Nicole arrives just before lunch the following day, and I send her through to entertain Mum. I'm busy in the kitchen. After a quick trip to the supermarket, I've been cooking all morning. If Matt is bringing the salad, I can at least make the desserts to show him – and everyone else – that I can cook perfectly well.

I have a blackberry and apple crumble all ready to go into the oven, and I'm busy whisking the egg whites for a chocolate mousse. A pan of fresh custard simmers and thickens on the hob. I'm just grating the last curls of chocolate onto the mousse when the door opens and Matt puts his head around.

'Anna!'

He steps inside and hugs me. I stiffen and hold the grater away from him, and he lets me go at once. I want to explain that I didn't want to mess up his jacket, but he's already inspecting the dishes on the kitchen counter.

'It all looks great,' he says. 'Does this mean Nicole's already here?'

'I made them!' I snap, outraged that everyone thinks I'm helpless.

'I'm sorry. Well, they look good.' He smiles warmly. 'And it's lovely to see you. You're looking well.'

'So are you.'

I say it rather grudgingly. He's dressed more casually than usual and seems relaxed. Nicole's influence, perhaps?

'You didn't go to Manchester after all, I hear?' I try to keep my voice in neutral.

'No, I decided against it.'

He doesn't add anything, and I decide not to dig further and open up the whole thing again.

He looks at the custard. 'Most impressive. Who taught you to cook?'

I shrug. 'I picked it up while I was away.'

I don't add anything more. I don't want to think about the Coromandel right now.

Matt seems to sense my need to change the subject.

'How have you been?' he asks. 'I heard all about the travelling from Nicole and Janice. Glad to be back?'

The question hits me like a sledgehammer. I think of everything I've left behind. I think of Ethan, Helen and Jim and of Nora and Patrick. I think of the sun rising across the gulf and setting behind the mountains. I remember swishing barefoot through the dew at dawn and drinking wine in the rose garden as dusk fell.

Not only can I not put any of this into words without crying but I don't want Matt interfering in my secret other world. It's a place and a life I made for myself, however temporary. Sharing even the smallest slice of it would tarnish it.

'It's fine,' I say at last.

It's the best I can offer. He doesn't pursue the subject but reaches into his carrier bag.

'I've brought some ready-made salad and new potatoes. They're pretty easy. You can just throw them into a pan of water.'

'I think I can manage potatoes,' I say. 'I've roasted and carved the chicken this morning.'

I nod towards the plate of neat slices on the countertop. 'And now I'm going outside to find some herbs for the butter.'

I brush past him on my way to the door and wonder whether I've annoyed him. That would be par for the course with us.

He just smiles and waves a hand. 'That sounds great. If you're all sorted, I'll go through and say hello.'

I snip furiously at the chives. He's as annoying as ever – assuming I can't cook and not even apologising when I show him how wrong he is. Perhaps he doesn't see me as someone worth getting annoyed with any longer. I certainly used to bother him. Apparently that's all over now, which is of course great.

Things improve a little over lunch. Unlike previous lunches with Mum and Matt, during which I sat waiting for uncomfortable topics to be raised and sank into increasingly sullen resentment, the conversation flows briskly. Mum seems surprisingly cheerful. Matt and Nicole discuss a film they saw together last week and a new Italian restaurant they went to afterwards. Mum raises her eyebrows at me, but I ignore her and go to the kitchen to check on the crumble.

Matt follows a moment later. 'Are you ok? You're very quiet today. Still jet-lagged?'

'Maybe a little,' I acknowledge, desperately wanting to ask him about Nicole. I stir the custard into bubbles, avoiding his eye. 'How's everything going for you?'

It's the nearest I can get to a direct question.

'Oh, much the same,' he says. 'Life's fine. I seem to be quite busy.'

'You always were.'

'I suppose so,' he says.

I give him the oven gloves and gesture to him to retrieve the crumble while I lift the mousse out of the fridge. It looks pretty good. The frothy bubbles have frozen into a smooth, brown sheet. I scrape a few more curls off the chocolate bar and reach for the bowl of whipped cream.

As I turn to leave the kitchen, Matt puts out a hand to stop me. 'Anna, would you have lunch with me one day?'

I give a nervous laugh. 'In case you hadn't noticed, we are having lunch. That's why I've been cooking all morning in the heat.'

He smiles but persists. 'I meant on our own. I'd like to talk to you without your mother sitting and listening to every word.'

'She never bothered you before,' I snap and suddenly hear myself – that same defensive tone I always use with Mum. What's wrong with me?

Matt's face is unreadable, and I'm ashamed enough to mutter, 'Yes, lunch would be fine. I don't know what I'm doing this week. I have to settle Mum in and sort out the physiotherapist. Do you want to give me a call sometime and sort it out?'

'I'll do that,' he says, and I wonder whether he will.

I want to ask what he plans to talk about. I'd like to warn him that any discussion of what happened between us is off the table. But Nicole comes in at this moment with a pile of dirty plates. She gives me a quizzical look behind Matt's back, and I glower back at her.

'Am I interrupting anything?' she asks mockingly as I push past her into the dining room. I hear her voice raised in a question as I leave. I can't hear what he answers.

Even Mum enjoys the desserts. Nicole is full of praise and passes her bowl for a second helping of mousse.

'I'm going to get so fat,' she says comfortably. It's the meaningless remark of someone who has been slender for her entire life. She ought to be. She never sits still for more than two minutes.

'Nonsense, dear, you have a lovely figure,' says Mum. I stare at her, but she ignores me. 'Don't you think so, Matt?' she presses on.

Although her face is bland, I'm sure I detect a faint air of triumph as she needles me. Or perhaps I'm reading something into nothing. I look at Matt and see he's grinning at Nicole.

'She looks lovely, as always. You both do,' he adds, turning to me, and I can't help pulling a face.

'You do look well since you came back,' agrees Mum. 'I suppose it's all that sun and sea air and hard work. She's been working as a maid in a lodging house,' she explains to Matt.

I start to speak, then catch his eye and subside as I see his air of amused understanding. 'So I heard, Janice,' he says gravely.

I frown at him, looking for the usual signs that he's scoring off me to curry favour with Mum. But he isn't. He's simply not engaging with her. He probably doesn't see the point in arguing with someone who's being deliberately obtuse. But I can never help myself. If I feel unjustly attacked, I have to defend myself. Matt's way is certainly more peaceful, and I wonder what I think I'll lose if I don't take her on.

Mum has already moved her attention back to Nicole. 'You've been doing nicely since Anna left. You'll be settled at that school for a few more years. Until you get married, I suppose?'

I open my mouth to point out that feminism has reached even into the darkest recesses of the teaching profession. That it is, in fact, entirely possible to have a job and a husband. And that this hypothetical husband could even take some time out of his career to look after his own children. Nicole gives me a broad smile, and I'm sure she reads my thoughts.

She answers before I can. 'But who'd have an old maid like me, Janice? I think I'd better stick to the job for now.'

Far from being offended, Mum smiles and clicks her tongue.

'Now you're being silly, dear,' she chides. 'The right man will come along, just you see. Perhaps he already has?'

I can't be the only one to notice her eyes hover over Matt.

He pushes back his chair and stands. 'That was a lovely lunch, Anna. Thank you very much. Why don't I clear up and bring us all some coffee?'

Nicole flickers a wink at me as we settle Mum into her recliner.

'Well done,' she whispers. 'You were most restrained.'

I smother a laugh. 'You certainly know how to handle her. I'm taking notes.'

We sit on the sofa and watch Mum begin to doze. Nicole waits until she's breathing deeply before speaking in a lowered voice.

'I think you make it harder for yourself sometimes. I know she likes to have a go, but you shouldn't always feel you have to fight your corner. You've made your own life, and no one can touch that unless you let them.'

Of course, she's right, but it's so much easier for her. She doesn't have our family history of Mum always thinking she knows best and my finely honed passive resistance. But she's right that I've made my own life, and I'm determined to hug it to me. I'm unwilling to share it with anyone around me in case they tread on it too heavily. I'm not sure how resilient it is.

Matt brings in the coffee, and the three of us sit and chat while Mum dozes. I don't go into too many details about my time in Queenstown or mention Ethan, but I talk a bit about the bed-and-breakfast. I describe the garden and the walks I took down to the harbour in the evenings. I don't talk about the plans Patrick and I were making for the restaurant. That will never happen now, and I can't explain it, even to friends. I'm terrified the idea will sound stupid once it's exposed to the scrutiny of others.

Nicole sighs as I describe the pine floors and sloping ceiling in my little attic room. 'It sounds perfect. I don't know how you tore yourself away.'

She stops abruptly, and we all look over at Mum, who's still asleep.

I'm guiltily aware of the resentment I struggle with each day, but I try to explain.

'Family comes first, and Dad would never have forgiven me if I'd permanently abandoned Mum.'

Matt shifts in his chair when I say this. I turn and wait for him to speak. We lock eyes for a long moment before he shrugs and smiles.

'It's not so bad being home,' I hurry on, not sure which of us I'm trying to convince. 'I'll find a job once Mum can get around again, and New Zealand will be like a dream – a long holiday I once took and tell my children about.'

I stop on a sob and glare hard into the distance. 'Sorry, I'm quite tired from the journey and the jet lag. Don't take any notice.'

Nicole doesn't press me further. She starts talking about the school now that Bentinck has gone and Graham is back in charge.

'It's amazing how little impression Bentinck made in two years,' she says. 'It's almost as though he never belonged there, so he couldn't make a dent. It always was Graham's school, and it still is.'

'That must have been pretty hard for Bentinck,' I say. 'Imagine having to follow a class act like that, with all those expectations to live up to. It's no wonder he failed.'

'You're sticking up for Bentinck, the Butcher of St Jude's, the terror of teachers everywhere?' she asks. 'Seriously, Anna, that man cost you your job.'

'No, he didn't, not really. It was the right time for me to leave. He made it easier, that's all.'

'No regrets?' she asks, and I see Matt glance at me again.

'No, everything worked out for the best.'

I feel a faint tingle in my cheeks as Matt keeps his eyes fixed on me – still without speaking.

'I was getting a bit lost,' I say. 'I felt swallowed up in everyone else's plans for me, and I needed to find my own way.'

I feel myself blushing furiously. It's partly with anger at Matt, I tell myself. He shouldn't be putting me in the position of having to explain to him what I don't understand myself.

'Are you going back?' he asks at last.

'How can I?' I snap, angry with him for the blunt question.

I keep one eye on Mum to make sure she's asleep. 'What's the use of kidding myself? Mum has to come first, and she needs me here, not faffing about on the other side of the world.'

He holds his hands up. 'I only asked. Peace?'

I sigh. 'Don't be stupid. I'm not trying to fight with anyone. It's just … complicated. You of all people should know that.'

'Have you met Martin yet?' asks Nicole, very obviously changing the subject.

'Martin?' I say. 'Martin who?'

She looks surprised. 'Janice hasn't mentioned him at all?'

'Hasn't mentioned who?' I say, feeling left out, as so often since I came back home.

'He's just someone we met in the new year,' says Matt. He looks as though he might understand how I'm feeling.

'He's a friend of your mum's,' he adds. 'I'm sure you'll meet him soon.' He glances at his watch. 'It's time I made a move.'

He looks at Nicole, who stands. 'I'll give you a ride. Thank Janice for us when she wakes up, Anna.'

I walk to the door with them, and Nicole hugs me goodbye. I turn to Matt to hug him too. Possibly put off by my earlier greeting, he's already standing on the front step, his hands in his pockets, so I just smile at him. I go back to check on Mum and watch through the window as Nicole reverses expertly and at speed off the drive and down the road.

I sit down to drink my cold coffee, wondering about this Martin and where Mum might have met him. I didn't expect the world to stop entirely while I was away, but things seem to have gone on perfectly well without me, which is disorientating. In fact, I'm not sure I like it very much at all.

Chapter Twenty-Five

Mum becomes more mobile every day, and I'm pleased to see she how seriously she's taking her physiotherapy. She sleeps downstairs, and I help her upstairs each morning and evening to wash. She always takes the chance to peer into the bedrooms to check I'm keeping them clean. But Nora has trained me so well that Mum can't find fault.

I've prepared her room ready for her to move into next week. She frowns when she sees the pile of towels lying on her bed.

'Clean towels go in the airing cupboard,' she says. 'You should know that, after all these years.'

'I thought it would be more convenient for you to have them on the bed to save you going up and down the landing. They look nice there, don't they?'

I take a leaf from Nicole's book and turn away before she can answer. The towels do look nice – all fluffy from the tumble dryer and neatly folded into a snowy pile. I must remember to extract the sprig of lavender I've tucked between them before Mum moves in. I might get away with changing the towels' location, but I hate to imagine her face if she ever saw bits of the garden on her bed.

One step at a time, I remind myself. She approves of the bathroom and has actually said so. I scrub it each morning out of habit, and even the grout sparkles in the sunlight. Jess isn't coming in while I'm here, but she's offered to give Mum a few hours once I move back to my own house, and I'm determined not to be upstaged when she returns.

Mum wrinkles her nose as she walks past me into the bathroom. 'What's that smell? Did we run out of my usual cleaner? You know which brand I like. You should have bought that.'

I'm surprised how easy it is to adopt Nicole's strategy of ignoring the implied criticism.

'I use white vinegar,' I say. 'It's great for getting everything clean and shiny, and it's much better for the environment.'

I can tell she'd love to argue, but there's no denying the place is spotless, so she waves me away so she can wash.

I go downstairs to check on tonight's dinner. Patrick gave me a lovely recipe for pork braised in cider and sour cream. I hum as I slice the apples and onions and toss them into the sizzling butter to caramelise. The kitchen door is open, and the drone of bees drifts in from where they're rootling among the lavender flowers. The sun falls brightly across the counter, so I move the pastry to a cooler spot to roll it out.

I swiftly top and tail a punnet of gooseberries and pile them onto the pastry. I sprinkle them with sugar and fold the edges over the fruit, leaving a few fat, striped gooseberries uncovered. I brush the crust with beaten egg, sprinkle it with more sugar and slide it into the oven. Patrick showed me how to do this when he had a glut of raspberries over the summer.

'It's lazy man's pie,' he said, 'but tell people it's rustic, and they'll love it.'

Mum bangs on the floor, and I run up to help her downstairs again.

'What's that smell?' she asks as she reaches the top of the stairs. 'Are you cooking something?'

'Tonight's dinner,' I say. 'I thought I'd get a jump on it so we can spend the afternoon outside. Perhaps we could go for a gentle walk?'

'I thought we'd have shepherd's pie today,' she says. 'There's some mince in the fridge that needs using up.'

I don't react. 'Maybe tomorrow. I've made a lovely casserole for tonight. You'll enjoy it.'

I walk away before she can answer and go back to the kitchen to start wiping down the work tops. The phone rings, and I run through to the hall before Mum can push herself out of her chair. My heart jumps when I hear Matt's voice.

'Hey, how's it going?' he says.

'Um, yeah, fine.'

I feel stupid being caught off balance like this. I thought he'd given up on the idea of calling me. After waiting for two weeks for the phone to ring, I decided I'd put him off with my rudeness over our Sunday lunch, and he'd sensibly decided to leave well alone. But he doesn't sound too put off.

'I was wondering about that lunch,' he says. 'Are you free today, by any chance? I know it's short notice, but I have to be in town this morning. I thought we could meet at Max's. Only if you'd like to, of course.'

My instinct is to refuse on the grounds of the short notice, but I've agreed to have lunch with him sometime, and I may as well get it over with.

'That would be fine,' I say, 'but aren't you working? You never have enough time for lunch.'

There's a pause. 'Not today,' he says. 'Would one o'clock be any good? There's someone I need to see first.'

We agree to this, and he rings off. I find Mum to let her know I'll be out for lunch.

She looks pleased at the news. 'Matthew called? How kind of him.'

I bristle. 'Kind?'

'Don't be so snappy, Anna. He obviously doesn't bear you any ill will. That's all I meant. Don't take me up like that.'

I remember a little too late my resolve not to engage, so I smile at her. 'Yes, it's a restaurant we both like. It's called *Max's*. Have you ever been there?'

She hesitates, and an unusual pinkness stains her cheeks. 'I believe so. I think I went there for dinner with a friend sometime over the winter.'

I won't get a better opportunity than this, so I ask as casually as I can, 'Would this be the mysterious Martin, by any chance?'

I immediately realise I've made a mistake in calling him mysterious, so I meekly accept the frown she bestows on me.

'I went there with Martin, yes.'

'That's nice,' I say. 'It's lovely there, isn't it? They have tables outside with big, striped umbrellas, and you're surrounded by chestnut trees.'

'I wouldn't know,' she says repressively. 'I prefer to eat inside. And as I said, it was winter.'

'So, who is this man?' I ask.

There's no way to ask about him without seeming nosy, but I've been dying to find out. It's most unusual for Mum to have a friend I don't hear about on a regular basis. There's Daphne who runs the gardening club and picks up Mum each week to take her to the meetings. There's Marjorie, with her perfect twins who both have high-flying jobs in London and dutifully visit their mother every other week. And there's Sue Peakes, who runs beetle drives at our local church and is always pressing Mum to bring me along to meet the fuzzy-haired curate.

'Martin is a man I met in the new year,' she says at last. 'We have dinner occasionally. He's away until the end of July on a trip.'

I realise this is the sum total of information I'll get right now. 'That's lovely. Will I meet him sometime?'

'Perhaps,' she says, and I know better than to persist.

I settle her into her new deckchair in the sun. I lie on the grass beside her, watching the clouds and imagining the hum of bees is the sound of Dad mowing the lawn, shirtless and sweating in the lunchtime heat. Everything was so simple when he was around. Mum, although never a restful person, was, I realise in retrospect, much less snappy and watchful.

'Do you still miss Dad?' I ask without thinking.

She turns her head against the striped material and presses her lips together. 'Of course, I still miss your father. What an odd question. What's brought all this on?'

'I don't know. I was remembering him doing the garden at the weekends. He kept it beautifully, didn't he?'

She nods. 'He did. I haven't been able to keep it up as much as I'd have liked. The man comes and cuts the grass and keeps it weeded, but it isn't the same.'

'Nothing is,' I agree. 'But I suppose everyone moves on.'

She gives me a sharp look. 'Is this about Martin? Are you trying to tell me something?'

I'm genuinely shocked. 'No! That was the last thing on my mind. I haven't even met him. I was just … missing Dad, that's all.'

'Yes, well,' is all she says, but her face is pinched into lines of misery.

I reach over to pat her hand. 'Forget it. I didn't mean to upset you. You still have me. I'm not going anywhere, am I?'

'Aren't you?' she says. 'I often get the feeling you'd like to be in New Zealand right now.'

I can't lie to her. 'Mum, I had a wonderful time out there. It's a gorgeous country. But I always knew it was just a holiday. I couldn't leave you on your own, and I wouldn't want to. Dad wouldn't have wanted me to.'

'I managed perfectly well while you were away,' she says. 'I won't hold you back from doing anything you choose.'

I feel the familiar rising irritation. She doesn't mean this.

'You couldn't do without me,' I say. 'We both know that. I won't abandon you.'

She peers at me, squinting in the sunlight. 'I couldn't do without you? What sort of nonsense is that? Who's been putting such silly ideas in your head?'

I sit up and shade my eyes so I can see her face more clearly. 'No one. But, since Dad left us –'

'He died, Anna. He didn't leave us.'

She's speaking crisply, but she doesn't seem hostile. In fact, she's inspecting me as though I've come from some alien planet.

'I know that,' I say, 'but it comes to the same thing in the end. He isn't here to look after you, and I am.'

There's a long pause, and I wonder whether I've made her angry. It doesn't usually take much.

She sighs. 'It was a difficult age for you to lose your father, so I made allowances when you didn't seem to grow up as fast as all the other girls. I understood why you might not want to go too far from home while you were coming to terms with losing him. But you've never seemed to put it behind you and find a focus of your own. I often wonder if you ever will.'

This makes no sense and also feels horribly unfair.

'You'd have hit the roof if I'd left home when Dad died!' I say hotly. 'I stayed for your sake – and for his too, if you must know.'

She looks at me with something like pity in her eyes. 'Your father always said you'd go far and do wonderful things. He had such great faith in you. I'm still waiting.'

I shake my head, fighting the angry tears that threaten to spill down my cheeks.

'What are you saying – that I should have walked out on you right after you lost your husband – that I should have abandoned you too?'

She sits up straighter in her chair. 'He did *not* abandon me, Anna, or you either. Get that out of your head. Your father had cancer, and he died. It happens. There was nothing you could have done – nothing any of us could do. None of us could save him. Have you not yet realised that? It was nearly ten years ago. You should have moved on.'

'*I* should have moved on!' I gasp. 'What about you? You stay in this house, even though it's far too big for you. You let me do your shopping and cleaning and behave like a skivvy. Each time I go on holiday, I worry myself sick about you alone at home without me. Most of the time, I feel there's nothing I could ever do that would please you. Do you realise that, Mum? Are you telling me now that you've never appreciated a single thing I've done for you?'

She ignores my raised voice. 'Of course not. You're a kind daughter, and you have a good heart. Perhaps there was a time after your dad died when I was glad you stayed home. But I never intended you to put your life on hold like this. Dad would have been horrified if he'd thought I was even trying to. But you seemed quite happy at St. Jude's, and I began to think you would marry Matthew and settle down and make a life for yourself that way.'

'You did a bit more than think, didn't you?' I say hotly. 'You pushed him at me at every opportunity. He couldn't do anything wrong in your eyes, and I couldn't do anything right.'

I'm crying now, but the tears are angry tears and don't stop me shouting at her. The past ten years flash before me, apparently meaningless in her eyes, totally wasted. On top of that, she's telling me I would have disappointed Dad – the man I loved more than anyone in the world.

'I like Matthew very much,' she says calmly. 'He's a lovely young man, and I think you're perfectly suited. You obviously don't, which I think is a pity, but it has absolutely nothing to do with me.'

She ignores the harrumphing sound that escapes me.

'I hoped you might move up to Manchester with him and try for a more independent life, but you didn't. Then you went off on this holiday and had a good time. Whether you realise it or not, it's changed you.'

'For the better?' I ask, through my tears, hating myself for caring what she thinks.

'Yes, I think so,' she says. 'You're more sure of yourself – happier even. I honestly thought you'd be making plans to go back there soon.'

I wipe my eyes on my sleeve and lie back on the newly mown grass, exhausted.

'You've given me a lot to think about. I wish I'd realised some of this before it was too late.'

'*What's* too late?' she interrupts. 'My goodness, Anna, you're twenty-six, not fifty six. You have all the time in the world.'

I can't drop this until all our cards are on the table. 'But *why*? Why weren't you more encouraging when I said I was going to New Zealand? You were quite cold about it.'

Her face softens as she looks at me. 'You didn't seem to have thought it through very well, and I didn't think it would last. I thought you might come back in a worse muddle than ever and have even more trouble deciding what you wanted. It all happened so suddenly, and it *was* rather a shock when I realised how much I was going to miss you.'

She smiles at my started expression. 'Go and wash your face if you're meeting Matthew. You can't turn up looking like that.'

I haul myself to my feet and look down at her lying calmly in her deckchair.

'Fine, I'll go and clean up. I wonder what bombshell *he* has for me? Announcing his engagement to Nicole, I expect.'

I say it as truculently as I dare, and she sighs.

'You need to decide what you want and stop blaming things on other people. Now, go and do something with your hair.'

I run upstairs to change into a clean shirt. I catch sight of my face in the mirror on the landing. I look truly terrible. My face is blotched, and my nose is red and shiny. It's hardly the perfect look to meet an ex-boyfriend, especially one who probably wants to tell me he's moved on with his life in a way I haven't managed to in ten long years. Well, good for him. I'm really happy if he's found someone new.

Chapter Twenty-Six

Forty minutes later, I pay the taxi driver and jump out at the nearest traffic lights. I dodge around a group of camera-carrying tourists and land breathlessly outside the cafe. Matt is waiting for me at a table outside. He stands and pulls back my chair for me, and I feel the familiar flash of unjustified annoyance at his unwanted helpfulness.

'Thanks,' I say, shifting the chair to the other side of the table so I'm facing him.

'This place seems to be under new management,' he says. 'Max has gone, and I got my head bitten off when I asked where he was. But I expect the food is the same. Are you still drinking cappuccino?' He waves to the server.

I'd love a cappuccino, thickly laced with foam and chocolate, but I won't give him the satisfaction of proving my predictability.

'It's hot today,' I tell him. 'I think I'll have iced tea.'

He waves again to the server, and I'm pleased to see her ignore him. I wave more firmly until she's forced to catch my eye and acknowledge me.

She returns a minute later and slams two glasses in front of us. She clearly takes this whole *having to serve the customer* thing as a personal insult.

Matt and I face each other in silence for a moment, then he pushes his frosty, dripping glass across the table to clink mine.

'Cheers!' he says. 'It's good to see you again, Anna – just the two of us.'

'Uh huh,' I say cautiously.

'I mean it,' he says. 'I've really missed you.'

I have to know why he's still seeing Mum. Is it for my sake or for Nicole's?

'I didn't know you were still visiting Mum,' I say. 'She never mentioned you in her letters.'

'Nothing at all?' he says. 'Well, she invites me over for lunch sometimes, and I occasionally drop in after work to check how she is and see whether there's anything she needs doing around the house.'

'Why are you such a nice person?' I ask him grumpily. 'Why on earth did you keep going to see her?'

'She was my last link to you,' he says, and I immediately feel annoyed.

He sees my frown. 'I'm not trying to make you feel bad, but did you think I'd just drop her when you left and not even keep an eye out for her?'

If I'd thought about the subject at all, I would have thought exactly that. But I can't really say so.

A thought strikes me. 'Wait a minute! It wasn't you who painted the front door, was it?'

He looks amused. 'Yes, with Nicole. We did it one Saturday afternoon, and your mum cooked us lasagne – after we'd thoroughly cleaned up after ourselves, of course. It was quite a day.'

'You never liked Nicole before,' I blurt before I can stop myself.

'Why would you say that?' he asks. 'She's a really nice girl. I never understood why you and I didn't spend more time with her when we were together.'

I'm completely taken aback. I can hardly tell him that Nicole couldn't stand him when we were a couple. I'm assailed by a vision of the pair of them slapping paint on the door and laughing.

'You'd make a good pair,' I say as calmly as possible. 'She'd liven you up and make you take some risks, and you'd stop her from doing anything too crazy. So, are you two …?'

The waitress slaps down two panini in front of us, frowns heavily and withdraws. The moment is lost.

I break the lengthening silence. 'You ordered mozzarella and tomato, and I asked for roasted vegetables and feta cheese. Which is which?'

Matt peels back the edge of one sandwich and inspects it. He peers inside the other one. 'They're identical. Should we risk calling the server from hell or draw lots?'

'Let's split them,' I suggest.

'I'm up for that.'

I dump half of my sandwich onto his plate and saw a chunk off his. We chew in silence.

'Nope, still no idea,' he mumbles through a mouthful of lukewarm bread.

I feel myself relax. This may not be as bad as I expected. When Matt asks me more about my time in New Zealand, I talk about Nora and Patrick and *The Feijoa Tree* and the idea I've had for a restaurant. He sounds genuinely interested, and I end up telling him far more than I'd planned. I talk about Miriam, the campsite by the lake, the Coromandel and the sunlight across the Gulf. I tell him about drinking coffee on the deck each morning, the air washed with the scent of jasmine.

'You loved it there, didn't you?' he interrupts at one point.

'I did. I'm not making a good job of describing it. There really aren't words.'

I'm assailed by the sharpest stab of homesickness yet. I shrug, to keep him at arm's length.

'But things change. People get ill. I knew it couldn't last forever.' I gently touch his hand. 'And thanks, by the way. It was nice of you to keep seeing Mum after I left.'

'Of course,' he says, and I wonder how much Nicole has had to do with his frequent visits.

'You could have written to me,' I say. 'Then I wouldn't have had to rely on Mum for news.'

I don't mention Nicole's regular emails. I'm still wondering why she never mentioned the painting party.

He smiles. 'I could have. Would you have replied?'

'Probably not,' I say honestly, 'but I might have done.'

This makes us both grin.

I push my unfinished sandwich away, defeated. 'This was certainly an experience.'

'The panini?' he asks.

It's a treacherous question, so I ignore it and push back my chair. 'It's been nice to see you again, Matt. I'm glad you called.'

'You can't be full after that awful thing,' he says. 'Can I buy you a proper dinner tonight?'

'Oh no, thank you. This was just … I mean, I only met you to …'

'I understand,' he says. 'Thanks for coming. I've missed you.'

'You've had Nicole.' I feel my face redden instantly at my pettishness. 'I mean, you've had lots of company by the sound of it.'

'Indeed,' he says, but he doesn't contradict me.

'Well, I'll just –' I'm suddenly furious with him and with myself.

He stands too. 'Hang on a minute, Anna. There's something I want to ask you if you have time.'

'What is it?' I say. 'I need to pick up some groceries.'

'The supermarket will be open until tonight,' he says.

'You're such a know-it-all!' I burst out, and his face freezes. 'Why, why, *why* do you have to correct me all the time? If I say I'm going to the supermarket, why can't you just accept it? If I want to go to the supermarket, I will!'

I sit down again with a thump. I didn't come here to fight, but if he's going to start treating me like a child again, it's time that he sees I've changed. It's time that *I* see I've changed.

He dabs a grain of salt off the red checked tablecloth, and his face puckers as he licks his finger. We sit in silence, not meeting each other's eye.

'Was that it?' he asks at last. 'Was that the real reason you finished it? You thought I was stopping you from making your own choices?'

'Yes! Well, no, not exactly.' I feel my face flush again. 'But maybe a bit. You've always treated me like a child. Just like Mum does. Just like everyone does. If I wanted to choose where to go, you always found a reason why your choice was better. And when I said your ideas were wrong, your ears turned as red as that stupid car of yours.'

I stop abruptly, hearing how childish this sounds.

'My ears turned red?' he interrupts in amusement.

I half laugh but feel a flash of anger that even now he isn't taking me seriously.

'You're doing it again,' I say. 'This is exactly what I mean. I'm trying to tell you how I feel, and you're laughing at me.'

He takes my hand. 'I'm not laughing at you. I'm really not. It's just that I've beaten myself up for months now, wondering what I said, what I did, where I went wrong. And now you tell me that my ears were the wrong colour.'

I don't pull my hand away, but it feels stiff and awkward clasped in his. As if he senses my discomfort, he lets it go.

'You've beaten yourself up?' I ask. 'But I told you why I thought we should finish.'

'You did,' he says, 'but I didn't believe a word of it.'

'There you go again –' I begin.

He interrupts at once. 'You told me you couldn't move to Manchester because of your mum. You said I should be free to make my own choices without having to worry about you. You said you were holding me back, and you felt guilty about it. Of course, I didn't believe you. It was clearly about you, not about me. That was fair enough, but you seemed to want to pass it all off onto me.'

'But you didn't argue with me,' I say. 'You didn't say anything at all. Come on, Matt, admit it. You were as relieved as I was.'

I smile, wanting to finish the conversation on a friendly note and escape.

'I could see that *you* were relieved,' he corrects me. 'And there was nothing more I could say. You clearly weren't telling me your actual reasons, and there was no point in dragging it out. You'd only have hated me more.'

'I didn't hate you!' I say, startled. 'I just didn't think it was working out very well. I thought – I still think – that we were both in it out of habit. If anything, I thought you were too good for me, which made me furious. But I never hated you.'

He looks at me directly. 'Is that the real reason? You thought I felt I was too good for you, that I looked down on you? Is that why you used to get so chippy with me?'

This silences me. Surely, he was the chippy one? I think back, trying to find a good example to prove how right I am. But it's all a jumble, and I can't.

'You can't deny you were horrible about my job,' I rally. 'And you thought yours was so amazing. You boasted about your promotions, and you thought teaching was a part time job for me. You expected me to uproot and move without a second thought because your career was so important and mine wasn't.'

His face darkens. 'That isn't fair, and it isn't remotely true. I thought you hated your job at St. Jude's. You never seemed happy there after what's his name – Bentinck – arrived. I thought you might like the chance to move and start somewhere else. I didn't think your mum was an insuperable problem, but clearly you did.'

He's giving me an out here, but I can't bring myself to take it.

'No,' I say slowly, 'she wasn't really the problem. If I *had* wanted to move, we could have worked something out with her. But I didn't want to go, and I didn't like the fact you assumed I'd pack up and leave just because you clicked your fingers.'

'No, that wasn't fair of me,' he surprises me. 'But I hadn't had time to think it through that day. I'd wanted that promotion for years. You knew that. I was so excited about it, and I thought it would be great for us both. When Paul told me the good news, I never thought I'd lose you over it. That pretty much took the shine off it, but it was too late by then.'

'I'm sorry,' I say, and this time I really am. 'All I was thinking about was escaping something that was going to make us both unhappy. Why didn't you tell me how you were feeling?'

He laughs. 'You didn't just dump me. You went twelve thousand miles across the world to escape from me. I got the message from that.'

'I wasn't only escaping from you,' I say. 'It was everything – Bentinck, the job, you, Mum, everyone knowing what was best for me all the time. I wanted to find out who I am and what I want without everyone else telling me and knowing best.'

'I got that,' he says. 'Did you find what you were looking for?'

He looks genuinely interested, so I consider the question before replying.

'Not really, but that's fine. I found out that I can cope by myself, that making mistakes doesn't matter if you can put them right, that maybe some people don't have a particular path they want to follow. They just sort of wander.'

I break off, wondering why I'm telling him this. This is Matt, the guy who never makes mistakes, who has a career plan and life mapped out to his entire satisfaction.

He places some money on the table next to the menu. 'I like the part about mistakes that can be put right. Thanks for meeting me, and thanks for telling me all this. It helps.'

'You mean, like, closure?' I venture, and he smiles.

'Yes, I think that's a good word. Thanks again, Anna. There's a bus in three minutes if I run.'

He leans over, kisses my cheek, and walks away. I watch him thread his way between the tables, and he's gone.

Chapter Twenty-Seven

I meet Martin at the end of August. Mum has had several calls each week since I returned home, about which she's said nothing. Then Martin returned from his work trip, and she informed me he'd invited us both out for the day. I wonder which of the three of us is the most nervous.

He's apparently suggested we go to see some gardens in the New Forest, well known for their herbaceous borders. Mum has been poring over the brochure all week. It's a good choice. There will be enough to see there to stop us from staring at each other in silence, and we can talk about the flowers if things get sticky. Other than that, I don't know what to expect.

I meet Nicole for a drink on Friday night and tell her about the invitation. She gives an annoying smile and refuses to be drawn about Martin.

'Judge for yourself,' she says. 'How would you like it if you were meeting someone for the first time and everyone had given them a run-down on you beforehand?'

I sip my apricot cooler. 'I bet Mum's told him all about me. This is great, by the way. I could get used to drinking cocktails.'

She grins. 'Very retro, aren't they? I think I'll buy myself a shaker and have a go at home.'

We chat for a while about school and drink two more cocktails before she suggests that I stop.

'You don't want to be hung over the first time you meet your future stepfather.' She giggles and pokes me with a paper umbrella.

'Oh, come on!' I say, startled. 'Please tell me you're joking. She barely knows the man.'

'I'm joking, I'm joking!' she says. 'Don't look like that, Anna. But would you mind?'

She looks at me curiously, and I stare back, wondering whether my cheeks are as flushed as hers.

'I've had too many cocktails,' I say. 'I thought you said stepfather.' And we burst into fresh giggles.

I tiptoe upstairs when I get home so Mum won't hear me and call me in to her room to check how much I've had to drink. I lie on my bed and think about what Nicole said. She was probably winding me up. It's the sort of thing she'd find amusing. I expect I'll find out tomorrow that this Martin has a wife and six children and just does Mum's taxes for her.

However, the thought that Nicole might have been serious sifts gently through my night. I dream and doze fitfully, waking at dawn with a dry mouth and a headache. It's a typical August day – warm and sultry with that faint, dusty feeling that signifies summer is thinking of packing up for the year.

Martin arrives promptly at one o'clock, which is surely a mark in his favour as far as Mum is concerned. He's in his early sixties, tweedy and grey-haired with modern square-framed glasses. The only notable thing about his appearance is his eyes, which are a startling blue in contrast to his general greyness.

He greets me pleasantly and without apparent embarrassment and kisses Mum's cheek. She's been on edge all morning. If it were anyone else, I'd say she was fluttery, but that isn't a word which could ever, by any stretch of the imagination, apply to Mum. She's looking very nice today, wearing a light, flowered dress I haven't seen before. I'm almost sure I can detect a trace of lipstick and powder, also something I haven't seen on her for a while. She rarely approves of tampering with nature. I remember venturing downstairs at fourteen with sky blue eye shadow smeared hopefully across my eyelids. The almighty explosion that greeted me ensured I didn't dare wear makeup again until I went to university.

We reach the gardens without incident. Martin takes the handles of the wheelchair and wheels Mum solemnly around the parts of the garden she's checked off in her brochure as best worth seeing. The rhododendrons, for which the gardens are famous, are long over, but Mum has never liked those anyway. Dad loved them and insisted on keeping just one, but she clipped at it ruthlessly and grumbled at the brevity of its flowering and the tatty, papery edges of the blooms.

I loved them and picked a few each spring, putting them in a cup of water on my desk for the few hours they would tolerate it. But we're here today to see the borders, which even I can see are truly gorgeous. They spill out of their beds in a lavish sprawl of colour so unbridled that I'm surprised Mum is so taken with them.

We tour the lower gardens in near silence before Martin suggests a cup of tea. We find a sheltered table in the little courtyard, and he orders us all a cream tea. We sit with our drinks, making awkward small talk about flowers.

I take a scone, pushing thoughts of afternoon tea in the Coromandel to one side. That part of my life is over and done with. I need to find a new place for myself back here. The crisp, golden scones are as delicious as Nora's, but they're a protocol minefield, served with a bowl of nearly liquid jam and another of oozing cream. In deference to the occasion, I'm wearing a freshly ironed white shirt with my jeans. I don't need jam down the front of it to make me feel even younger and even more unsure of myself than I already do.

Ever since I heard we were coming here, I've been hoping to see the famous rose beds. But they're up a steep, grassy slope, and the wheelchair isn't managing the narrow, wood-chipped paths too well. Mum decides to sit in the courtyard for a while and enjoy the sunshine, and when Martin offers to accompany me to see the roses, she insists I accept. I'd prefer to go alone, but I don't want to appear rude to Martin, so I agree.

We leave her next to the shelter of a sunny brick wall, wrapped in her rug and in no danger of being targeted by even the lightest breeze. I check her brake several times before wandering down the nearest path with Martin. As we walk, I watch him curiously out of the corner of my eye. It feels completely surreal to be vetting a potential boyfriend for Mum – if that's what I'm doing. He seems unconcerned by our silence and clearly isn't about to break it.

I clear my throat. 'So, Martin, I haven't heard how the two of you first met.'

He looks vaguely surprised at what I now worry may be considered an intrusion. But he seems to have excellent manners, so he ponders the question for a moment. I watch with some amusement. How difficult can it be to recall where you met someone? Unless, of course, it was somewhere strange that they'd prefer not to talk about – an identity parade, perhaps, or a morgue?

'We met at our ballroom dancing class,' he says at last.

I gape at him. Ballroom dancing class? What ballroom dancing class?

'Ah, dancing,' I say thoughtfully, as though that clears everything up. But it's no good. I can't leave it at that, so I probe further.

'How long have you been ballroom dancing?'

'For several years now,' he says. 'I used to go with my wife. After she died, I carried on going each week. I didn't know what else to do. Janice started lessons in the new year. Neither of us had a partner, so we just … joined forces. She picked it up terribly quickly – far more quickly than I did.'

'Really?' I say, picturing Mum floating around a dance floor in a swirl of pink taffeta and clotted mascara.

I blink to clear the ridiculous vision. 'Why did she start going to the classes? Did she ever tell you?'

He considers. 'I think it was that friend of hers, Nicole. She came along with a young chap a few times, and they brought your mother with them. When they stopped coming, Janice came by herself. I told her she mustn't stop the lessons on any account. She's such a quick learner.'

I try again to picture the pair of them waltzing solemnly around a dance floor. Even more incongruously, I imagine them tangoing in a moonlit garden with roses between their teeth. Grow up, I tell myself firmly. A new interest like this is exactly what Mum needs.

'Who was the guy who came with Nicole?' I ask. 'Did you meet him?'

'Yes, a few times, but I forget his name now. Your mother seemed fond of him. Pleasant young fellow.'

I mentally grind my teeth. Matt! It couldn't possibly have been anyone else. Mum isn't fond of too many people. I suddenly wonder whether she's fond of Martin.

'Do you see Mum … er, Janice … very often?' I ask.

I feel that I owe it to her to discover the extent of their relationship and whether he's on the level. He doesn't look like a con man. He has wavy, greying hair brushed neatly behind his ears and a dull, tweed jacket. But it could all be a ploy. She has a reasonable amount of savings, and he might see her as fair game for a scam, or simply as a retirement meal ticket.

'We see each other each week at our dance classes,' he says, 'and we go out for dinner most weekends.'

'What exactly is your job?' I ask, and he starts at my abruptness.

'I'm an accountant. I'm a partner in Broughton and Smythe in Winchester. I'm the Broughton half of it. Last year, my oldest son joined us as a junior partner, so there will still be a Broughton when I retire in a few years' time.'

'You have children?' I ask.

I'm not sure why I should be surprised at the idea. After all, plenty of people seem to have them. Martin just seems rather vague to have produced anything as definite as children.

'Yes, indeed,' he says. 'I have two boys. David is thirty-two and married to a nurse. They have no children yet. James is twenty-five. About your age, I suppose? He's an anthropologist. He's nearly finished his PhD in Birmingham.'

His face shines as he mentions them, and I feel petty interrogating him like this.

'In fact, James is coming to stay with me next weekend,' he adds.

I immediately sense danger. The last thing I need right now is someone telling me I have *so* much in common with their son or brother, and we really *must* meet up.

'How nice,' I say repressively. 'You must be looking forward to seeing him.'

He beams. 'Oh, indeed I am. It's always lovely to see him and his partner.'

That gets me off the hook at least.

'What does she do?' I ask. 'Is she a student too?'

'*Peter*,' he lays a slight emphasis on the word, 'is an editor with a small publishing house in Birmingham. That's how they met, when James was looking at getting some of his research published.'

'It would be nice to meet them both sometime,' I say.

I wonder whether Mum knows about Martin's children yet and if so whether she has an opinion, filed neatly alongside the opinions she has about everything else. Hopefully, other people's children are exempt. She didn't mention them to me when she told me about Martin, but she didn't mention the accountancy firm either.

'They must both be very bright,' I say at last.

Try as I might, I can't think of a single interesting thing to say about two people I've never met yet who surely form the largest part of this stranger's life. How big a part does Mum now form, I wonder? Perhaps she'll merge imperceptibly into Martin's family as time goes on, especially as his children seem to be so successful and such a source of pride to him. It will make a nice change for her.

'I suppose they're bright,' he says. 'Their mother certainly was. She was a doctor at Southampton General – an orthopaedic surgeon. I always thought the boys took after her rather than me. They were so focussed and decisive, while I just bumbled along after them all.'

He smiles at me again, clearly not minding. He has a lovely smile, all creases and folds. I'm suddenly reminded of Miriam.

'Doesn't Mum mind that about you?' I say.

'Mind what?' he says.

I catch myself. 'I'm sorry. I don't really know what I mean. She's just, you know, quite a decisive person herself.'

'There isn't generally room for two decisive people in a relationship.'

He smiles, and I freeze. Hearing him use the word *relationship* so casually feels almost shocking, especially when he's referring to my mother. Maybe this is how parents feel when their children start dating and set out on the first part of their trajectory away from them. Is this why Mum encouraged Matt so strongly, seeing him as someone unlikely to take me away from her?

But these concerns are ridiculous. Mum is a fifty-nine-year-old widow, not some teenager with their first boyfriend who needs keeping an eye on. I can think back now with hard-won amusement to my humiliating parental curfews. They were of course the earliest in my entire class and the reason, I'm still sure, that Gareth McPherson asked Susie Mann to the graduation disco and not me.

We walk on a little further. Martin solemnly inspects the fading roses, as though checking for greenfly, while I close my eyes and breathe in their glorious scent. I remember Patrick's garden and keep my eyes closed for a moment longer to hide their dampness.

As though he can read my mind, Martin asks me about my trip to New Zealand, and I give him the edited version I keep for strangers to whom I have no inclination to elaborate. He listens closely. At various points, it seems as though he might like to ask questions, but I finish my narrative firmly and give him my best smile-as-full-stop.

He seems to accept this. 'It all sounds most exciting. Elizabeth and I travelled a lot before the boys came along.'

'Really?' My tone is unflattering, but he looks like such a static person.

'Oh, yes,' he says. 'We started with a six-month honeymoon right after university and travelled around Asia. We had hardly a penny between us once we'd paid for the airfares, but she had her internship lined up, and we knew we wouldn't get the opportunity again for a while.'

I try to picture him tramping around Thailand in his tweed suit, clutching a briefcase. 'What was it like?'

He gives a reminiscent smile. 'We had a wonderful time. We stayed in hostels and in huts on the beaches and sometimes with local families. They were terribly kind.'

He's certainly shattering a few of my preconceptions.

'I thought New Zealand was a challenge,' I say. 'I wouldn't have dared to start with Asia.'

'But you went by yourself,' he says. 'I thought it was very brave of you when your mother told me about it. Don't forget we had each other.'

His face shuts briefly, but he looks up and smiles cheerfully.

'We always said we'd prefer to collect memories than possessions. And we had a very happy thirty-four years and two lovely sons together. I don't know that anyone could ask for more than that.'

'Mmm,' I agree, through a slightly thickened throat. 'Did you keep on travelling when the boys were born?'

'As much as possible,' he says. 'We mostly went camping in Britain when they were young. Once they were old enough, we went further afield.'

I think back to my childhood trips with Mum and Dad. We spent weeks in various guesthouses during my summer holidays, where meals were served at exactly the same time as at home and the only difference was that none of my friends were there for me to play with.

We also spent one freezing spring weekend in Holland so we could see the tulips. I remember how thrilled I was to be going abroad and how disappointed I was to be put on Mum's passport – *'Because it's cheaper'*. I wanted my own little book to wave at uniformed officials to demonstrate my world citizenship. I hated being an appendage to Mum, always tethered to her plans.

On my eighteenth birthday, I applied for my own red and gold badge of freedom and carried it around with me for days after it arrived. I wanted to be completely prepared in case someone unexpectedly had to drop out of a trip and offered me their tickets. Whenever I went away with Matt, he took charge of the documents, including, at Mum's insistence, my passport. I think she had visions of me being stranded in far-flung places without a British Embassy. The memory still annoys me.

I shrug it off and ask Martin more about his family holidays. He obliges with a string of destinations that make me dizzy. He has a much better sense of humour than I expected, and I laugh at his stories of the boys during a cruise they took to the Caribbean. He tells me how David followed the steward around as he prepared the cabins each evening, and no one could understand why there were never any chocolates on the pillows.

'A ship isn't the best place to be when your son's crimes are discovered,' he says. 'There's absolutely nowhere to hide, and we were shunned in the dining room for the rest of the week.'

But he smiles fondly at the thought.

I ask for more memories, and he describes the time they berthed in the island of St. Thomas and woke the following morning to see several pirate ships staging a mock battle in the glassy harbour. After that, they put the boys into a pushchair so they could wander away from the tourist strip and see the island properly.

'It was such a hot day,' he says, 'and the children were grizzling. So, we set off up the hill in case there was a breeze higher up. David jumped out and ran on ahead. We came around a corner to find him talking to an elderly woman in her garden. Everyone always took to little David, and she invited us in. We drank fresh lemonade, and she gave us leaves from her Bay Rum tree so we could take the smell of the islands with us when we returned to real life.'

'That's lovely,' I breathe, thinking of Patrick's herb garden and simultaneously pushing the thought away. This is something I manage more easily with each day I slide between myself and New Zealand.

Martin talks for a while longer of New England in the fall and the maples splashing their crimson and gold across the landscape. He tells me about a train they took across the Australian outback one spring and how the boys watched the kangaroos bounding easily alongside whenever they pulled away from a station.

I can't help breaking into these stories at one point. 'Accountancy?'

He smiles as though he's been asked this before. 'I'm sorry, doesn't it fit?'

'It fits your appearance, but you're an adventurer underneath. You have a romantic soul.'

He laughs. 'Not really, but I do like to see things for myself. But I like order as well. It's quite exciting to take a jumble of figures and make sense of them.'

Maybe this is the part that appeals to Mum, although I wonder what she makes of this other side of him. Perhaps she keeps the various parts neatly pigeon-holed and only looks at what she wants to see.

'We didn't travel very often,' I say, watching him to see how much he knows about our family. He nods, not giving anything away. I press on, trying to explain the three of us to him.

'Mum likes familiar things. She isn't a great one for change, and Dad always seemed happy to go along with her. He was diagnosed with cancer when I was fourteen, and we didn't go anywhere after that. He had all the treatments and went into remission, but it came back after a couple of years, and it had spread.'

I shrug helplessly. Why I'm telling him this, I don't know, but he seems so serene and unjudgmental.

'It's a tough time for everyone, isn't it?' is all he says.

I nod. 'How did your wife –?'

'Breast cancer,' he says. 'Like your father, she was treated, and we had five more wonderful years. But she wasn't surprised when it came back. I think she always knew.'

My eyes are full of tears now. 'How did she cope?'

'She was magnificent,' he says quietly. 'I'm still so proud of her. I was the one who went to pieces, and she and the boys had to pick me up. I couldn't imagine life going on without her. We'd been so happy, and I couldn't bear to think of her suffering. But in the end, it was quick and calm. We were lucky that way.'

'I suppose you were,' I say. 'Dad wasn't so good at the end. He was in a lot of pain some nights, but he didn't want to go into a hospice. He was determined to stay at home with us, and it was hard for them to get his pain relief right.'

I think back unwillingly to those last few days – sitting with Dad day and night, not sure whether he could hear me. I told him

I'd look after Mum, that I'd make him proud of me and tell his grandchildren all about him. But I never told him I loved him. That would have been too much like goodbye, and I wasn't ready for that.

Martin is patting my hand gently, and I'm surprised to feel the tears slipping down my cheeks.

'I'm so sorry,' I gulp. 'I've never done that to a complete stranger before. I didn't mean to embarrass you.'

'Maybe it's time,' he says. 'Janice tells me you never talked to her about your father's death.'

This stings me. 'Neither did she! We don't talk about personal things in our family. We never have.'

I can't help feeling curious. 'What else has she told you about me?'

He opens his hands. 'Not much, not much. But we've both been through it, and perhaps it's easier to talk to someone you know will understand.'

'She could have talked to me,' I say, wiping my eyes. 'I knew him all my life. Who else could understand as well?'

He hesitates before answering. 'But it's a different pain – that of losing a husband and losing a father. The boys and I were terrified of hurting each other for a while. I felt guilty that they'd lost a mother, and they didn't know what to say to me. I think Elizabeth understood that. She left each of us a letter.'

I'd love to ask what the letters said, but I have no business intruding.

'I wish Dad had left me a letter,' I say. 'We never talked about him dying. When he did, Mum was in such a state that I had to arrange the funeral by myself. I still don't know whether I got it right or whether he'd even have liked it.'

He nods. 'I hardly remember Elizabeth's funeral. It felt like something that had been arranged for everyone else, when all I wanted to do was hide somewhere until the pain went away. I expect you did just fine.'

He pats my hand again. 'It was a tough age for you, wasn't it? Janice told me that you and your father adored each other.'

I'm shocked, although I'm not sure whether this is because of the sentiment or because it's Mum who said it.

'I adored him,' I say hesitantly. 'He wasn't someone who said much about how he felt. He and Mum were both alike in that way.'

I hardly notice that Martin is still here. 'It's funny, but I found myself thinking more and more about Dad while I was away. It was as though I couldn't think about him while I still lived at home. All I could think of was how it had been at the end. While I was in New Zealand, I remembered some of the things we did when I was a child, and I was able to remember him without remembering the medicines and the pain and Mum crying.'

Martin smiles. 'I can understand that perfectly. After Elizabeth died, I wanted to sell the house. Each time I put the key in the door, it was like a physical pain. David, bless him, took me to a cottage in the Lake District for a week just because it was somewhere I'd never been with Elizabeth. I spent the week walking miles in the pouring rain to exhaust myself because I hadn't slept properly in weeks.'

He stares into the distance. 'After a few days, I started to remember the better times, and I could picture her face without bursting into tears. When I got back home, I decided to keep the house for a while. She was still there, you see. Now, I think of her when certain flowers come into bloom or when her favourite music comes on the radio, but it's all very gentle, and the pain has gone. I feel as though she flits in and out to check on me. That may sound silly, but it's how I like to think of it.'

'Not silly at all,' I say. 'It's been nearly ten years, but I don't think I'm quite there yet. It sounds like a long time, but it only feels like yesterday that Dad was here and looking after us both. Once he'd gone, it felt as though the only thing I could still do for him was to keep on looking after Mum.'

Martin nods again. 'I can only go by what Janice has said, but it sounds as though you were very close to your father. Maybe that was difficult for your mother? I wouldn't know. I never had a daughter. We'd have loved to have one, but we were delighted with our boys.'

'I'd like to meet them sometime,' I say, and this time I mean it. He looks so pleased that I feel able to ask him something else to see whether he can assuage some of the hurt I'm still feeling.

'I had the weirdest conversation with Mum the other day,' I say. 'I told her that I won't leave again because I know she needs me to look after her. I was trying to reassure her, but she said she'd far rather I'd gone and made my own life.'

The hurt wells up again, and I pick at my sleeve so I don't have to look at him directly. 'Do you know whether she meant that?'

He waits until I've recovered a little. 'Anna, your mother has never said a bad word about you. Believe me, she knows how lucky she is that you've been such a dutiful daughter. But perhaps …'

I lift my head at the *perhaps*, and he smiles again. 'Perhaps she feels, as all parents do, that there's a natural order of things. We'd love to keep our children close for ever. We have a tendency to think we know what's best for them, but we need to let them go at some point.'

'She could have said something,' I say. 'She never once gave the impression that she wanted me anywhere she couldn't keep an eye on me.'

I try to joke, but the subject is still incredibly painful.

He considers this for a long moment, and I realise he's a very restful man.

'It's possible that your mother wanted two things at once,' he says at last. 'We feel terribly protective of our children, and it's hard to think of them as adults. She recognised what a terrible loss it was for you when your father died. Maybe she both wanted to keep you close and let you go.'

'She didn't do a great job of communicating any of that,' I say. 'I thought she'd be lost without me.'

He nods. 'Sometimes our children have to take the first step and pull away before we can see they're ready to leave. I was terrible when James left home.'

His mouth curves at the memory. 'I made a dreadful fuss. I was fine when David went, but James was the baby. The thought of him fending for himself out in the wilds of darkest Guildford had me waking each night in a sweat. In the end, Elizabeth had to tell me to get a grip before he ran away to Peru to escape me fussing. She told me the most respectful thing you can do for anyone is to give them their freedom. Underneath it all, I knew she was right, so I calmed down.'

I think about this. I can't imagine Martin making a fuss about anything, but then I hardly know him. If he could behave like that with his younger son, I can see how difficult it might have been for Mum, with an only child and no husband to reassure her.

'Would she cope without me?' I ask. It's a blunt question, but we'll have to go back to Mum in a moment.

He doesn't answer directly. 'We poured so much of our lives into bringing up the boys that I was a little frightened we wouldn't have any life of our own once they left. I needn't have worried. We had a very different life, but it was no less wonderful for that. We still travelled and took our dancing classes and got to know each other all over again. Your mother didn't have any of that. You hadn't left home when your father died. I wonder whether it's time for her to make that new life now you're making yours.'

He doesn't sound judgmental, so I tuck away this thought for later perusal.

'I'm glad she met you,' is all I say, and he thanks me gravely.

'Perhaps it's time to see how Janice is doing?' he suggests.

'Did I pass?' he asks suddenly as we make our way back past the roses. I'm taken aback to see him smiling comfortably at me.

'Pass what?' I ask, deliberately stupid to buy time.

'Weren't you checking me out to see whether I'm acceptable suitor material for your mother?'

I'm silent for a moment before accidentally catching his eye and laughing. 'Yes, but you weren't supposed to notice. And if you did, you weren't supposed to say anything.'

'Oh, many apologies. Point taken.'

He takes my elbow to guide me around the edge of the stone wall to where Mum is waiting. I catch an exchange of glances between them and smile inwardly. We all seem to know what this meeting was about, yet none of us will open it up for discussion. There are some major pluses to being British. All the same, there seems to be an unspoken understanding between them that excludes me and makes me feel slightly uncomfortable.

I'm glad when Mum looks at her watch and says it's time we went home. I don't know whether to invite Martin back for dinner. Inviting Mum's friends to her own house is an area of etiquette that hasn't arisen for me before, so I decide to wait for her lead. We certainly have enough casseroles in the freezer for several visitors. But Martin politely refuses when she suggests it, saying that he's promised to help David move his things into his new flat.

He helps Mum out of the car and wheels her to the door. I step inside, wondering whether he's going to kiss her goodbye and not wanting to find myself in their way. But he just squeezes her hand and thanks us both charmingly for a lovely afternoon.

I help Mum out of her wheelchair, hand her the crutches and head to the kitchen to check on dinner. There are an increasing number of subjects I have no wish to discuss with her, and this is definitely one of them.

Chapter Twenty-Eight

It feels strange to be climbing the school stairs to the first floor once more. I haven't been near Bentinck's office since I stormed out in November. I notice that the autumn leaf-prints along the art corridor have been replaced with spring leaf-prints. I push through the swing doors to the admin corridor and pass Mike Glover coming the other way, clutching a cardboard box. He glances at me curiously but doesn't speak. I wonder whether he even recognises me.

Graham's door is wide open, as always. There's a friendly tumble of ornaments and photograph frames spilling across the desk where Bentinck sat so many months ago. Graham has his back to me. He's struggling to pin up a massive year planner for the next school year, but I'd recognise the back of his balding head anywhere.

'May I help you with that, sir?' I ask demurely, and he spins around.

'Anna, what a lovely, lovely surprise!' he booms, folding me into an enormous hug.

His sweater is prickly against my cheek and smells faintly of cigarettes. I remember his total disgust when the staffroom became smoke free, and the smokers were consigned to an airless hole on the third floor. Hugging him feels like I imagine hugging a grandfather might do, although I never met either of mine.

This reminds me. 'Congratulations, by the way! I hear you're a grandfather now. How does that feel?'

'Gosh, yes, indeed I am!' he says. 'They're popping them out like mad now. Jenna's pregnant too. She's due in October. We haven't been permitted to meet the father yet, but we live in hope. And Paul and Alicia rang last night to say they're expecting twins on Christmas day. I can't keep up with them all. It's going to cost an absolute fortune in birthday presents.'

He can't keep the elation out of his voice, and his face creases as he tries to suppress a huge grin.

'That's wonderful,' I say. 'Congratulate them all for me. So, what are you doing back here? Surely, you have enough to keep you busy for quite a few years.'

He shrugs and grins. 'Ah, well, there's life in the old dog yet. Jenna's due at half term, and Alicia's having the twins in the Christmas holidays. Very thoughtful of them to consult my timetable. Coffee?'

'Lovely,' I say.

He disappears into the outer office, reappearing a moment later with Lesley, who gives an excited squeak when she sees me. I feel a little guilty about the way I behaved when I last saw her, especially as none of it was her fault. I doubt she was any fonder of Bentinck than the rest of us.

'Anna!' she says. 'How lovely. It's been so long. What have you been up to? Nicole was telling me you went to Australia for the winter, you lucky thing.'

'New Zealand,' I say. 'Yes, I had a great time, but I'm home now.'

'And will we be seeing you back here? I do hope so.'

I glance at Graham, who nods at her. 'Lesley, that coffee would be very welcome now.'

She bustles out again, and he laughs. 'I missed her when I left. Always a smile, and never a long face. I get the impression that your friend Bentinck didn't appreciate her many fine qualities.'

I laugh too. 'He'd have preferred a robot, I expect. The place wasn't the same without you, Graham.'

'I was on the board that appointed him,' he says, 'and I had my doubts even then. However, as an outgoing old fogey, I had little influence. Charles Freeman was dead set on him. He said the chap was a moderniser. And as you may have noticed, what Charles wants, he generally gets.'

'Except for having the shoplifting suspension lifted,' I remind him.

'I was forgetting that. Perhaps that Bentinck chap wasn't as bad as I thought.'

I nod. 'I feel quite grateful to him, in a way.'

'Yes, you've seen the world. I've been hearing all about it from your friend. She's been bending my ear about re-employing you. I expect you already know that,' he says.

'That was nothing to do with me,' I say quickly. 'I'd be in New Zealand right now if Mum hadn't broken her hip. I haven't come here angling to get my job back.'

'Of course not, but I suppose you're looking for something now you're home. Do you still have that house of yours?'

'Yes, Nicole's renting it and paying the mortgage, and I'm living with Mum while she finishes her physiotherapy.'

He nods. 'Well, now, I have several English classes who are about to be teacher-less, poor little dears. Molly's going off on maternity leave for a year, starting at the end of this month. I wonder whether you might consider helping us out?'

I stare out at the leaves starting to turn on the chestnut trees and the late summer flowers scrambling over the groundsman's hut, hiding the cracked windows. It wouldn't be too bad to work here now that Graham's back, and I've really missed Nicole. I'm surprised how easy it is to picture myself back at the school now it's returned to how it was when I first started.

'Graham,' I start, then stop. Maybe I should accept his offer just for a year. He's looking out of the window. I assume he doesn't want to pressure me.

'No,' I say suddenly. 'Thanks very much, but no.'

He turns to face me again. 'Good girl. I'm not a bit surprised.'

I give a half laugh. 'You expected me to refuse? You don't want me back?'

'Not at all,' he says. 'I'd have you back like a shot if that's what you wanted. But it isn't, is it?'

I shake my head. 'I still don't know why not. I enjoyed teaching here, and I'd love to work with you again, but no.'

This is the second time I've burnt my bridges here in this very office, and I wonder, as I did the last time I was here, what I'm doing. I wait for a moment, willing my heart to come into line with my head and allow me to stay, but it won't.

Lesley appears with the coffee, and I sit in front of Graham's desk in the same chair I've sat in so often during these past four years – the first time sweaty-palmed for my job interview, and the last when I was suspended. I'd like to feel a sense of history, of connection, but I don't. It's only a chair.

I take a gulp of the scalding coffee. 'Nicole will kill me.'

'Does that really matter?' asks Graham. 'She knows what she wants, and she goes after it. Why should she decide for you as well?'

'Oh, she doesn't, not really,' I say. 'It's just that I have nothing more permanent, and she's gone to all this trouble for me.'

Graham stirs several teaspoons of sugar into his coffee while he thinks about this. 'I've gone with my gut instinct all my life,' he says slowly. 'Sometimes, it's got me into trouble, but not too often, and I've always slept well at night. You're terribly afraid of making mistakes, aren't you, Anna? Now, why is that?'

'Because no man is an island,' I say without thinking. 'If you make mistakes, other people can get hurt too. You can't only think about what's best for yourself.'

'I didn't say that,' he says. 'At least, I hope not. But following your gut doesn't mean steamrolling everyone else. Anyway, I think you're a person who would always be too empathetic to make decisions that hurt the people you love.'

My mind flashes to Matt, and I flinch at this undeserved praise.

Graham doesn't appear to notice me pulling a face as he presses on. 'But there's a big difference between not hurting people and letting them take control of the things they have no right to control. You do them a disservice if you allow them to behave like that. Goodness knows, I've made mistakes, but they've been my own. And if they've needed paying for, I've tried to do it without complaining.'

He smiles. 'That's something we've both tried to instil in our children, and don't think I haven't wondered why at times. There's a granddaughter on her way who won't have a father around, as far as we can tell. All we can do is to be there for her mother and keep our mouths firmly shut. And you know what, my dear, it will all pan out in the end. She'll grow up just fine because things have a habit of working out one way or another.'

'But you'd have preferred Jenna to make different decisions, wouldn't you?' I say. You can't want her to face extra difficulties right from the start.'

'What I want for her and what she wants for herself don't have to match,' he says. 'And who's to say I'm right, anyway? Plenty of single mothers do just fine. Some of the nicest children in this school have been raised by just one parent. No, we had our chance to do things our way, and she must have the same chance. Fair's fair, after all.'

I gaze out of the window while I consider this.

'It would be so much easier if I knew what I wanted,' I say at last. 'Jenna's obviously made her decision, and she's lucky to have you two as parents. If I had a serious plan for the rest of my life, it would be easier to go ahead, even if everyone hated it. I have a few ideas, but they're all rather vague, and I don't know whether they could ever work. I've never had much in the way of career goals. Everyone around me seems to know what they want. Why can't I?'

He stands and walks over to the window. 'It takes some of us a little longer to get to know ourselves. Hopefully, we keep changing throughout our lives anyway, or else we stagnate. We need to go through the entire process again and again.'

He turns to look at me. 'I didn't go into teaching until I was thirty, and that was a complete fluke. My father was an electrician, and he took me on as an apprentice at eighteen. I was jolly lucky to get such a good job straight out of school, and I worked with him for seven years. But it was never for me, and one day I told the old man I was off. It broke his heart, but he let me go.

I tried a few different things for a while, and then I met Martha. Her father owned a preparatory school in Shropshire. Horrible place it was – all boiled cabbage and early morning runs. But he offered me a term's work covering for someone's sick leave, and I was bitten by the bug. I never looked back and eventually ended up here. I'm not sure my father knew what to make of it all, but he was happy enough for us, and I've never had a day's regret. I wouldn't change a thing.

Maybe something like that will happen to you, and you'll find the one thing you want to do with your life. Then again, maybe it won't. Some people never let themselves become defined by what they do, which can be a good thing. One thing's for sure, you'll never know unless you get out there and try a few things – and fail too, if need be.'

I pour myself some more coffee. 'So, what was this all about, Graham? First you offer me a job, and now you tell me you're glad I didn't take it.'

He laughs. 'I don't think that friend of yours would ever have forgiven me if I hadn't made the offer. She's been on at me ever since I came back, and I quite agree with her. You were shamefully treated. Of course, that fellow Bentinck had to remove you.'

All the shame and frustration wells up again, and I open my mouth to protest.

He lifts his hand. 'He absolutely had to remove you. The guidelines are clear. So far, he acted correctly, but he appears to have made little effort to discover what went on in that classroom. And given all the trouble that young man has caused everyone over the years, a few words of support to you might have gone a long way. Am I right?'

I feel the searing anger all over again, surprised to find it as fresh now as it was on that horrible day.

I almost stamp my foot. 'To believe Simon Denny over me and humiliate me by bringing in Charles Freeman to patronise me too. It was unforgivable!'

He's watching me with interest. 'But your reaction was, shall I say, surprising? I have to say that when I first heard about it from Nicole, I couldn't quite grasp what had gone on. You should have been supported, informed of your rights, encouraged to contact your union. Those are the first things I would have said to you.'

'I know you would,' I say, 'which is why it was doubly hard when Bentinck was so unsupportive. I knew that if you'd still been there, you'd have sorted it all out for me.'

'You were reinstated,' he reminds me, 'which was an acknowledgment that guidelines had been followed and you were found to be innocent. I can make allowance for hurt feelings, but you resigned, you went across the world. Some might say you ran away. Now, why was that?'

I stare at him angrily. I'd never have thought that Graham would be anything other than supportive. I relied on him so heavily when I started at St. Jude's, and he never once let me down. But he's waiting for me to answer, and I can't let him know how hurt I feel.

'I left because I didn't like the way my life was going,' I say slowly. 'I was just plodding along, and I didn't feel that any of the things I did were by choice.'

'I see,' he says. 'Is there any coffee left?'

He tips the cold, thick dregs out of the pot and grimaces. 'Too late, I'm afraid. Now, tell me, why did you let young Nicole pack you off to the other side of the world? Was that your choice or hers?'

'Mostly hers,' I say. 'She's hard to resist. You've seen that for yourself.'

He chuckles. 'A young woman of conviction, indeed. She's talked me into putting Spanish in the timetable as a year nine option, and she's already looking into exchange trips. I don't suppose I'll get much say in it all. I'm dreading the day she insists I start attending yoga classes.'

He chuckles again and drains his cup. 'But I must say, I like to see all this enthusiasm. I admire someone who knows their own mind. She reminds me of my Jenna.'

I feel as though he's slugged me in the stomach, and it's a moment before I can answer. I always thought that Graham was fond of me – that he was a father figure in a way. I wonder now whether he thinks of me as an indecisive drifter. Maybe he prefers Nicole. But I try not to let my insecurity show. It's ridiculous at my age.

'It might have been her idea,' I say, 'but it's the best thing I ever did. I got away and saw a bit of the world. I met new people …'

I hesitate as I remember Ethan, but I've trained myself not to think about him for more than a few seconds.

I plough on. 'I turned my life around, and I'm not going back to what I was before. That's why I said no to you.'

I finish with a flourish, hoping to goodness I've convinced him.

'I'm glad,' he says. 'You're a bright girl, and you should be able to make your own decisions. How's your mother doing?'

His face shows nothing but a genuine interest, but I suspect this isn't an entirely disconnected query.

'She's doing a lot better,' I say. 'She's having physiotherapy each day. The doctor said she'll be walking on her own in no time.'

'Good, good. So, what's next for you?'

I shrug. 'I'll stay with her as long as she needs me. After that, I don't know. I'm trying to think of it as exciting. I don't have to decide right now.'

'Indeed you don't,' he says. 'Just make sure that when you finally decide, you know whose decision it is. I'm afraid I have to get going. Martha and I are accompanying Jenna to her ante-natal appointment. I never went to any of Martha's. Apparently, this was a heinous omission, for which I need to do penance this time around.'

His face is still wrinkled with suppressed pride at the thought of the new baby, so I don't feel too sorry for him.

This time, as I walk down the grey stone steps and through the playground, I know it's for keeps. There's no going back. I have wonderful memories of the children who taught me so much and colleagues who were mostly great. But I also have the confidence that comes from turning my back on it all and taking another path. After pushing St Jude's and everything connected with it to the back of my mind for so long, I'm glad I came back today. I've reclaimed the good memories, junked the bad ones, and said goodbye.

It's taken me far too long to appreciate the vast difference between running away and walking away, but I think I've finally got there.

Chapter Twenty-Nine

By mid-September, Mum is walking well and managing the housework by herself. She seems much happier to have her renewed independence and appears to be doing even more than before she broke her hip. I called Jess last week, and she said she's happy to take on a few extra cleaning hours whenever we like. With Christmas coming, she could use the money.

Mum meets Martin one afternoon to take the ferry over to Hythe while the weather holds. I clean the house from top to bottom and roast a joint of beef. She arrives home at five o'clock and sniffs delicately.

'That smells good,' is all she says as she goes to hang up her jacket. She no longer questions my place in the kitchen and has given me several useful tips as I try out new recipes. At seven thirty, I pour us both a glass of wine, and she helps me carry the vegetable dishes through to the dining-room. I've also made four little Yorkshire puddings because I know how much she loves them. I help her to carrots, glazed with butter and sprinkled with parsley, and offer her the gravy.

'You really enjoy this, don't you?' she asks.

I nod and take a deep breath. I won't get a better opening than this.

'I really do. I'll never be a famous chef, but I love cooking, picking things I've grown myself and feeding guests.'

'You like to look after people. You always did.' She stares into the ruby depths of her wineglass.

'Maybe too much?' I ask, and she smiles.

'It isn't a fault. I'm glad you didn't grow up only thinking of yourself.'

I cut a sliver of beef, enjoying the way the iridescent pink shades into the crisp brown of the crust. I chew for a moment, then gently lay my fork down so it doesn't clink and distract her.

'I'm not going back to teaching, Mum. It isn't me.'

'I'm not surprised,' she says. 'You turned down Graham Staples' offer.'

'How did you know that?' I say.

'Nicole told me, but that's all she told me. We haven't been gossiping about you.'

I smile. 'I don't suppose you have. She wouldn't tell *me* a thing about Martin before I met him either.'

Mum turns faintly pink, as she often does when I mention his name. I'm so pleased for her. Whenever I've met him, he's been exactly the same – calm, friendly and unflappable.

'I'm really happy for you, Mum,' I say. 'He's lovely, and you're looking ten years younger.'

'That's all very nice,' she says, 'but I believe we're talking about you.'

I smile at the rebuff. It isn't personal, and I'm not sure how I'd feel discussing my new boyfriend with my adult daughter.

I change the subject. 'I learned to cook in New Zealand.'

'I've noticed,' she says. 'It's made a lovely change from those frozen desserts you used to buy.'

'*The Feijoa Tree* – that's the place where I was working – is in the most gorgeous location. It's on the Coromandel peninsula, just across the bay from Auckland.'

'I know perfectly well where it is,' she says. 'I bought a map of New Zealand so I could see where you were.'

She's been so full of surprises recently that it isn't worth antagonising her by reacting to this one.

'It's the most beautiful place I've ever seen,' I say. 'The bed-and-breakfast is on the edge of the town. Nora and Patrick don't want to expand the business because they're coming up to retirement age, but they own a small house next door. I always call it *The Feijoa Branch.* Patrick uses the garden, but the house itself is empty at the moment and pretty run-down.

He and I were talking about fixing it up – making a flat upstairs and turning the ground floor into a restaurant. Really more of a cafe, I suppose.'

I glance at her to see whether she's realised where I'm going with this. My heart sinks when I see her frown.

'Are you saying you'd like to open a cafe here?' she asks.

'Not here, no. I'm saying I want to open *that* cafe.'

Her face snaps into understanding, and her eyes widen.

I feel a flash of sympathy for her. 'I'm sorry, Mum. I don't mean to upset you, but I'm going back, at least for a while.'

'I'm not shocked,' she says, although she clearly is. 'It's a little sudden, perhaps.'

'No, it isn't.' I take her hand, and she doesn't pull it away. 'I've been thinking about it for months. Each time I cook something new, I wonder whether it would be a good fit for the restaurant. Each time I see a new line of bed linen or towels, I wonder whether they'd fit in at the bed-and-breakfast. I really want to do this. I've been looking into it, and I think I could apply for an investment visa to start a business. I'd employ local people and start small. Patrick said he'll help me with doing up the house.'

'You have it all planned out,' she says.

She seems to have shrunk as she perches on her chair opposite me, her lips tightly pinched together.

'Mum, you told me I should leave home. Have you changed your mind?'

She lifts her chin. 'Of course not.'

She nearly gets away with it, but her face suddenly crumples. 'I'll miss you so much.'

I stare at her. 'I thought you wanted me to go and make a life for myself and let you make yours. If that isn't the case, why were you so aggressive when we talked about it in the garden?'

She almost shouts at me, and I jump. Mum never shouts.

'Because it was the right thing to do, and the only way I could force myself to say it was straight out. You wouldn't have taken any notice otherwise. You'd already thrown everything up and come rushing home as soon as I was ill. Someone had to give you a push.'

She's crying properly now. I kneel by her chair and hug her.

'It isn't forever, Mum. I'll visit you often, and you can visit me any time you like. Nora will always find you a room, and there will be two spare bedrooms in *The Feijoa Branch* once I've decorated. You can bring Martin if you like. One room or two – I don't care.'

I hope I haven't gone too far in saying this, but she gives a shaky laugh and wipes her eyes.

'Of course, you must go. I think it's a wonderful idea.'

'Thank you,' I say quietly.

I realise this is a big sacrifice for her, and I appreciate the way she's taking it. For my own sake, I'm also happy to know it isn't as easy for her as she seemed to imply only a few weeks ago.

I show her some photographs of the house. Patrick emailed them to me last week after I phoned them to tell them both the news. '*I'm coming home!*' was all I managed before bursting into noisy tears. Patrick quickly passed me over to Nora, who made soothing noises for a while before crying herself.

They're looking into planning permission for me, and Patrick says he may have found someone willing to help with the cooking. I don't want to get too tied up with that, much as I love it. I'd rather help Nora out as needed and learn more about the gardening. I've also been thinking of setting up a lunchtime sandwich business in the town.

I have so many ideas, and I explain some of them to Mum as we sit over coffee. She listens carefully and at one point even offers me a start-up loan if I need one.

'That's so kind,' I say, touched. 'I wasn't expecting you to do anything like that.'

'I wouldn't have offered if you had been,' she says. 'It's your inheritance, anyway. Dad left everything to me, but it will be yours one day.'

'Not for a long time, I hope. And I'd like to think you'd have spent it all on riotous living before then.'

'I doubt it,' she says crisply, and I subside.

It's a lovely offer, and I'm grateful for the confidence she's showing in me. I know I can trust Martin to protect her from any disastrous decisions. It's amazing how quickly I've grown used to the idea of him. He clearly has no idea of trying to replace my father, and he seems genuinely fond of Mum. I stop myself mid thought. I'm only just breaking out of my role as protector. I should respect her ability to look after herself and not immediately start looking for a replacement.

The next few days are exhausting. I buy myself a ticket for the following Friday. I'll be travelling economy this time, and alone, but I don't care. I'm going home. I run up a huge phone bill talking to Nora and Patrick. They've sent Mum pictures of the house and the garden, and she seemed pleased to see them.

I finally get her to the point where she can use my old computer to send and receive emails directly, and I trust that Nicole will continue to help if necessary.

She, of course, was unsurprised by my news when I told her.

'I'd love you to stay,' she said, 'especially now that Graham's back. But you have unfinished business, haven't you?'

'I suppose so,' I admitted. 'I'm ready to take a few risks and see whether I can make something of this restaurant idea. You'll come out to stay, won't you?'

She agreed to look into flying out at Christmas or Easter. With that promise, it felt as though there was one more tiny link between my two worlds, connecting both my lives, even if the threads are fragile as yet.

It's far more difficult to decide whether to contact Matt. I've heard nothing from him since we had lunch. In some ways, it might be better to forget it, but I don't want him to feel I'm ignoring him. In the end, I send him a card to tell him that I'm flying to New Zealand on Friday and wishing him well for the future. I hold it halfway through the letterbox slot, withdrawing my hand several times before finally dropping the card in, telling myself it's the best way to draw a line under everything for us both.

Martin has been invited to an early lunch on Friday. I'm leaving for the airport straight afterwards, and I want to avoid any long drawn-out farewells. I'm scared they could still have the power to turn me back. Nicole has volunteered to take me to the coach station, which seems somehow fitting to close the circle.

I'm glad to be saying goodbye to Mum while I know she has someone with her. Martin and Mum refuse to let me cook, so I go upstairs to check I've packed everything I want. I've already sent a few boxes by sea so I can have a few more of my belongings with me in New Zealand. I've shipped my comforting puffy quilt, all my books and my winter clothes. It's spring again out there, so I can keep my suitcase light for the journey.

It's surprising how little I've amassed since university. Perhaps my feeling of rootlessness has had something to do with that. All my furniture is staying here. Nicole has again mentioned buying the house, and I'm considering it. Even if things don't work out with the restaurant, I don't want a house tying me down and forcing me to return before I'm ready.

I take a last look around my empty room. It isn't really mine any more, although I know Mum will keep it for when I come to visit. It's the room in which I spent my entire childhood; the place I ran to hide and scream into the pillow after Dad's death; the place I came back to so reluctantly each night from university. So much history, but it's all past now. It slipped away when I stopped holding onto it and clutching the memories painfully close.

I can no longer see my younger self in here as I look at the single bed and the new green carpet Mum had fitted while I was away. It's both familiar and strange, but the ghosts no longer linger. Dad is fading from the house too. I probably felt as close to him in New Zealand as I do here, or even closer, which is a good feeling. I'll always carry a small piece of him with me. I don't need the physical reminders anymore. I raise a hand in a silent farewell to both of us and bump my suitcase downstairs.

We have a pleasant meal, and the fact that some of the jollity is forced doesn't hurt the occasion.

Martin has brought champagne. 'Not to celebrate your leaving,' he explains anxiously, 'but to toast your courage and your new venture.'

We raise our glasses, and I touch Mum's hand. Her lips are trembling, but she nods, blinks and takes a sip.

'Mum's been great,' I tell Martin. 'I couldn't have done this without her.'

I see her reluctant smile, but she doesn't comment.

'Of course, of course,' he says. 'Janice is a very organised woman.'

'Have you ever been to New Zealand?' I ask him and see Mum frown across the table at me.

He shakes his head. 'I've travelled around Australia but never made it over to New Zealand.'

'If you can get around Australia, New Zealand's a snip,' I say. 'You can drive from the top of North Island to the bottom of South Island in two days. You should come with Mum. I think you'd like it there.'

'Coffee!' announces Mum, standing up and marching to the kitchen, her back showing her outrage at my inappropriate behaviour.

Martin's mouth is twitching as he clears the plates. I decide not to push it any further.

We drink our coffee in silence. The seconds are ticking by all too quickly as I think of all there is to say and all I can't say. Nicole will be here any minute, although she's said she won't come in and join the grief-fest.

Mum understood when I explained that I need to make this journey by myself. She's even managed not to ask me whether I've booked the flight correctly. I look out of the window as the mantelpiece clock chimes one o'clock. Amazingly, I see Nicole pulling up outside, on time for once. Martin carries my suitcase to the front door, and I turn to Mum. She's smiling tightly – the same smile I used to think meant she was annoyed.

She purses her mouth hard. 'Well, goodbye, then.'

'I love you, Mum!'

I step forward and hug her before she has a chance to answer. I can't remember when I last said that, even as a child. Dad was the person to whom I ran for hugs, the person onto whose knee I climbed at the end of the day. I wonder now whether that hurt her.

'Call us as soon as you get there,' she says. 'Don't worry about the time.'

'I will,' I promise, wondering momentarily about the *us*. But who cares what she means, I chide myself. She's as entitled to her privacy as I am.

Tears are pouring down my face now, but I don't care. Why shouldn't they both know how I feel? There's nothing to be ashamed of. Martin puts the suitcase by the door and kisses me gently on one cheek, then steps back and takes Mum's hand. They stand close together as they watch me pick up my case, wipe my eyes and step out into my new life.

Chapter Thirty

Nicole pulls into the coach station, and we sit in silence for a while. Neither of us wants to move. I'm still tear-splotched, and she's biting her lip. When I left last time, it was only the whirl of anger and disappointment and Nicole's relentless energy that propelled me along until I found myself at the airport. This time, it's something I have to do alone, and there's no one encouraging me to go. In fact, I'm pretty sure Nicole thinks I'm being ridiculous.

I ask her this directly, and she laughs. 'There are times when I ask myself what I've started. I only imagined it being a sort of holiday for you to get over the breakup and get some perspective on your relationship with your Mum. I thought you could take a break from Bentinck and see the world. I never imagined you'd get bitten this badly. I've been dying to ask you all summer – is it a man? Have you met someone out there?'

I laugh. 'You won't believe me when I say no, but it's true. I met someone briefly, but he turned out to be a bit of a loser. Actually, that's not fair. He wasn't for me, but no bones were broken. Maybe I should think of him as my wild oat.'

'Do I get the gory details?' she says.

'Not a hope.'

She sighs. 'So, what *is* this all about? It's a pretty big step you're taking, and all for what? You don't have a proper job out there, and Graham's offered you one on a plate here.'

I shake my head in bemusement. 'Listen to you! What about all those times you've said I should break out and travel, let Mum fend for herself, have some fun? You've changed your tune.'

I feign a sudden enlightenment and lower my voice. 'Is it a man?'

She gives an annoying smile. 'Would you care?'

'That depends. Who is it?' I see her mocking smile and quickly cover myself with a casual, 'No, of course not. I'm joking. That's great. Are you going to tell me?'

She mimics me. 'Not a hope.'

'Oh, forget it,' I say. 'The coach is leaving in ten minutes, so I'd better get moving.'

'I'm sorry,' she says. 'I was only messing with you. There's no one in particular right now. I'm just settling down and quite enjoying it. It's been lovely having a place of my own, and work has been a lot better.

'Thanks for all you've done for Mum,' I say sincerely. 'I mean you and Matt.'

'And there it is,' she mocks me again. 'That's what you really want to talk about, isn't it?'

I stiffen. 'No. I'm glad that Matt's fine, and I'm glad you two seem to get along much better than you used to, but that's it.'

'You're right,' she says. 'We do get along much better. It's a bit like Pride and Prejudice, isn't it?'

'Except that Matt never disliked you,' I point out, and she grins.

'Don't get so defensive. I've admitted I was prejudiced. He always seemed such a stuffed shirt, and you never seemed yourself when he was around. I've been wondering whether that was because I saw him through your eyes.'

'And now?' I ask.

She gives a mysterious smile, but I don't care. I can't help probing. If I'm going away for another year or two, I don't want to wonder every day what's happening back here.

'He's great,' she says. 'We've had a lot of fun, and he's been brilliant when your mum's been off on one of her … having a … I mean, when she's …'

I touch her hand. 'Not many friends would have done everything you two have. I really am grateful. I hope you know that.'

'She's been fine,' she says quickly. 'Once you get the hang of her, you find her bark's worse than her bite. After a couple of flaming rows, we got along very well.'

'Flaming rows?' I gasp. 'Nicole, you didn't!'

She shrugs. 'Just a bit, early on. Come on, Anna, you've been letting her get away with murder for years. You know you have. But I treat her like a human being, and she returns the favour. And of course, she's always loved Matt. He can do no wrong in her eyes. It drives me mad.'

'Well, he's very good to her …' I begin but break off as she grins again. 'You're right,' I say. 'I have no idea why I'm defending him, especially to you. He obviously doesn't need it.'

'No,' she agrees, 'but I think you've got the wrong impression about him since you came back. That's partly my fault. I was trying to clarify things for you.'

I'm not sure what she's saying, but I don't want to pursue it and risk an argument before I leave. Whatever happens in the future, Nicole's my best friend. She's stuck by me through all this, and I owe her so much.

She gives me a quizzical look. 'I wish you'd talked to Matt before leaving. Your relationship didn't end too happily, did it?'

'I have talked to Matt,' I say defensively. 'I had lunch with him a few weeks ago. Hasn't he mentioned it?'

'Yes, he has,' she says. 'What did you talk about?'

'You mean he hasn't already told you?'

Her face snaps in surprise at my acid tone, and I back down. 'Oh, I don't know – this and that. I told him about my plans for the restaurant. He seemed quite interested, which surprised me.'

'And what did he talk about?' she says.

'Not much. I tried to stay away from contentious subjects, and he didn't drone on endlessly about his job like he used to.'

She sits bolt upright and stares at me. 'That might be because he doesn't have a job to talk about.'

'What do you mean? I know he turned that Manchester thing down, but that was ages ago.'

'You really are hopeless,' she says. 'Didn't you ask him what he's up to?'

I shake my head. 'No, I didn't want to discuss any of the subjects we used to row about. Not row, exactly, but all the things that used to annoy me so much.'

She puffs out her cheeks. 'Didn't he tell you he'd quit his job without having anything else to go to?'

'Why on earth did he do that?' I ask. 'Are you trying to say it was my fault?'

'Yes,' she says. 'I mean, I don't know. You probably started it. He was pretty fed up when you left, and he seemed to lose interest in things. A few weeks before you came home, he quit, just like that.'

'Why didn't he tell me?' I say.

'How would I know? Maybe he didn't want to put pressure on you. You haven't been too friendly to him since you got back, and he says you never wrote to him when you were out there.'

'Neither did he!' I explode, and she shrugs again.

'Anyway, there you have it. I'm not sure what he's going to do next. He's doing some consulting right now, but it's patchy. I expect he'll find something.'

'What about the Red Monstrosity?' I ask.

'Gone!' she says. 'It went with the job, and he hasn't got another one yet that I know of.'

That would explain him getting the bus the other day when we had lunch. I'd assumed the car was in for a service.

'I still think he could have told me,' I say stubbornly. 'I didn't ask him to quit his job or get rid of the Red Monstrosity. Anyway, it can't have been because of me. He hasn't mentioned a word of this when we've met.'

She shrugs. 'He might have done if things had been different.'

'If *I'd* been different, you mean? Well, that's too bad. I can't be responsible for his happiness and his job decisions, can I?'

She relents. 'I suppose not, but I still think you should talk to him.'

'That isn't going to happen. I'm leaving for the airport in a minute. Maybe I'll write to him when I get there.'

'All right,' she says, 'but it's a shame.'

'In your opinion.'

I wonder guiltily whether I've been as unreasonable with Matt as Nicole thinks.

She looks as though she wants to say something else. Instead, she glances at her watch, and we climb reluctantly out of the car and lift my cases from the boot.

'Keep in touch,' I say. 'I want to hear all the news.'

'Yeah, you too.' She gives me an enormous hug before holding me away from her for a moment. 'Look at you – all grown up. I still don't know what I've started.'

My eyes start to flood, and I rub them on my sleeve. 'No vodka this time?'

'You can buy your own vodka,' she says. 'You're a big girl now.'

She hugs me again. As with my first journey, the last thing I see through a blur of tears is Nicole looking anxious.

'*May they never become past friends,*' I murmur to myself and grin at the surprised look of the passenger in the next seat.

This time, when I jump down from the coach at Heathrow and the driver slings my suitcase onto the concourse, everything seems familiar. I lug my cases to the departures hall, where I stand in line for ages and finally check them in.

I turn to look at the screen for my gate number and am barely surprised to see Matt getting up from a nearby seat. He's wearing the jacket I bought him two Christmases ago. I thought he hated it, but then again I thought he hated a lot of things. All of which is irrelevant to the question of what he's doing here.

'How did you know?' I demand. Then the penny drops. Nicole, of course.

'I might have gone straight through passport control without you seeing me, and you'd have come all this way for nothing,' I point out.

He smiles. 'I took a chance. It seemed worth it. I wanted to see you before you left.'

'I don't have long.' I'm annoyed with myself for feeling even a little pleased to see him.

'I know,' he says, 'but your flight doesn't have a boarding time yet.'

'Know-it-all,' I mutter, and he grins again.

'Can I buy you a coffee, a plastic-filled sandwich, whatever?' he asks.

'Coffee will be fine, thank you.'

I lead the way to the coffee shop where I first met Miriam – to where it all started.

'What would you like?' he asks.

'Cappuccino, please, lots of chocolate.'

'Not iced tea?' There's a smile behind his eyes.

'Just a cappuccino, thank you.'

I watch him threading his way over to me, carrying two coffees. As he reaches the table, I stand and pull back his chair for him. His face doesn't flicker as I sit down again.

There's a long silence while we sip our cappuccinos. I'm not sure how I feel about letting Matt into my new life. I've kept everything separate so far, and I don't know how far I can mix my two lives without losing something – perhaps losing a part of myself.

'Do you mind?' he asks at last. 'I can leave if you don't want me here.'

'No, it's fine. You're here now. You'd better not be checking up on me for Mum to see whether I've forgotten anything.'

His mouth twists, and I relent. 'It's fine, Matt. It's very kind of you to come and see me off. That is what you're doing, isn't it? You aren't flying somewhere yourself?'

'Not today,' he says.

'More closure, then?'

He laughs out loud. 'Did anyone ever mention what a pain you can be?'

'Thank you,' I say. 'Why didn't you tell me you were coming?'

'I thought about it,' he says, 'but I no longer have the Red Monstrosity, so I couldn't have given you a ride.'

I laugh uncomfortably. I didn't know he was aware of that nickname. 'I don't have Daisy any more, so we've both lost something precious.'

'Indeed we have,' he says. 'Anyway, Nicole said she thought this was something you needed to do by yourself, and I could see her point. You've been giving a pretty good impression of someone who wants to make all her own decisions.'

'Nicole said that? You talked to her about it?'

He gives me a wary look. 'Yes, is that ok? I only wanted to ask her whether you'd mind my coming here.'

'And judging by the fact you're here, I'm guessing she said I wouldn't.'

'Something like that,' he says. 'I got the impression that she felt guilty about talking you into this the first time. She knows you were in rather a state, and she feels she may have been a little pushy.'

'Pushy?' I say. 'Nicole? No, you've lost me.' I bite back a grin, and he smiles too.

'She wasn't remotely wrong to send me to New Zealand,' I say. 'I expect you'll be seeing her soon, so you can put her mind at rest. It's the best thing anyone ever did for me, and I'll always be grateful to her. And I'm going back there, aren't I? It's my choice this time and nothing to do with her. She wanted me to stay here and teach at St. Jude's.'

'Yes, she told me that too,' he says. 'For what it's worth, I think you've made the right decision.'

I'm completely taken aback. 'You do?'

He nods. 'I do. As I say, that's just for what it's worth. It's nothing to do with me anymore, but it seems to me that you've found your way. I don't know how I can put it any more patronisingly than that, so please don't ask me to try.'

He has a line of chocolate powder across his upper lip. I lean across and flick at it with a serviette.

'Sorry, these cappuccinos obviously need practice,' he says.

'Yes,' I agree, 'but they're worth it.'

'Clearly. And what are you heading back to, if you don't mind me asking?'

I hesitate. 'There's a job waiting for me in the Coromandel. I'm going to help Nora and Patrick until they find someone more permanent to replace me. Then Patrick and I will have a go at doing up next door, and we'll look for someone to help me get the restaurant up and running.'

'Sounds good,' he says, and I'm grateful he doesn't push it further.

He stares at his cappuccino before asking, 'And will there be anyone waiting for you when you arrive?'

His eyes are serious, so I choke back the sort of flippant reply that rises automatically to my lips whenever anyone asks me a personal question. He deserves much more.

'Patrick's meeting me,' I say. 'He's heading into Auckland for some supplies, so he'll swing by and pick me up from the airport on his way back.'

'And how about when you get to the Coromandel?' he says.

'Friends. No one special, if that's what you're after?'

'It was, actually.'

'And you?' I ask in return. 'You haven't told me anything about your plans. You didn't even tell me you'd left your job. Nicole only mentioned it this morning.'

I feel the same wash of hurt as when she told me, assuming I must already know.

'Mum didn't tell me either,' I add. 'Don't let her hear about it or you'll be off that pedestal before you can blink.'

He shrugs his shoulders, unperturbed. 'She knows. I made her promise not to breathe a word to you. She didn't like it, but she finally promised. I'd have told you myself, but I didn't want to put pressure on you or make you feel I quit the job because of you.'

'Did you?' I ask bluntly, and he laughs.

'Partly, I suppose, but you mustn't let it bother you. I don't think you realise how much it shook me when you left last year. I'd been with you for so many years, thinking everything was all right, that we were all right, making plans for the future. I often felt you were angry with me, but I was never sure why. You pulled away from me so often, and I tried to give you space. But you never said anything, and I didn't want to.'

I brush my eyes with the back of my hand. 'I'm so sorry, Matt. I know I messed things up. I messed *us* up. You were right. I did need some space when everything was pressing down on me. But I can see now that I was hitting out at all the wrong things, and you got hurt in the process. You and Mum weren't the problem, and neither was Bentinck if I'm honest.'

'Does it have to be too late?' he asks, still looking down at his mug.

I want to reach out and touch him, to make him feel better, but I resist. If I owe him nothing else, I owe him complete honesty in case this really is goodbye.

'You have to understand that I've made a new life,' I say. 'It's something I've done by myself, and I love it. I've found my path, even if I don't know where it's leading me. It isn't that I won't miss you, but I'm still frightened I'll get sucked back into everything I've worked so hard to shake off.'

'I understand,' he says, 'and I certainly don't have the right to push you.'

I smile at him gratefully. Unlike Ethan, Matt deals in a currency I both recognise and value. Even if I leave him penniless, he has the integrity to accept it. He won't steal.

'And you?' I ask. 'Will there be anyone meeting you when you get home?'

'You know there won't.'

'I thought …'

'No, you didn't,' he says. 'If this is last time we see each other, let's not play games.'

'Ok.' I apply myself to my fast-cooling cappuccino.

He glances at his watch again. 'Is this a permanent thing or more like a gap year?'

I think about this for a moment. 'Does it matter? I'm having fun and trying something new. Who cares whether I come back or not?'

He shoots me a swift look when I say this but still doesn't speak.

'I'm saying that I don't want to plan my life out in detail …' I trail off, not sure I'll ever be able to explain.

'Me neither.' He must see my surprise because he flushes. 'I tried it the other way, and it wasn't as fulfilling as it seemed. So, I think I'll let the dust settle a bit before I look around.'

He concentrates on tracing a pattern in a patch of spilled cocoa powder, not raising his eyes. I try to visualise him in New Zealand and am surprised to find the image is nowhere near as incongruous as I would previously have thought. Maybe what I've built for myself – what I still plan to build – will not only stand the light of day but will prove resilient enough to allow other people in without damage. Only time will tell, and I'm grateful I have plenty of that.

'If you don't find another job at once, you could visit me,' I say without giving myself time to think and over-analyse.

He looks up and smiles. 'I'd love that. I've never visited that part of the world.'

I snort. 'Like I don't know that! You only ever wanted to go skiing.'

'Yes, that's what I meant,' he says. 'There's some excellent skiing in New Zealand.'

He catches my horrified look and grins. 'Hey, I'm kidding! I'd love to come and visit you. I'd like to see your restaurant if you start it. I could wash some dishes for you and maybe see a bit of the country too.'

'You have my email – or Nicole does,' I say. 'Let me know.'

'I'll do that, if you're sure.'

I look into his familiar hazel eyes for a long moment. 'I'm very sure. You can always go home again if you don't like it.' I smile as I hear Nicole's voice echoing down the tunnel of ten long months.

I glance up at the banks of screens, and there it is – my flight – finally beginning to board.

I jump up. 'I have to go!'

Matt hugs me warmly, and I take his hand as we walk past the shops towards passport control. New Zealand suddenly seems an immense and frightening distance away. Then again, so does the UK. I have a foot in both and a home in neither. Just for a second, I waver.

'What's wrong?' he asks teasingly. 'Have you forgotten your passport?'

'I haven't forgotten anything at all,' I say, reaching up to kiss him.

I tug my passport out of my pocket, wave it cheerfully and walk slowly away from him into no-man's-land.

I hope you enjoyed this book. If you did, please consider leaving a review on Amazon. It helps new readers find my books, and I really appreciate it.

Join my mailing list to receive a free short story and be the first to receive special offers and notifications of upcoming books.

rosemarywhittaker.com/signup

The Cinnamon Snail

She's found the love of her life. He just hasn't realised it …

When Christian moves from Copenhagen to London, Kate quickly tumbles into love. He's the most handsome and charismatic man she's ever met, and she's all set for her Happily Ever After.

Until he announces that he's returning to Copenhagen, and he doesn't want her to go with him. Nothing Kate can say will change his mind. All she can do is plan a new future without him. And if that future happens to be in Denmark, that's entirely her own business.

She gets a job at The Cinnamon Snail Cafe and sets out to win Christian back. His new girlfriend is a slight problem – but when true love is on the line, anything goes.

Kate has a year to prove she can settle into a new country and persuade the love of her life she means business. A piece of cake!

A delightful new story of Danish pastries, romance, and lots and lots of hygge.

Available now in paperback and Kindle ebook

Sunshine State

When life gives you lemons …

What should you do when your ex-husband still works with you and is trying to date most of your co-workers?

Emily Martin is struggling with the aftermath of a bitter divorce. All she wants is to be left alone to rebuild her life. But that's an impossible dream as long as her ex-husband is hanging around. So, when she's offered an assignment in Florida, she jumps at the chance for a fresh start.

She's escaping Jack for a year, but she still needs a way to get even. Her new office mate suggests online dating, and Emily realises the perfect revenge is to find the man of her dreams and take him back with her to the UK. That way, Jack will see she has not only moved on but traded up.

But as the year passes, she starts to wonder whether revenge really brings happiness. If not, can she discover a new way of being and finally achieve her very own sunshine state?

A feel-good story of sunshine, speed-dating and Mai-Tais.

Available now in paperback and Kindle ebook

The Wattle Birds

Sam has met the man of her dreams – and he's just proposed!

But Josh's home and business are in Australia. When Sam agrees to join him there, she quickly discovers the challenges of her adopted country – starting with her workaholic fiancé and her prickly and hostile new sister-in-law.

But the biggest obstacle of all is Josh's ever-present, glamorous ex-girlfriend. Sam is taken aback to find that Lauren is Josh's business partner and possibly the reason he's happy to work such long hours.

It may be time to admit defeat and return home. Josh is working so hard that he probably won't even notice.

But Sam is surprised to discover that, while she fell in love with Josh in the UK, she's fallen in love with the rest of his family in Australia. She's quickly faced with the choice between love and reality – unless she can find a way to make a new life that includes them both.

A feel-good story of one engagement, two cultures, and a small but very adventurous koala!

Available now in paperback and Kindle ebook

About the author

Rosemary Whittaker wanted to be an author as soon as she was old enough to hold a book the right way up. From that moment on, she was the despair of her teachers, who attempted to impart the basics of an education while she stared out of the window, making up characters and situations.

Having accidentally absorbed enough to graduate and become a teacher, she spent the next few decades moving around the world with her husband, children, and menagerie of unexpected pets.

She accidentally found herself in Australia some years back and intends to stay there for a very long time. She currently spends her time writing, sourcing English marmite and salad cream and wrangling her two determinedly destructive house bunnies – Pumpkin and Midway.

Rosemary has written several light-hearted romance novels set in the different countries in which she has lived. She also writes children's books as R J Whittaker – in particular a series of books about a recalcitrant monkey named Pom Pom, who is not in any way, shape or form based on her experience of raising her own four boys.